Have a
Little
Faith
in Me

Have a Little Faith in Me

Sonia Hartl

PAGE STREET
PUBLISHING CO.

PAGE STREET
PUBLISHING CO.

For Kaitlyn and Rylie

To my beautiful baby girls, as you journey through this life
I hope you'll always have friendship, compassion, and wisdom
to light your way

Chapter 1

If I hadn't made such a big deal about my virginity, I might not have spent a valuable portion of my summer checking nosebleed tissues for images of Jesus. I blamed society. Virginity had always been viewed as this monumental thing, like you gave away a piece of yourself just because you got tired of saying "no" or curiosity got the better of you. A whole piece of your heart, soul, or whatever. That mentality was how I ended up poring over brochures for Camp Three SixTeen a week after my junior year ended.

Sun streamed in through my partially closed curtains, a single beam of light stretching across the Camp Three SixTeen pamphlet on my pillow. Some would've said it was a sign from God. In my mind, it was a way to get my ex-boyfriend back, and that single slant of sunlight was all the justification I needed.

I put my feet up on the wall and let the row of wildflowers I'd tacked above my headboard tickle my toes. A few browning seeds clung to the end of a dandelion head, from the time Ethan had brought me to a puffy white field so I could make unlimited wishes. My mom called it my Garden of the Dead. My dad called them dust collectors, but I couldn't bear to get rid of them. Without the flowers, I'd have nothing left from my relationship with Ethan, other than the empty place inside me that never stopped aching.

Camp Three SixTeen could make us right again though. Ethan always said he left camp feeling closer to God, and if I wanted to be with him, I had to get closer to God too.

I tucked the camp application into my top drawer, next to the condoms that claimed to be ribbed for my pleasure. A purchase I made a little too late. Ethan had broken up with me in order to restore his virginal heart before I could take them out of the Walgreens bag. Even though I didn't need them for sex anymore, they could still be used for my pleasure. I peeked out my bedroom window, where my best friend, Paul, lay on his backyard trampoline, wearing his earbuds. Probably listening to a band I'd never heard of.

I ripped open one of the condom packages, filled the condom with water in my bathroom sink, and tied a knot around the end. My window hadn't had a screen since the night Paul had climbed a ladder to our second story so we could split our first beer.

I slid the glass open and launched the water condom toward the trampoline. "Incoming!"

The condom sailed over Paul's head, hitting the grass behind him. It burst open. Damn. Not only had I missed, but I'd given away my position.

Paul pushed his sunglasses up on his head. "Weak!" he shouted. "Try again."

He put his sunglasses back on and lay with his fingers linked over his chest. Like he wasn't about to get a face full of water courtesy of Trojan. I filled up a second condom, threw it out the window, and it burst six feet to the right of the trampoline. Paul faked a yawn.

Now he was in for it.

I filled up the last condom in the pack and stood at the window, my arm raised high above my head. Paul gestured for me to bring it on. As I was zeroing in on his smug expression, I hadn't noticed his mom coming out onto the back patio. I let the condom fly, too far to the left, where it hit Paul's mom smack on her shoulder and exploded.

She looked around for the source of her unexpected soaking while Paul rolled with laughter, safe and dry, on his trampoline. I debated ducking and hiding, but nothing got past Paul's mom. She'd raised five boys and knew all the tricks. I gave her a sheepish wave.

She put her hands on her hips. "CeCe, what on earth are you doing?"

"Sorry, I was trying to hit Paul," I said.

"In that case, carry on. I'm sure he deserved it."

"Hey." Paul sat up. "You're my mom—aren't you supposed to be on my side?"

"Sorry, kid. Girls have to stick together. I just made a fresh batch of lemonade," she called up to me. "Come on over and have a glass."

Paul's mom was the best.

I raced downstairs, letting my mom know I'd be next door as I passed by her in the living room. Once I was outside, the sun baked my shoulders, bringing out all the little freckles I had only in the summer. I'd tugged my long brown hair into a sloppy bun to keep my neck from sweating, and it flopped around on top of my head as I jogged over to Paul's.

He pulled out his earbuds as he opened the back gate for me. "My mom is going to have a lot of questions if she discovers you weren't throwing water balloons."

"Who says balloons can't be ribbed for her pleasure?"

"Ribbed for Her Pleasure would be a great band name." He slung an arm over my shoulder. "Just so you're prepared, even though you didn't hit me, expect certain retaliation."

"You have to catch me first." I ducked out from under him

and ran to the other side of his trampoline. "Because I'm fast. You're no match for my catlike reflexes."

"When's the last time you beat me in a race?" He strolled around the edge of the trampoline. "Third grade?"

"And I'm still riding that high." I side-shuffled to keep him on the opposite side.

"I let you win." He picked up his pace.

"Oh really? Is that why you cried when you lost?"

Before I could get my feet to catch up with my brain, he pounced. He caught me around the waist, and I hooked my leg under his, sending us both crashing onto the grass.

Light danced in his dark eyes as he pulled off a piece of broken condom that had clung to the front of my tank top. "One of these days I'm going to find a way to guard myself against your classic move."

"Impossible. I've been perfecting it for years."

Paul's mom brought out a pitcher and two frosty mugs, setting them on the patio table. Paul jumped to his feet and helped me up. His palm already had callouses from helping his stepdad out at his flooring company for the last week.

We sat under his patio umbrella, which his stepdad had hooked up to spray mist on hot days, sipping lemonade while puffy clouds drifted across the lazy sky. Summer didn't get any better than this. I'd miss hanging out with Paul for three weeks while I went to camp, but I had a plan to win Ethan back, and I wouldn't be deterred.

Paul ran a hand through his shaggy dark hair. "My stepdad said we can help out at his Habitat for Humanity gig this summer, to get our community service hours in before we start senior year."

"That's cool of Brad, but I have a different plan."

"What plan? You don't plan." He lifted his mug to his lips.

Here went nothing. "I'm going to Camp Three SixTeen."

Paul choked on his lemonade, pounding on his chest as he coughed. "I'm sorry, what?"

"I'm not in yet, but I'm applying for their rising senior leadership program." I picked at the flecks of purple polish left on my thumbnail from junior prom. "So. I'll be getting my community service done there."

"CeCe. No." His forehead wrinkled between his brows, like it did whenever he worried over a chem exam or his latest breakup. "You have no idea what you're getting into."

Paul had gone to Camp Three SixTeen between eighth grade and freshman year, right before his pastor father left his mom for the half-his-age church secretary. Paul's mom got on okay after he left. She was the toughest woman I'd ever met, and everything I aspired to be, minus the whole abandoned-after-five-kids-and-twenty-eight-years-of-marriage thing.

Paul hadn't taken it as well. He'd been the picture-perfect pastor's son his whole life, but when his father left, he gave up church, God, and everything he'd ever believed in, finding his pleasures . . . elsewhere.

"I'm not going for Jesus; I'm going for Ethan," I said. "And before you tell me this is ridiculous and won't work, hear me out."

"Ethan is a douchebag and not worth three weeks at that place. Trust me." To say Paul wasn't a fan of my ex-boyfriend would've been a huge understatement.

"Listen. It's perfect." I drew little hearts in the melting frost on my mug. "He said in order to become born-again, he had to end things because he couldn't keep his hands off me."

Paul raised his eyebrows. "And you bought that piss-poor excuse?"

"Well." I smiled to myself over my mug. "He really couldn't keep his hands off me."

"Since he's claiming he's a virgin again, does that make you a virgin again too? Because I'm pretty sure you didn't have sex with yourself."

"I don't know." I frowned. "Is that how it works?"

"No. That's not how it works." Paul ground his teeth. "He's not a virgin and neither are you, and whatever line he fed you about being born-again is a bunch of bullshit."

"You're mad. Why are you mad? I know Christianity isn't

your cup of tea, but it's Ethan's." Not that I'd known Jesus would be some kind of roadblock when we'd first started dating. "If I want to get him back, it has to be mine, too."

"I'm not mad." Paul rubbed his hands over his face. "I'm worried about you. What if you follow him to camp and he has another girlfriend already?"

"Ethan wouldn't have another girlfriend." My voice froze over. "He's not you."

Last month Paul had broken up with Bree Newman before her red hair dye had washed out to a light pink, then he showed up to a party with Sydney Lamb the next night. And I would've totally missed his fling with Ella Holt in between if she hadn't bragged in the locker room about the ladyhead he'd given her after lacrosse practice. Paul meant more to me than anyone in the world, I'd defend him with my last breath, but secretly I had no clue why all these girls tried with him in the first place. He didn't do meaningful or long-term relationships.

"Isn't that a blessing?" Paul's tone matched mine. "But let's assume Ethan isn't like me. What happens if you go to camp and get him back? Will you start going to church, quoting Scripture, carrying a Bible around?"

"I could suffer through church. What's an hour out of my day once a week?"

"Suffering is exactly what you'd be doing. For a guy who

doesn't care enough to value you for who you are. I don't know what you think that is, but it's not love."

"That's mean." I hadn't expected Paul to be all rah-rah about my plan, given his feelings about Christianity, but I hadn't expected him to be so harsh about it either.

"No, that's truth." He stood, grabbing the pitcher and his mug. "You better get comfortable with it, because you're in for one hell of a rude awakening." He went into his house, slamming the patio door shut behind him.

So much for winning the support of my best friend. Not that I should've expected him to understand. Paul breezed through girlfriends, never getting close enough to get hurt. He didn't know what it felt like to give yourself completely to someone, or how bottomless the pain could be when they gave it all back and walked away. If I didn't act, I'd sit and stew in all my ugly feelings. Ethan told me exactly why he ended our relationship. As far as I was concerned, that was an open door. All I had to do was fake my way through a few weeks at Jesus camp.

Seemed simple enough to me.

Chapter 2

A week later, Mom and Dad sat at the dining room table with their joint laptop open. My dad sorted through bills while my mom plugged numbers in to her budgeting spreadsheet. After my parents bought our house from a nice old couple, they racked up thirty thousand in credit card debt to remodel the kitchen and both bathrooms. They paid it off years later with my grandmother's estate, becoming allergic to debt in the process. They tried to make it sound cool by saying they lived off the grid, but it really meant cash or nothing. I still had no idea how my parents met, but I'd heard the "how they got out of debt" story fifty billion times.

I grabbed a banana from the counter and pulled up a chair. "Are you sure there's room in the budget for camp?"

"I already sent the check and your mom got you some of their shirts. They still need your recommendation letter, but that's just a formality. Everything else is in order." My dad scanned the electric bill, looking for any discrepancies. A weird hobby of his. I had no idea if he even knew what to look for or what he'd do if they had overcharged us.

"Okay." I chewed on the banana as my argument with Paul ran through my mind. He'd made it sound like I'd be walking into a torture chamber. "Do you still think this is a good opportunity to build character while I commit to finishing my community service before senior year?" That's how I'd pitched it to them. One of my finer moments.

Mom shut her laptop. "Are you having second thoughts? Because if you're having second thoughts, we can put a stop payment on the check."

"It already cleared," Dad said. "Second thoughts or not, you're going to camp. We made a lot of sacrifices for this to happen, and we're hoping it'll be a good influence on you. It's high time you grew up and finished something you started."

"I want to go." This was my best chance to get Ethan back, and he loved the place. It was all he'd talked about right before we broke up. "I think I let Paul get in my head."

"It's no surprise he doesn't want you to go, but three weeks isn't that long," Mom said.

"What are you two going to do while I'm gone?"

"We were thinking of hosting an orgy, and maybe even giving crystal meth a try." My mom had an oddball sense of humor.

"Why are you like this?"

"Come on." She laughed and poked my side. "What do you think we're going to do? Between school, yearbook, and your friends, you're hardly home as it is."

She had a point. Even during the summer, I spent way more time at Paul's than here. He had a misting umbrella and a trampoline. "Will you miss me?"

"We always miss you when you're not here, Fancy girl."

I hugged my mom and went back up to my room. The camp handbook I'd skimmed through last night lay on my dresser next to the Bible I hadn't gotten around to cracking open. I still had another week. If time got away from me, I could always Google the best quotes and hope it would be enough to get by.

The pink-and-white striped suitcase I never got to use, because I never went anywhere interesting, sat at the end of my bed. I'd tucked a red satin-and-lace bra-and-underwear set into a secret compartment. Just in case. Camp Three SixTeen had a strict no phone rule, in bold black lettering at the beginning of the handbook, but they didn't mention other electronic devices. I could probably stash my iPad behind my sexy underwear.

A rock hit my window, and I ignored it. I was still annoyed with Paul for getting pissy about camp. I debated between a floral summer dress and a navy skater skirt before throwing both of them into my suitcase. Another rock hit my window.

I slid the glass open. "You can always knock on my—Oh."

Paul had draped every sheet in his house over his trampoline, creating a secret hideout underneath. Something we used to do every weekend until we got too old for make-believe. But when his father left, we revived the tradition. It turned out we still needed a place where we could forget reality for a little while.

The night his father had packed his last bag and driven away, I'd re-created the hideout. I drew a hundred stars with a silver Sharpie on the underside of the trampoline and told him a story about a boy who was too good for this earth, so he'd been chosen to live among the stars. When things got hard or scary, we always had stories for each other. He put the hideout up the day after Ethan had ended things with me. Paul drew a bunch of little fish and told a story about a girl who created an ocean with her tears and learned how to swim.

I ran over to his house, letting myself in through his back gate. Per tradition, I put my arm in through an opening between his old Spider-Man sheets and pretended to knock.

"What's the password?" he asked.

Whoever made the hideout decided the password. A rule I sincerely regretted agreeing to. I rolled my eyes and deadpanned my way through the spiel. "Paul is a king among men, desired and envied, and known the world wide for his great taste in music."

"You may enter." He'd spread a flannel blanket over the grass, and lay on his back with his hands laced under his head.

I crawled next to him and mimicked his position. He'd drawn a hill made of daisies with a little house on top that had smoke curling out of the chimney. "Who lives there?" I asked.

"A lonely boy. While he enjoyed the company of his twelve cats, he missed his best friend. Though he long suspected she only hung out with the boy to take advantage of his misting umbrella and his mom's lemonade."

"It's not the girl's fault the boy's mom makes such good lemonade."

"And so his suspicions were confirmed. However, the boy still enjoyed her company for reasons that often escaped him. But one day the girl told the boy she'd be traveling to a faraway land, a dark place with no Wi-Fi."

"Is that no Wi-Fi thing for real?" There went my plans to smuggle in my iPad after they confiscated my phone. "Sorry. Go on."

"Though the boy was mad at the girl for taking on such a foolish quest, he also thought about how boring his summer would be if he were left alone with his twelve cats."

"What's with the cats? You're allergic to cats."

His lips twitched, though I couldn't tell if he was annoyed or about to laugh. "The girl had a tough goal ahead of her, even though she thought she knew everything. Which left the boy with two choices: He could see her go on her own and get a small amount of satisfaction from saying he told her so, or he could go with her and help. For who better to guide the girl on her foolish quest than the boy who already knew the lay of the land?"

My heart sped up. Of all the ways his story could've ended, this would've been my last guess. Having Paul with me would make the whole thing a lot less scary, but I'd be furious if he was messing with me. "Has the boy made a decision?"

"The boy has decided to join the girl. Because she'll need all the help she can get."

"Are you serious?" I sat up, bumping my head on the underside of the trampoline. "Don't get me wrong—I want you to come with me—but are you going to be okay with that?"

"I'm not worried about me. I still know what to say and how to act to pull off the believable Christian shtick. You, on the other hand? They'll eat you alive." Every time Paul talked about camp, he made it sound like a slow and painful ride through Dante's Inferno. If that was his way of trying to get me to bail, it wouldn't work. I'd seen the brochures. The only fire I'd be getting close to would be the one toasting my marshmallows.

"What's in this for you?" As much as I wanted Paul to come with me, and he certainly knew his way around Christianity better than I ever would, it seemed like a huge waste of his time. "I doubt you're going to find your usual sort of fun there."

"Watching you fall on your ass after one of your crackpot ideas blows up in your face is my usual sort of fun." He tugged on the end of my ponytail. "Plus, I need my community service hours too, and this is way easier than framing houses."

"First of all, name one crackpot idea that blew up in my face."

"That time you joined PETA to get out of dissecting a fetal pig in biology."

"Because it was disgusting. They wanted us to cut open baby pigs. Piglets. And it's not like I knew all those protestors were going to show up." The school had to cancel the whole dissection just to get them to go away, which earned me a week of in-school suspension and a spot on junior prom court.

"When you joined the ski team because that one guy smiled at you in the hall."

Austin. He was pretty. Sadly, he did not feel the same way about me after I twisted my ankle and hit myself in the face with my own ski. "Sports are hard."

"Or, more recently, when you joined yearbook to make sure there was at least one picture of you on every page, but the editor didn't like you, so all the pics are of you making this face." He closed his eyes and let his tongue hang out of his half-open mouth.

"Are you done now? Because I think you've made your point."

"This is more involved than all those other schemes combined." He reached his hand toward mine, letting it fall on the blanket before making contact. "I don't want you to get hurt."

"I'm hurting now, so what's the risk?"

The heavy weight that had settled on my chest the night Ethan had told me he couldn't be with me anymore increased in pressure. Paul laid his arm out, and I rested my head in the crook of his shoulder. I hadn't cried since the night he'd held me and told me the story about the girl who'd learned how to swim in the ocean of her own making, and I wouldn't cry now, but that didn't mean I was okay. Sometimes the hurt made me so numb, crying would've been a relief.

"I hate Ethan," he said.

"I know."

"Why don't you?"

I'd asked myself that a lot when Ethan had first broken up with me. Every time I got angry, I'd think about when we'd first met. His parents let him go to public high school after years of homeschooling, and he didn't quite fit in. He wore an ugly tan shirt with ferns or something on it. After a couple of senior guys tripped him in the hall by his locker, I took his hand to help him up. It was warm and soft and molded perfectly against mine. After I'd dated a string of guys who'd only wanted one thing, Ethan had come along like the antithesis of the typical asshole. A genuinely nice guy with kind eyes and a terrible sense of fashion.

I didn't know who I was without him. His friends all called me "Ethan's girl," and I wanted so badly to belong somewhere, instead of constantly trying and failing to find my place. I hadn't done enough to make us work while we'd been together, but I could fix it. Ethan wanted a relationship with Jesus more than he wanted me, but there was no reason why he couldn't have us both.

"He didn't want to break up with me," I said. "He had to."

"According to who? Jesus? Give me a break." Paul propped himself up on his elbow, taking away my headrest. "You're worth so much more. Why can't you see that?"

"Are we going to do this all summer? As much as I adore you, and I do want you to come with me, I don't want to fight the whole time. I don't pick at you about your ex-girlfriends, so why can't you do the same for me?"

"I've never pretended to be someone I'm not to get back

together with any of them, and if I had, you would've knocked some sense into me. Because that's what friends do."

"To be fair, you never dated any Christians."

"See that spot up there?" He nodded to the underside of the trampoline right above where I was lying. "It's the point. And it went right over your head."

"No, I got the point. I just chose to ignore it." I crawled over to the opening in the sheets. "This has been fun, but I've got a Bible to read. Because that's what Christian girls do."

"God help you."

"Thanks, but I think I've got this one."

If I could fake faith as easily as I faked confidence, I'd have this in the bag.

Chapter 3

I stared out the bus window, watching the countryside roll by. Every farm we passed reminded me of the field where Ethan used to take me. Where he'd pick wildflowers for me and tell me how jealous the guys in his youth group were of his hot girlfriend. Where his hand trembled the first time I let him touch me under my bra. He used to make me feel powerful and in control, and without him, I'd been left floundering.

Paul pulled out his earbuds. "Why do you look so forlorn?"

"Just remembering." I picked up his earbud and stuck it in my ear. Some guy with a nasally voice sang about purple streets and unwashed dreams. "Speaking of forlorn."

"Blister Park. They're really abstract, but they have great bass lines." Another one of Paul's underground bands no one had ever heard of. For good reason. "Did you get a chance to read any of the Bible?"

"Yep." Nope. "I'm almost done with it now." I'd fallen asleep before I'd made it past the first page. "It's a neat story." So boring.

"Neat, huh?" Paul turned toward me in his seat. "Which part is your favorite?"

"Noah's Ark. I liked the big boat and all the animals."

He settled back in his seat with a serene smile. "I like the one where Jesus tames a dragon and shoots laser beams out of his eyes. It's got more action in it than the one with the big boat."

My expression froze for a half a second before I scowled, ruining any chance I had of convincing him I'd done my homework. "You're hilarious."

He put his earbuds back in but kept that knowing smile. I was sure he thought of this as some big joke, but the closer we got to camp, the more I worried. If Ethan saw through me, I'd just be a sad and desperate girl who'd followed him to camp. Like one of Paul's twelve imaginary cats that'd been fed once and wouldn't leave the back porch.

I yanked his earbud out. "You're still going to help me, right? I know you get some kind of weird kick out of seeing me screw up, but you're not going to quiz me about the Bible in front of people, are you?"

He looked at me like I'd called him by the wrong name. "You think I'd do that?"

"No." I flopped back on my seat. Paul gave me crap for my less-than-brilliant mistakes in private, but he'd never humiliate me or give other people the opportunity to do so. "But if I can't fake it, he's going to think I'm a stalker."

"Where would he get an idea like that?" Paul rubbed his chin between his thumb and index finger. "It's not like you lied about your religion to get a leadership position at a camp you have no interest in to impress a guy you have nothing in common with. Oh, wait."

"I'll look even more pathetic than the night he dumped me," I said in a small voice.

I'd clutched Ethan's hand, tears streaming down my cheeks, while he explained, over and over again in a low and patient voice, his resolve to restore his virginal heart. Like I was a child. After what we'd shared, he wanted to erase it all, as if we'd never happened. He left me alone and crying on my sidewalk. If he'd looked in his rearview mirror when he'd driven away, he would've seen me like that. A sad lump of a girl, pouring her heart out to the cracks in the concrete.

"Hey. You're not pathetic." Paul gathered me against his chest. "I'll help, okay? I don't like this idea or support it in any way, but I hope you know I won't leave you to the wolves."

"I don't tell you enough how much I love you." I rubbed my nose and inhaled the spicy scent of soap and sandalwood. "Are you wearing a new cologne?"

"That was a terrible segue. And yes."

I patted his shirt and sat up. "It's very manly."

"Thanks?" He gave me a funny look. "We should go over some of the more basic stuff. You'll be in a cabin with three other girls."

"Mandy, Sarina, and Astrid." I'd gotten my cabin assignment after my parents' check had cleared, and done a little digging to see who I'd be sharing a bathroom with.

Mandy had no social media presence, not even an old Facebook profile. Sarina had an Instagram account set to private with a profile picture of a Precious Moments angel. Astrid used every social media outlet on the face of the planet, but I only picked her out by narrowing her down to the one person who was in every picture posted. Her stream was filled with massive group photos—not a selfie in sight.

"They give you a few hours to unpack and get to know your cabinmates before dinner," Paul said. "I'm not allowed in the girls' cabins, so you'll have to wing it. Try not to talk."

Insulting, yet helpful. That was practically Paul's tagline.

"No problem. It's not like I'm itching to form lifelong bonds with a bunch of uptight church girls."

I doubted I'd be able to relate to them outside of polite niceties anyway. Even Astrid, who appeared to be the most normal, papered her social media profiles with Bible quotes and daily affirmations. They'd probably bust out the smelling salts if they got a look at my Instagram. My last post had been a news article about a guy who'd tried to hump a shark.

The bus pulled to a stop and let us all out in front of a small brick building. We'd only traveled an hour north, but the trees had grown taller and the sky looked closer, like you could reach up and grab one of the clouds. Even the air smelled cleaner. I took a deep breath and choked on a mouthful of bus fumes.

While the driver got our bags out of the travel compartment, Paul stood next to me, surveying the scene. His lip curled the moment he spotted a college-aged guy in a crisp white polo holding up a Camp Three SixTeen sign. "Tell me again why I volunteered to do this?"

I hooked my arm around his and batted my lashes. "Because you'd do anything for me."

He responded with a short grunt.

Ethan hadn't been on the bus—his mom probably drove him—but it didn't stop me from looking around as I dragged Paul toward our waiting van. The college guy introduced himself as Michael, not Mike, and led us to where two other people our age waited.

"These are going to be some of your leadership peers this summer," Michael said. "We need to do a roll call before we ship out. Paul Romanowski."

Paul nodded.

"Good to have you back, brother," Michael said. "Peter Lipscomb."

"Here." A fidgety kid who looked about twelve raised his hand.

"Mandy Pardee."

The infamous Mandy with absolutely no digital footprint raised her hand. I'd assumed she'd be a sullen girl in a British boarding school uniform who carried a Bible everywhere, but she didn't come close to how I'd imagined. Her blond hair shimmered in the sunlight and she had enormous blue eyes that reminded me of tropical beaches. Her nose turned upward, but it didn't make her look snotty. Probably because she had such an earnest expression.

"And last, but not least, our newcomer, Francine Wells."

"I go by CeCe."

Michael frowned, as if going by anything other than your given name was a sin. "All right then, CeCe. Mandy here is a third-year vet and she'll be able to show you around."

Mandy gave me a warm smile. They should've put her on the brochure.

Peter shook Paul's hand. "Are you related to Pastor Romanowski?"

Paul stiffened beside me. "He's my father."

Peter's eyes bugged out of his head like a squeeze doll.

"He was a guest speaker at my church this winter. The passion that guy has is nothing short of amazing. Brought church attendance up by twenty-five percent. Do you think he'll come visit?"

"No." Paul pinched his lips together. "We're not on speaking terms."

"Oh. I didn't realize." Peter shuffled his feet. "Sorry, dude."

"We're really excited to be here." I clapped my hands together, desperate to break the tense silence. "Is this your first year at camp, Peter? Or are you a vet like Mandy?"

"A vet." Peter turned as red as the acne dotting his jawline. "I almost didn't make it this year, but my mom thinks I need this place."

Michael threw open the van side door. "Let's go. Girls in the second row, boys in back."

We shuffled in, and I turned around to Paul. "Is this typical? Boys can't sit by girls?"

"It's just for the ride up," Peter said.

"So Michael can concentrate on driving," said Mandy.

Paul leaned forward, whispering loud enough for everyone to hear. "They're saying Michael can't check for undercover hand jobs if he's trying to keep his eyes on the road."

Peter coughed, beating on his chest as his eyes watered. And Paul was supposed to be the one helping me. I may have lacked Christian prowess, but at least I knew enough not to talk about hand jobs in the Jesus camp van.

Mandy's pale cheeks turned a light pink. "What brought you to camp this year, CeCe? Did you hear about it through your church?"

"Oh, um, yes." I'd been so busy getting ready to attend camp, I hadn't actually gotten around to going to church. "They had brochures. Next to the doughnuts."

Paul snorted in the seat behind me. The one time I'd gone to church with him when we were kids, before his father bailed, I fell asleep during the service. But I remembered the doughnuts. It was the first and last time Paul invited me to hear his father speak.

Mandy nodded as if I'd just said the most fascinating thing. "That's how I found out about camp. Two years ago, I just wanted to have a parent-free summer. I thought it would be no rules, fun in the sun. But I came away from camp with a deeper understanding."

"A deeper understanding of what?" I asked.

Paul shoved his knee into the back of my seat. We had to come up with a better plan for him to communicate my many failings. Fortunately, Mandy took it as a sign of genuine interest and continued on as if I hadn't asked a completely ridiculous question.

"Of Jesus, of my purpose on this Earth, what God expects from me. I went home and threw myself fully into youth group, gaining all the knowledge I could until I felt ready to lead. This is my first summer in the leadership program, and I'm so excited to pass on everything I've learned over the years. What about you? Are you pretty involved in your youth group?"

"Yes." Paul's mom had done me a solid by slightly exaggerating my involvement in her church for my recommendation letter, but I think she did it more for Paul's benefit than mine. She'd been trying to lead him back to Jesus for years. "Though not as long as you."

"We all have different experience levels, but it's not a competition. I've been rooming with Sarina and Astrid since we were sophomores. We interpret our personal faith in different ways, but our common love for Jesus brings us together in the end."

"I'm sure," I said. Paul told me the less I talked, the better off I'd be, but I had to do some talking. "What's your favorite thing about camp? Besides sharing a love for Jesus and all that."

"The lake is a lot of fun. We have a giant Blob that can launch you ten feet into the air. Campfire testimonials are always the best bonding experiences." Mandy turned pink again, which I found oddly endearing. "And there's this one guy I'll be happy to see again."

"Summer boyfriend?" The most tragic of relationships.

"For the past two summers." She beamed. "We've always gone our separate ways at the end of camp, but he thinks God has a plan for us."

"That's sweet." If God had a plan for me, I hoped it involved leading me back to Ethan before the end of summer. I couldn't stand the idea of going into senior year without him.

"Camp Three SixTeen, straight ahead," Michael said.

I leaned forward in my seat. A weatherworn wooden sign bearing the camp name hung between two posts on the dirt road. A thick tangle of woods surrounded the open property. Dirt trails wound around the open space dotted with dozens of log cabins on either side of the lake. Sun shimmered off the water, and a huge flotation device I assumed to be the Blob bounced lazily on the waves. A small church sat on top of a hill, and an enormous wooden building stood at the center of camp, with a cluster of smaller ones around it.

"That's the big house," Mandy said, pointing to the structure. "We eat meals there, and have dances and the talent show there too. Daily devotions are in the chapel, of course, and we have bonfires over there." She pointed toward an open spot by the water with a huge fire pit at the center and plenty of fallen logs for seating.

"How many kids are there?" I asked.

"It depends on attendance. The campers run from rising freshmen to seniors, but the younger years have more kids. Like, thirty each in the freshman and sophomore years. There are eight of us rising seniors who are all in the leadership program."

"Makes sense." The older kids got, the more likely they were to question their upbringing. Paul was a prime example.

"Our cabin is up there." Mandy pointed toward the back of the woods. "The boys' cabins are on the other side of the lake."

"Does that really keep everyone separate?" I asked.

"No." Mandy giggled, and it sounded like a tinkling bell. Everything about her was charming. "But we behave ourselves for the most part."

"That's because anyone caught having sex gets thrown out and has to explain it to their parents," Peter piped up. He'd been so quiet on the way, I'd almost forgotten about him. "It happened last year, and it was pretty embarrassing."

"I can only imagine." I sank lower in my seat. I wondered what the treatment of non-virgins would be in a place like this. Maybe Ethan didn't count because he was born-again, or whatever. "Keep my panties on. Check. Anything else I should know?"

"No fighting or drinking or swearing." Mandy ticked them off on her fingers. "It's not like any of us engage in that sort of thing, but they have to lay down rules."

"Understandable." I turned around to Paul and smirked.

"You going to be okay with the no swearing thing?"

"I'll live," he said, keeping his eyes out the window.

Michael pulled up to the big house and parked. "Everyone out."

We stumbled over each other as we exited the van, our bags forming a small mountain around us. Paul nudged me. "Ready to go home yet?"

"No. I think I'm going to like it here." The scent of clean air and pine trees filled my lungs. Everything about this place was beautiful. The setting, the lake, the people. No wonder these kids walked away feeling closer to God.

"The rest of the seniors should be here already. You're the last group," Michael said.

As I searched for Ethan, all my fresh insecurities surfaced. What would he say when he saw me? Would he be angry I'd invaded his little sanctuary? I'd played the happy scenario over so many times in my mind, it hadn't occurred to me to think of an alternative. He had to be happy to see me though. Now that I was getting in with all the Jesus stuff, there wouldn't be anything to stand between us. This would be okay. I'd be okay.

A high-pitched squeal from Mandy made me jump, and that was when I saw him. Ethan. His square frame, only a few inches taller than me, already golden from the sun, a sweep of light hair shading his confused eyes. I squeezed my fists together, practicing the speech I'd prepared for my sudden appearance, reminding myself for the billionth time that I wasn't sad or desperate.

Mandy took a flying leap into his arms, planting a series of kisses over his cheeks and mouth. The mouth that had kissed mine only a month ago.

And with that, everything inside me shattered.

Chapter 4

My bottom lip trembled and my breath came in fast gasps, as if I could physically suck my building tears back in. I closed my eyes and opened them again, but Mandy and Ethan's reunion didn't go away. If anything, it got worse. The way he looked at her sent sharp pains through my chest. The awe and tenderness in his eyes used to be for me.

And I'd done everything to keep it.

Ethan turned his head, and I searched for myself in his gaze, the powerful, beautiful, in-control girl who'd helped him to his feet in the hall. But he couldn't see me anymore. The girl I'd been before he broke my heart no longer existed.

Paul leaned down. "Now is probably not a good time to say I told you so, but . . ."

"Can you not right now?" Despite my best effort to feign nonchalance, the pressure in my lungs tightened. "I think I'm going to be sick."

Paul tucked me against him and led me away from the campers who belonged here. I hadn't been this close to Ethan in weeks, and at the same time, I'd never been further away. He called my name as Paul steered me behind a small wooden building, but I couldn't look back. If I did, I wouldn't be able to hold the dam from breaking free.

Under the hum of a window air-conditioning unit, Paul sat me on a tree stump and rubbed my back while I held my head between my knees.

"I'm so stupid," I said behind a gulp of air. "Of course he has another girlfriend. A nice Christian girl he can be proud to take home."

Ethan's mom was probably thrilled. She'd give Mandy one of her limp hugs, and they'd play hymns together on the family organ. Maybe every once in a while they'd make a joke about that one time Ethan sowed his wild oats with a girl who had a loud mouth and loose morals.

"I tried to warn you," Paul said. "This idea was terrible from the start."

"I know you get a buzz from being able to say you told me so, but can you put that away for a second and at least pretend to be my supportive best friend?"

Paul wrapped his arms around my shuddering frame. "Do you want to leave?"

"I can't leave." I looked at Paul in horror. "He'll think I only came here for him."

Paul scratched his head. "I'm ninety-nine percent sure that cat is out of the bag."

"I have to put it back in the bag."

I couldn't walk away. If I left, I'd be the person Ethan saw when he looked at me now. The sad and desperate girl. My plan had taken an unexpected detour, but I could still find my way back. I hadn't Googled all those Jesus facts and convinced my parents I was headed down a path of good moral judgment just to roll over at the first obstacle.

"What's going on in there?" Paul tapped my head. "You had the same look on your face the night we soaped Principal Higgins's hot tub."

I smiled at the memory. Paul and I had snuck into our principal's backyard at two in the morning and dumped five containers of Tide into his hot tub. One for every day of suspension I'd received for the PETA protest. We turned on the bubbles and watched the foam overtake his patio from the safety of the woods behind his house. Still the best night of my life.

"I'm fine." I wiped away the smudged mascara from my eyes. Seeing Ethan with Mandy hurt, but I had to get it together. I didn't want to spend my senior year wondering what could've been if I'd tried. "How do I look?"

"Like you just had your heart broken."

I rearranged my features. "How about now?"

"Like you're going to make whoever did it pay."

I needed to work on my facial expressions, but it was better than sad. "I'm going to talk to him, try to gauge his reaction when I tell him how much Christ-ing I've been doing."

Paul tilted his head back and took a deep breath. "I don't recommend leading with Christ as a verb."

"You know what I mean."

We headed back to rejoin the group of leadership campers, who hung out by the big house in a tight group. Sweat gathered under my palms. Back at home, Ethan had been the one out of place. The shy guy who got tripped in the halls. The one who had a sweet smile but owned a fine collection of the world's ugliest clothes. Today was no exception. He wore a black T-shirt covered with bolts of lightning and a wolf on the front.

But as I watched him make jokes and laugh with the other campers, he became someone else. Someone confident and in his element. The first time he asked if he could kiss me, he stared at his feet. Here, he stood up straight, looked people in the eye. It unnerved me.

"Where did you two disappear to?" Mandy asked in a wink-wink, nudge-nudge tone.

Ethan glared at Paul for an instant before his face quickly

melted back to polite interest. Maybe I'd imagined it. I gave Ethan a fingers-only wave, not fully trusting myself to speak yet. I just had to get through this initial awkwardness.

"Hey. Wow." Ethan's Adam's apple bobbed up and down. "It's surprising to see you here. A good surprise, but yeah. Can I talk to you for a second?"

"Sure." That sounded casual. Cool. I could do this. I followed him up a gravel path, past the big house and a row of cabins near the edge of the woods. "Funny seeing you. One hell—heck, one heck of a coincidence.

"What brought you to camp?" He was so close, I could count the gold flecks in his eyes, just like I'd done the first time we'd kissed. I looked for myself again, and found nothing.

"I'm fulfilling my community service, and spending three weeks in paradise getting closer to God. Isn't that why you're here?"

"If that's why you came, I'm happy for you. This is a good place for those who seek. But if you're here for me, I'm sorry, but—"

"I'm not." I'd practiced this conversation in my head so many times. It was now or never. "You know Paul? I know you know Paul. Anyway, when you broke up with me, it opened my eyes to all I'd been missing in my life, which was great, because Paul had been trying to get me to go to church for ages.

His mom introduced me to his youth group, and that's when I found the Lord and all that good Christian living."

Ethan looked up at me through lashes so long, his mother said they were made from angel's wings. "I thought you said you and Paul were just friends."

This scenario hadn't even crossed my mind. "You're jealous? Of Paul?"

I tried to keep my face from betraying this little light of mine. He still cared. Maybe not in the same way he used to, but it was something. I could work with something.

He kicked at the gravel under his feet. "No."

His nostrils twitched like they did whenever he lied. Like that time he'd told me his mom still liked me after the family dinner where I stubbed my toe and dropped an f-bomb in front of his ten-year-old brother, or when he said I wasn't that bad at bowling after I got five gutter balls in a row. Or when he dropped me off the night we had sex and said he'd call me in the morning. I should've known then that was the beginning of the end.

My eyebrows drew together as a new plan formed in my mind. One I prayed Paul would forgive me for. "You're the one who broke up with me. I thought you'd be happy to see I've moved on with someone new."

Using my best friend to make my ex jealous wouldn't be

my proudest moment, but I'd already followed this guy to Jesus camp. Pride had gone out the window a long time ago.

"I am happy." Lies. "It doesn't bother me." More lies. "But since when is Paul the epitome of good Christian living, as you say?"

"His father happens to be a well-known pastor." Who abandoned his family for a much younger woman, but that was neither here nor there. "Without Paul's love and support, I never would've made it to this point in my life. He's the one who helped me find Jesus. In between all our awesome make-out sessions, of course."

"This is hard. Seeing you here. You know how much you tempt me." Finally, some truth. I resisted the urge to give a victory shimmy. "I'm here to work on my relationship with Jesus, and I'm afraid you might be a distraction."

"I'm not here to tempt or distract you." He still wanted me. Even if I couldn't see it in his eyes anymore, it was all the spark I needed. We could get back there. This was only a start. "I'm with Paul now, and it looks like you're with Mandy, so . . ."

"Why Paul? You know he just uses girls and discards them when he's done." He shuffled his feet. "I don't want you to end up as another notch on his bedpost."

"Don't worry about me. I'm not your problem anymore." My tone hardened enough to cut glass. Even if what he said was true, I drew the line with anyone who talked shit about Paul. "You don't know him like I do, so maybe you should keep your mouth shut."

"I'm sorry. That was uncalled for." He glanced back at the group. "Let's get through this summer and we can talk about us some other time when you're not all fired up."

"I'm not fired up. I'm fine." I turned around and blew him a kiss over my shoulder. "Nice seeing you, Ethan. I'm super-thrilled you're here this summer."

He wanted to talk about us. My plan was already working better than I'd hoped. Now I had to convince Paul to play along. I spread my arms and tiptoed across the figurative tightrope I'd created. One wrong move, and I'd go tumbling into the abyss.

As soon as I rejoined the group, Paul slung an arm around me and whispered in my ear. "How did that go? Did you gauge his reaction to all your Christ-ing?"

"Could've been worse," I muttered. "I might've gotten you into something you won't like, and I'm hoping you'll remember our decade-long friendship and not disown me."

"What did you do?"

I knotted my fingers together as I tried to work out how to present it to him.

"CeCe." He grabbed my shoulders and leveled his gaze, making it impossible for me to look away. "What did you do?"

"I knew you two were a couple." Mandy clapped her hands together as she approached. "Why didn't you just say so in the van? There're no rules against dating here."

Paul started to object, and I put my hand over his mouth. "We wanted to be low-key. So we could hang out without feeling like we needed to be watched."

The look he gave me could've wilted my mom's garden, and that thing had been dead for years. He'd bring it back just to watch it die again. This might've been a bad idea.

"They monitor you whether you're coupled up or not," said a girl who had the coolest eye makeup I'd ever seen. She'd painted mermaids over the lids and turned her eyebrows into the tail. This couldn't be the Precious Moments angel.

"Sarina, it's not that bad," Mandy said. Maybe this girl was the Precious Moments angel. Or I'd stumbled across a different Sarina Bean. "Maybe when we were regular campers, but we're in the leadership program now. We're practically counselors."

"Counselors who don't get paid," said Astrid. I recognized her from all her group photos. I thought she'd been using a filter, but with her rosebud lips, thick lashes, and a mass of curls framing her face, she actually looked like a living doll.

"Astrid is our grumpy-pants," Mandy said. "But she knows more Scripture by heart than anyone I know, and leads a youth group of two hundred back at home."

My jaw dropped. "Two hundred? I think that's the whole of our graduating class."

"I don't do it alone," she said in a tone that suggested otherwise. "We're a big church and really committed to bringing the word of God to the next generation."

"That's awesome. Isn't it, bunny?" Paul pulled me against him and nuzzled my ear. "I'm not very happy with you right now," he whispered.

"Just go with it. I'll explain later." I glanced at Ethan as he rejoined the circle. "Paul could've abandoned me before I became a believer, but he stood by me, helped me see the word of God as truth. So, he's getting some of us excited. One person at a time."

"That's how it's done." Astrid nodded. "All avalanches start with a single snowflake."

"Looks like everyone has been introduced." Ethan hauled his rucksack over his back. "We should probably go unpack before dinner call."

"I got Astrid, Sarina, Mandy, and who are you?" I asked a boy with shortly cropped hair who had meaty arms and oddly skinny legs.

"Jerome." He shook my hand in a super-formal way.

"Now you know everyone. Let's go." Ethan shoved Jerome to move him along.

"Where's Peter?" I asked.

Jerome let out a short laugh. "He's probably up at the cabin, trying to sneak porn, or he's being catfished by whoever he chatted up on a gaming forum."

I glanced at Paul, who had totally lied about the no Wi-Fi, so in my mind that made us even, but he had his eyes narrowed on Jerome. "He seemed like a cool dude on the ride up."

"You think so, huh?" Jerome puffed up his chest, but the effect was ridiculous with his little legs hanging out of his shorts.

Mandy stared between the two of them with her pouty bottom lip sticking out. "Guys. It's the first day. Do you think you could chill out a bit?"

Jerome jerked his thumb at Paul. "This guy shows up out of nowhere and thinks he can pass judgment on me? How do we even know he's a real believer?"

"'For in the same way you judge others, you will be judged, and with the measure you use, it will be measured to you,'" Paul said.

"Matthew 7:2," Astrid whispered under her breath.

My jaw dropped. I hadn't heard Paul quote the Bible in years, but it rolled off his tongue like water. Maybe Christianity was how other people described riding a bike. Not that I'd know. I'd never gotten the hang of bike riding.

"Come on." Mandy lifted my pink-and-white suitcase, even

though she already had her own rucksack to carry. "We're in cabin eight. It's the best."

Paul nodded at me to go. As I followed Mandy along the dirt path, it became clear I hadn't just taken a bus ride up north— I'd stepped into another world. One where I didn't speak the language and I couldn't have been more out of the loop.

God help me, indeed.

Chapter 5

Taking on the role of my summer best friend with more determination than actual appreciation for my company, Mandy insisted on covering my eyes before she would open the door to cabin eight. I had to assume a cabin was a cabin, though. I'd camped plenty of times as a kid, and we always stayed in cabins with electricity so my dad could hook up his sleep apnea machine.

Mandy giggled her little bell-like giggle and took her hands off my eyes. "Ta-da. What do you think? Isn't it the cutest?"

The cabin had plain white walls, with exposed wooden beams crisscrossing the ceiling. It smelled like mothballs and floor cleaner, but it was homey enough. Four twin beds with white sheets took up most of the space, save for a giant braided rug at the center of the open room. Each bed had a wooden cross above it and a set of shelves built into the wall, with drawers for storage underneath. A door to the back opened up to a small bathroom with one shower, one toilet, and one sink. That would suck in the morning.

"Since you're new, we decided to let you have first pick of the beds," Mandy said.

"When did you decide that?" I asked.

"When you ran off to make out with your boyfriend."

"Paul's not—" I'd gotten so accustomed to telling everyone and their dog that Paul wasn't my boyfriend, changing that particular trajectory would take some getting used to. "I mean, yes. Lots and lots of making out. You know. Before official camp begins."

"I'll tell you a little secret." Her blue eyes danced with mischief. "You can make out after official camp begins. Just don't get caught."

Did Christian kids even make out? Obviously they did on some level. They could even have sex as much as they wanted, so long as they claimed to be born-again whenever it suited their needs. But I didn't know if they talked about it out loud, or if it was one of those things everyone did but no one talked about. Since I was stuck sharing a cabin with Ethan's new girlfriend, I hoped it was one of those things they didn't talk about.

"I guess I'll take this one." I pointed to the bed tucked behind the door. There wasn't much of a difference between the beds, but I didn't want to get stuck next to the bathroom.

"Perfect." Mandy tossed my suitcase onto the bed. "You can personalize it any way you like. They even let us paint the walls if we promise to paint them white again before we go."

"That seems like a lot of work for three weeks."

"No one ever goes full color. They just paint crosses and butterflies and things like that." Mandy dumped her stuff on the bed across from mine. "How do you know Ethan? Do you two go to the same church?"

"Um . . ."

I hadn't figured out how to explain that one yet. Luckily, Astrid and Sarina barreled in behind us, providing a nice distraction. They did rock-paper-scissors to decide the fate of the last good bed, with Sarina's paper covering Astrid's rock. Astrid gave a long-suffering sigh and put her stuff on the bed next to the bathroom.

The girls caught up on their school year while I quietly unpacked my clothes and the few personal belongings I'd taken with me. They had the kind of easy rhythm with each other that came from spending every summer in the same cabin since they were sophomores. Even if they hadn't figured out I wasn't a Christian, there was more than one way to be an intruder.

I put my collection of romance novels on the shelf next to a picture of my parents. Probably not Jesus-camp-appropriate reading, but I'd die if I could only read the Bible for the next three weeks. The Beanie Boo elephant my dad got me for my birthday, because for some reason he still thought I was five, sat next to the Bible I'd run over a few times with my mom's car to make it look well read. I was sure I'd committed some kind of high-level blasphemy with that one, but in for a penny, in for a pound.

"She hit a line drive straight to my stomach," Mandy said, telling Sarina and Astrid about her homeschool community's softball team. "I still caught it, though, and you should've seen the look on her face. They thought they had the game in the bag."

"Nice," Astrid said. "I bet you had a welt the size of your head."

"Bigger." Mandy beamed as if this were a point of pride. "Do you play sports, CeCe?"

Other than my disastrous first day on the ski team, where I walked away with a black eye and zero chance of dating Austin? "No. Sports and I don't get along."

"Same for me," said Sarina. "Unless you count shopping as a sport. I'd be All-State in collecting Sephora Beauty Insider points."

"Speaking of which, how do you do that with your eyes?" I couldn't stop looking at them. The mermaids on her lids appeared to swim every time she smiled.

"My parents didn't let me wear makeup until I turned sixteen. Once they let me, I went a little overboard." She cast her eyes downward, like it shamed her for some reason.

"I think it's amazing," I said. "I'd give anything to have that kind of talent. Do you draw, too, or just do cool stuff with eye pencils?"

"Just the makeup." She folded and refolded the same shirt from her bag three times. "I'm really not that good. I'm still learning."

"Oh right." Astrid snorted. "That's why you've gotten fifty thousand YouTube subscribers in what? Six months?"

"Wait." I held my hand out. "You have fifty thousand subscribers and you think you're not that good? I'm all for a little modesty, but da—darn. You've earned the right to brag."

Her face paled. "Pride is a sin."

"It's a stupid sin." All three girls went suddenly still, and Paul's advice about not talking echoed in my head. "Well, it is." I huffed as I threw a stack of shirts in my drawer. "Girls get enough crap." Did they consider *crap* a swear? "The least we can do is be proud of our own accomplishments. Lord knows the world won't do it for us."

"I was proud when our softball team went to nationals," Mandy said as she stared at her clasped hands in her lap. "I don't think that's a bad thing."

"It's not," Astrid said. "I take pride in my youth group. And, Sarina, you should be proud of your YouTube channel.

Your tutorials taught me how to apply liner without stabbing myself in the eye, and that alone is a pretty phenomenal feat."

"My parents don't feel the same way." Sarina looked out the window. "They might make me take down my YouTube channel when I get home from camp."

"Then tell them Galatians 6:4 states that 'Each one should test their own actions. Then they can take pride in themselves alone, without comparing themselves to someone else.'" Astrid crossed the cabin to give Sarina a hug. "Pride is only a sin when you use it to put others down."

"Thanks." Sarina's cloudy expression cleared. "What about you, CeCe? Do you have any hobbies or extracurriculars you're involved with?"

"Not really." Unless they counted causing a ruckus at school on a regular basis, telling stories with Paul in our hideout, or pelting his mom with water-filled condoms. Which I'm sure they didn't. "I'm still trying to find my thing. Other than worshipping Jesus, of course."

"I checked out your Instagram," Astrid said. "You have a lot of pictures of Paul making goofy faces. That looks like a hobby."

"Oh. Well. That's kind of an 'us' thing."

Outside of the occasional shark-humping news article, Paul and I had pretty much dedicated each other's Instagrams to maximum one-upping. It started with a shot I took of him watering his mom's flowers. From the angle of my bedroom window, it looked like he was peeing. He fired back with an unflattering photo of me shoving half a Popsicle down my throat.

It devolved from there.

"I looked you guys up too. I thought you were a girl with a Precious Moments profile picture," I said to Sarina.

"That is me," she said. "My family one. I do all my makeup pictures under EyesAlive. It's not attached to my real name in case weirdos on the Internet try to look me up." Her face turned beet red. "I don't mean you. I mean, like creepers and stuff."

"Weirdos on the Internet would be a great band name," I said, before realizing that would only ever make sense to Paul. "I saw all your pics too," I said to Astrid. "You're always with a ton of people. Is that your youth group?"

She nodded. "Some of them. I try to show us having a good time, so people resistant to attending church won't feel like it's all stuffy and boring."

"I'm sure you didn't find anything on me." Mandy picked at the split ends in her sunny hair. "My parents think the Internet rots your brain. And their parents said the same thing about television, so we don't have one of those, either."

She didn't have Internet or Netflix? My heart wept for her. "What do you do for entertainment?"

"We have music, and phones with no data. I have seven

brothers and sisters, so there's always someone around to play board games with. I like to bake. Sometimes we invite friends over and play softball. We go sledding and ice-skating in the winter. Usual stuff."

It sounded pretty normal. Not for me, but I had friends who did all those things. No social media, though . . . I shuddered.

After I folded my last T-shirt and stuck it in a drawer, I turned back to the girls. "I know Mandy and Ethan are a thing." I somehow managed to get that out without a hint of bile rising up my throat. "Is anyone else here dating?"

"The only man I have an interest in committing myself to at this point in my life is my Lord and Savior, Jesus Christ."

Okay. So Astrid was no fun.

"What about you, Sarina?"

She blushed. The Christian girls did that a lot. Like the girls back at school who could make themselves cry on demand. A skill I envied.

"Last summer Jerome kissed me at the final bonfire," Sarina said. "I'm not sure if anything is going to happen this summer. Let's say I wouldn't be opposed to it."

"Really?" I said. "No offense, but that guy seems like a total dick."

"Why? Because he didn't come to the rescue of that little pervert, Peter?" Sarina's disposition had gone chillier than the window unit working overtime to keep our cabin a steady seventy-two degrees. "You're new, so you don't know he almost got kicked out last year."

"For what?" Peter was on the skinny side, kind of nerdy, but overall seemed harmless.

"He had a picture of a girl under his mattress," Mandy said in a hushed tone.

"A naked picture?" Gross, but not the worst thing teenage boys kept under their beds. I'd once found a week-old burrito growing fuzzy mold under Paul's.

"Not naked, but she might as well have been," said Astrid with a look of revulsion on her face. "It came from one of those calendars. The kind where the girl wears dental floss while she rides a muscle bike that is an obvious euphemism for a man's penis."

"And he almost got kicked out for that?" The people in charge were way more hard-core than Mandy had made them seem on the van ride over. "Seems a little extreme."

"It's disgusting and objectifying to women. He's lucky his parents made such a huge donation to the camp, or he would've been gone for sure," Astrid said. As if that settled it.

I sort of agreed with her about the objectification, but if a woman got paid to wear a short skirt and pose for photos on a motorcycle, that was her business. Hell, I'd probably do it too. It had to pay way more than babysitting, for a fraction of the work. Christian CeCe couldn't voice that opinion though. Christian CeCe had to toe the line to keep her ruse intact.

"It sounds like he could really use this place then," I said, recalling when Peter had mentioned something about why his mom wanted him to return to camp.

"We should get down to dinner." Mandy hooked her arm through mine. "The food is actually pretty decent here. And, as leadership campers, we'll have access to the kitchen keys for cleanup duty, so we can always snag some chips if we get hungry later."

"Isn't that stealing?" I asked.

"For all the work we're going to be doing for free?" Astrid's face puckered. "They owe us the chips, cookies, and whatever else we feel like eating, whenever we want."

And with that, Astrid had given me a pretty decent lesson in navigating Christianity. Outside all the Bible Scriptures I hadn't bothered to read. Turned out, any sin could be justified with a certain level of entitlement.

Chapter 6

We met up with the guys by the lake before dinner. They had an annoyingly long trek to get to camp, but I supposed it built character. Or at least better calf muscles. A cool breeze kicked up off the lake and mixed with the scent of wildflowers growing along the trail. A month ago Ethan would've picked some of those for me. Now he made a huge show of picking up Mandy and spinning her around. Hint taken. The younger kids who walked by oohed over the golden couple as I tried not to vomit.

Paul slung an arm over my shoulders. "Can I talk to you for a second?"

"He probably wants to ravish me before dinner," I said to Ethan as Paul dragged me away from the rest of the group.

"You told me you'd explain," Paul said. "I got the gist of it from the way Ethan talked while we unpacked, but I want to hear it from you. Why did you tell him we're dating?"

"It just happened." I rubbed my arms, wishing I'd grabbed

a hoodie before we'd left for dinner. "He wouldn't even look at me until Mandy made some offhand comment like she thought we were together. It made him jealous."

"I got that part." Paul crossed his arms over his chest. "What I don't get is why you're still actively pursuing a guy who A, has a girlfriend, and B, only bothers to notice you when his possessive jackass instincts kick in."

"He said we could talk about us after camp."

Paul closed his eyes and rubbed at his temples. "I'm trying to understand your point of view, and I'm not getting there. He's obviously keeping you on the hook."

"But if he didn't care, it wouldn't matter to him." Like Paul was one to lecture me. He hadn't even noticed when Jessica Hapgood started dating his lab partner to get his attention after they broke up. "Ethan still loves me. He can't stand the sight of me with another guy."

"No." Paul's lips thinned as he exhaled through his nose. "He's jealous because he's an asshole. He wants you to want him for his ego, not because he loves you. If he really cared, he'd either break up with Mandy now or let you go."

"It's not like that. He isn't aggressive or mean like the other guys I've hooked up with. He's awkward and shy and gets picked on at school."

Ethan was the nice guy. That was the whole reason why I'd

dated him in the first place. I was so tired of the guys who acted like they were doing me a favor by being seen with me, like Justin Counter, who only ate lunch with me so I'd pay for his Taco Bell. Or Tyler Volk, who wouldn't even make eye contact with me after I gave him a hand job. Later I found out he told a bunch of people I sucked at it and he had to walk me through the whole thing, so I told everyone his penis had been so small, I had trouble locating it in the first place. I considered us even.

On the other hand, Ethan wasn't hot or athletic or cool. He was kind of a dork. But he held my hand in the halls and picked me flowers and bragged about me to his friends. He got scared after we had sex. His upbringing traumatized him into believing he'd put his immortal soul in jeopardy, and it was hard for me to blame him for that. Burning for all eternity was some serious shit.

"Remember the summer before sixth grade?" Paul asked. "When we picked a bunch of blueberries on my grandfather's farm and set up a roadside stand?"

"Of course." We tried to sell the berries individually, thinking we'd make a huge profit, because we were eleven and didn't understand the concept of supply and demand. "It was really cool of your aunt to buy that one berry from us."

"Our first and only sale." He smiled. "But remember what happened after, when I tried to give you a celebratory kiss on the lips for our first dollar?"

"I punched you in the face."

"Yeah." He rubbed his jaw as he looked off in the distance. "I miss that girl."

"You do? I mean, I didn't know getting punched in the face was your thing, but if you want me to, I'm more than happy to oblige."

"I'm sure you would. Anyway, after that happened, my mom gave me a huge lecture about what it means to respect girls. She hasn't stopped lecturing me since that day. But I doubt Ethan got the same talk from his parents. They're probably the type who pretend sex before marriage doesn't even exist."

"It's a shame all your mom's lectures didn't sink in for you." Paul's mom was a cape-wearing Super Christian, but still a realist in a lot of ways. The number of girls he dated wouldn't have gone by unnoticed.

"Why do you think it didn't sink in? Do you think I don't respect girls?"

The troubled look on his face gave me pause. I'd been giving Paul crap about his meaningless relationships since freshman year, when I overheard Alisha Roth crying in the locker room. He'd dumped her shortly after they'd made out behind the gym during the Halloween dance. It never seemed to bother him before, or maybe I'd never pushed the right buttons. I never did tell him that Alisha had cried. Girl Code kept me from revealing how much damage he'd really done over the years.

"I think you appreciate girls." I had to pick my words carefully, because Paul wasn't heartless. Not on purpose. "But you think sex is just sex, like it's not a big deal to you. Which makes you a little dense when it comes to the emotional stuff."

"You make everything a big deal, and I'm the dense one? Nice try, but look at what all that emotional investment did to you. Now you're stuck faking it with me at Jesus camp." He took my hand, threading his long fingers through mine.

"You're going to do it?" I bounced on my toes. "You're not mad at me?"

"Don't get me wrong—I'm annoyed and frustrated with your total lack of awareness regarding Ethan. But you already told him we're dating. For better or worse, you're stuck with me as your summer boyfriend."

"I could do a lot worse." I wrapped my arms around him, squeezing all my gratitude for his friendship into my hug. I'd be completely lost without him.

As we headed back up the trail, I waved to some of the others from our group who were still talking by the lake. Paul and I made our way into the dining hall, which was packed with kids from ages thirteen to seventeen, and grabbed trays at the front of the long food line. The cavernous room made every clang of silverware rattle off the walls. College-aged counselors hung out in tight-knit groups against the walls as they scanned the crowd for any sign of a burgeoning food fight.

"How did unpacking go for you?" I asked.

"All right. Don't like Jerome. Never liked Ethan. They're bros, of course. Peter doesn't talk much, spends a lot of time in the bathroom. That's pretty much it."

"These next three weeks are going to suck for you, aren't they?"

"Yep." He gave me the kind of grin that reminded me why so many girls at our school asked me if I'd be cool with them asking him out. As if I cared. He wasn't hot in the traditional sense: he was tall and lanky and didn't have a six-pack or muscular arms, his nose was too big for his face, and his eyebrows were a little on the bushy side, but he had a way of looking at someone as if they were the only one in the room.

"I'm sorry," I said. "I don't think I've said that to you yet."

"It's fine." He nudged me forward with the line. "Do you think I'd miss the chance to watch you squirm this summer?"

"You wish you could watch me squirm."

"Don't I know it." His low voice sparked a warm tickle in

my stomach, making my head light. I'd become extra aware of the fresh bread on the line, and my mouth watered. I must've been really hungry.

"I'll have you know I handled myself like a pro during the whole unpacking." I put two rolls and a mini-baguette on my tray. "No one suspects for a second I'm not like them."

"Unpacking and getting to know your cabinmates is like riding a bike with training wheels, and you're about to enter the X Games." He loaded his tray with two sandwiches, an apple, a salad, and two bags of chips.

"Watch me double backflip on a half-pipe for Jesus."

"I'll pray for you." He chuckled.

"No, you won't." I passed the weird meat drowning in brown sauce as I moved down the line. "Speaking of riding a bike . . . what's up with that Scripture you laid down like a boss on Jerome? Do you just remember stuff like that?"

"This environment has a way of recalling it more clearly than back at home, but it's not like I can escape it there, either, with my mom and stepdad determined to save my soul."

"Aww, how sweet are they?"

Paul ignored me and added five cookies to his tray. With the way he ate, his mom probably had to go shopping every day. My parents wouldn't even let him come over for dinner anymore because his appetite didn't fit into the budget spreadsheet.

"Your mom is such a badass, I bet she could save your soul on sheer will alone."

His eyes shone with amusement. "No swearing."

"It says *ass* in the Bible. I'm calling a pass on that one."

"You're thinking of a donkey, unless I missed the part where Jesus referred to his disciples as a group of badasses."

"Language, Mr. Romanowski," said a stern-faced man who had more gel than hair on his head. "We don't tolerate swearing here at this camp, as you'll well remember."

"Yes, sir," Paul mumbled while my entire frame shook from trying to hold in my laughter. "Not funny," he said to me. "If I go, you're screwed."

"Language, Mr. Romanowski." I grabbed two wedges of Swiss and Colby cheese, debated, and took another Colby. We stopped at the drink station, and I stuck my glass under the purple Kool-Aid.

"Don't." Paul put his hand over mine to stop me. "The first rule of Jesus camp is don't drink the Kool-Aid."

"But"—I looked mournfully at the drink station—"it's Purplesaurus Rex."

"It's your funeral."

"Fine. Though if it's really that bad, they shouldn't even have it out." I filled my glass with iced tea, picked up my tray, and headed over to the leadership table.

I plunked down my food next to Ethan, who turned his nose up at my dinner. "I see you're still content to live off bread and cheese."

"It's true." I slathered a generous amount of butter on my roll. "I'd make an excellent old-world prisoner."

"They didn't get cheese." He bumped his arm against mine and smiled. For a brief moment it was like it used to be between us.

"Alas. Guess I'd have to be on my best behavior then."

"Your best would probably still get you a week in the hole." Paul set his tray next to mine and stretched his long legs under the too-short bench.

"That wouldn't be so bad." I licked the butter that had dripped off the end of my bread. "Depending on whose hole I got to spend a week in."

Across the table, Peter snorted, spraying milk across the table.

"Watch yourself." Ethan scowled as he wiped the droplets off his arm.

Paul pushed his glass to the side. "It's milk, dickhead. It won't kill you."

"What's your problem with me, Romanowski?" Ethan looked at me with an odd expression, like he'd bitten into a lemon expecting an apple. "Proverbs 5:20?"

"Careful, Jones. I'd hate for your choirboy face to get busted up." Paul kept his tone eerily calm, but I recognized the threat. I'd only heard Paul talk that way once. To his father.

"Paul, don't." I wrapped a hand around his upper arm. I had no idea what was going on, but the tightness there scared me, like it would take so little to trip his wire. "If you want to go for a walk, I'll walk with you."

Paul held Ethan's gaze, like in a game of chicken, until Ethan turned his attention back to his food. "Forget it, man. I'm not here to fight. I'm trying to get closer to Jesus."

"I'm not. Remember that the next time you breathe a word about CeCe to me."

The Bible verse Ethan had mentioned didn't mean a thing to me, but that unfamiliar warmth spread through me again, and I stuffed a bite of cheese into my mouth to get my jumpy stomach to relax. Across the table, Peter eyed Paul with puppy-like adoration. Poor kid. I bet no one had stood up for him in his life.

Mandy set her tray on the other side of Ethan. Even her sunny persona dampened under the tension at our table. "What did I miss?"

"Nothing," the four of us said at the same time.

Jerome arrived next, and Ethan glared at Peter until he moved down to make room for Sarina and Astrid. The gang was all here. And what a happy little family we made.

Mandy shoveled food into her mouth at steamroller speed. She barely chewed once before she grabbed another forkful of potatoes to stuff in next to the meatloaf she'd inhaled. It was like watching a snake unhinge its jaw and swallow a mouse whole. She caught me staring, put her fork down, and dabbed at her mouth with a napkin.

"How do you stay so skinny when you eat like a lumberjack?" I asked.

Paul coughed and elbowed my ribs.

Mandy didn't seem fazed. "Growing up in a home with eight kids, you learn to grab what you can, when you can. You don't have brothers or sisters?"

"Only child," I said.

"I'm sorry." She had a pitying look on her face, as if literally fighting to get full at every meal was some kind of life experience I missed out on. "We didn't get a chance to talk more about this at the cabin, but I was wondering how you and Paul know Ethan. Do you all go to church together?"

Ethan shot a glance at Paul. "No. Same school."

"That's so neat." Mandy beamed at us. "How fun to have friends from home here."

"I wouldn't call us friends," I said. "More like once-upon-a-time acquaintances."

"Once upon a time, huh?" She took down half her milk in one gulp. "That sounds like a story. I bet it's an interesting one."

"I bet you wouldn't think so if you heard it," I said in a singsong voice.

Astrid narrowed her eyes as she glanced between me and Ethan. I had to watch myself with her. She was a lot sharper than I'd given her credit for. "There will be plenty of time for stories at the testimony bonfire on Sunday night."

I lifted my glass in a toast. "Can't wait."

Once we finished eating, we had to make sure all the trays got picked up and there wasn't a bunch of trash or food left lying out. The kind of crap job reserved for counselors in training. It quickly became clear that "leadership program" really stood for "grunt work."

The actual counselors pushed the benches to the back of the room as the lights dimmed. Large speakers at the front of the stage blared the kind of hip-hop my mom listened to in the car whenever she took control of the radio. Very nineties. Colored strobe lights lit up the dining hall, and everyone started . . . well, I couldn't call it dancing, but they jerked their bodies around in an attempt to dance. Christian girls gone wild.

The stern-faced man who'd given Paul a lecture at the food line took the stage. You'd think a rock god had entered the room. He flashed his game-show-host smile, and all around me people screamed. Mandy had honest-to-God tears streaming down her cheeks. What fresh hell had I gotten myself into?

"Welcome to the X Games!" Paul yelled in my ear.

"What's wrong with everyone? Is this why you didn't want me to drink the Kool-Aid?"

Paul laughed so hard, I could actually hear him above the noise. "That's Pastor Dean up there. He runs the place, and people kind of think he's cool."

"Kind of?" A young girl in the front row fainted and had to be carried away by two counselors. "Good Lord."

"Amen." Paul leaned close enough for me to feel his breath on my neck. "Now are you starting to see why I left all this behind?"

"Give me a few days to process what I'm seeing here. I'm sure I'll get there."

"I'm sure you will." He smirked.

The strobe lights shut off and a single beam shone down upon Pastor Dean, making the generous amount of gel he'd slathered in his hair glow like a halo. "Welcome, new and old friends, to Camp Three SixTeen."

The crowd cheered and I clapped respectably, so as not to stick out.

"We're going to have another wild summer and I can't wait

to hear your testimonies. But before we get into the activities we'll be doing, who here is down with Jesus?"

The earth-shattering scream nearly split my head open.

Pastor Dean held a hand to his ear. "I can't hear you."

"What more does he want?" I asked Paul a moment before another cheer, impossibly louder than the first, shook the walls of the building.

"That's more like it!" Pastor Dean shouted. "You know what I see before me? Warriors. Strong, loud warriors for our man Jesus."

He could've stood there spouting gibberish and the crowd would cheer.

"I thought they said no fighting." I grabbed Paul's arm. "Are they training us to be actual warriors? I didn't sign up for combat."

Astrid shot a quizzical look over her shoulder.

"Might want to save your questions for when we're alone." Paul nodded to Astrid. Soft music started up, and Pastor Dean's voice hummed like slow molasses as he gave praise and thanks to the Lord for gathering us all here. "Just go with it. Act like you're mid-orgasm."

I rolled my eyes. "Oh yeah. As if I know what that's like."

"You don't?" Paul raised his eyebrows. "Isn't that interesting?"

"It's not that interesting in this situation." I glanced around at the people holding their hearts and swaying; they all had one arm raised to the heavens.

"Act like you just took a big bite of cheese." He got so close this time, his cheek brushed mine. "The best cheese you've ever had in your life. Brie."

"Oh God. Yes."

"That's the look." Paul lifted my arm to match everyone else in the room. His fingers trailed around my wrist and I shuddered. "Keep your hand in the air and think of Brie."

If only it had occurred to me to think of Brie while I'd had sex with Ethan. It would've been a whole lot easier to fake it. Astrid gave me another backward glance and, seemingly satisfied with what she saw, continued to sway and cry with everyone else.

Pastor Dean droned on for what felt like an eternity, but the crowd never lost interest. Not even the freshmen fidgeted, and I knew they didn't have thoughts of Brie dancing through their heads to keep them sated. The Lord truly worked in mysterious ways.

"Thank you all for sharing your passion, your love for Jesus," Pastor Dean said. "We've got everyone's favorite, the bonfire testimonies, set for Sunday night. Tomorrow after workshops we've got a fun treasure hunt lined up, so make sure you get plenty of rest tonight and keep your bodies strong for the Lord. It's going to be an exciting summer."

"What's this testimony bonfire thing people keep talking about?" I asked.

"It's where people overshare their most shameful sins that led them on the path to Jesus, thinking they won't be judged, but we all remember the good ones," Paul said. "The last time I was here, there was a guy who said he let his dog lick peanut butter off his—"

I held up a hand. "No need to finish that sentence, thanks. Testimonies sounds horrible. Amusing, but horrible."

"My advice is to listen. Don't be tempted to speak."

"What makes you think I'd be tempted to speak?"

He gave me a bland stare.

"Okay, fine." I mimicked zipping my lips. "No speaking. Just listening."

"Trust me, you don't want to get caught up in testimony night."

Chapter 7

After Pastor Dean left the stage and everyone woke up from their Jesus trance, we helped the counselors put the benches back for breakfast. The camp had a lights-out rule at eleven, and I had no problem with that. My whole body felt like I'd run a five-mile obstacle course. The combination of manual labor and faking the Christian spirit took a lot out of a girl. We finished cleaning up the big house at ten thirty, long after the younger years had already gone back to their cabins, leaving the leadership group alone on the grounds.

The air smelled of woodsmoke and freshly mowed grass. Gravel crunched beneath our feet as we trekked toward our cabins, with only the moonlight to guide us. Though the camp had a strict no phones rule, I wish I'd snuck mine in just to get a picture of the sky. I'd never seen so many stars at once. Not even on my family camping trips, which tended to be in heavily wooded areas without much open space for stargazing.

Paul held my hand, hanging back from the rest of the guys to walk with me. "Do you think there's a chance you can sneak out of your cabin tonight?"

"Sure, why not?" The other girls would probably be too nose deep in their nightly prayers to notice. "What did you have in mind?"

"We need to go over some of the workshops. Sometimes they split up the guys and girls for those, so we should probably figure out how we're going to get you through them without you making an ass of yourself."

I smiled sweetly at him. "Don't you mean making a donkey of myself?"

"That too."

An owl hooted in the distance as we got closer to the cabins. The light from the moon dimmed near the forest. A tight cluster of trees blocked out the stars, leaving the woods a twisted mass of dark leaves and unknown predators. Out here, no one could hear us scream. Except for maybe Jesus.

"Summer camps are a classic setting for all the worst slasher films." I shivered and rubbed my arms. "If there's a masked killer out there, we'll be the first ones to die."

Paul squeezed my hand. "Because neither of us are virgins."

"Might as well write our obituaries now."

He pointed toward the forest. "I'm going to hang a red

T-shirt from a branch on that tree right there, by the lake, the halfway point between our cabins."

"Oh right. That tree right there. So descriptive."

He gave a long-winded sigh. "Just look for the red shirt."

"What happens if we get caught sneaking out?"

"They'll threaten to kick us out. Unless we come clean and confess our sin to our parents, meaning they'll make us tell them we snuck out to have sex."

I'd die a thousand deaths if Pastor Dean forced me to tell my mom I'd had sex with Paul. She practically thought of him as the son she never had. "So. Don't get caught then?"

He nodded. "And if it looks like you might get caught, run for it. They won't hog-tie you or anything. They'll just spend the next few weeks laying the guilt on you."

"Sounds like you have a lot of experience in this area. How much sneaking out did you do with good Christian girls when you were a freshman?"

He wiggled his eyebrows. "Wouldn't you like to know?"

"You are such a pig." I shoved him. "And not even a modest one."

"That might all be true, but I'm still saving your bacon."

"And I'm forever grateful." I leaned up and pressed my lips against his cheek.

Mandy turned around right then and oohed, like the

kiss-track for a cheesy sitcom. If only she knew I'd done a lot more with her boyfriend than a chaste peck on the cheek. Ethan looked at me with regret, which made my heart leap into my throat, and he gave Mandy a real kiss on the lips, which made my heart promptly drop into my stomach again.

"See you at devotions tomorrow?" Mandy sounded as if the breath had been kissed right out of her. I knew the feeling. Literally.

"I'll be waiting for you by the chapel. Until then, I'll dream of you." Ethan used to say corny but sweet things to me all the time. That stung. He kissed Mandy's hand, and Paul pretended to stick his finger down his throat behind him.

The boys left us to go to their side of the lake, and we filed into cabin eight. Sarina immediately went to the bathroom to remove her eye design, which turned out to be more of a process than ladies-in-waiting dressing a queen. I sat cross-legged on the toilet seat with her giant tackle box of makeup as she plucked rhinestones out of her eyebrows. She had ten tubes of lipstick, from cherry red to dark purple; two concealers, both a few shades darker than mine; and twenty eye shadow palettes holding every color under the sun. The second layer of her box held eyeliners, mascara, stick-on jewels, and a bunch of other stuff that had some purpose beyond my comprehension.

"How long does it take you to do your eyes in the morning?"

I picked up a thin black tube and squeezed the end. Sticky gold glitter splattered in my face. "Sorry." I dropped the tube and tried to rub the glitter off, but I just ended up smearing it around.

"It depends," Sarina said. "Today was special, because of the first day of camp. I don't do mermaids or things like that every day. Usually it takes me a half hour."

"I never got the hang of eye shadow." I wore foundation and gloss and sometimes mascara, but every time I tried eye shadow, I ended up making myself look like a drug addict.

"I could show you." Sarina blushed. "No pressure. Only if you want to."

"Are you kidding?" I set the box aside and jumped up. "I'd love it. I don't need anything super-involved, like your mermaids, but it would be cool if I could wear eye shadow without looking like I'd just walked away from a weeklong heroin bender."

"We have an hour free before dinner tomorrow. Let's make it a date."

"Bless you." I flung my arms around her from behind, sending us both tumbling into the rim of the sink. "One day I'll sing songs and write poetry in your honor."

She patted my arm with a bemused expression on her face. "It's not that big of a deal."

"It is to me." Who knew I'd actually learn something of value at this camp? I checked the time on the clock above the towel bar. "Crap. I have to go."

I grabbed a black hoodie out of my open drawer and tugged it over my head.

"Where are you going?" Mandy asked.

"Just meeting Paul for a little bit. Don't wait up, Moms." I dashed out the door, leaving the screen slapping against the wood frame.

Once I made it under the cover of the trees, I found a narrow, not camp-made trail to follow. Generations of boys and girls must've worn this path thin trekking to and from the other side of the lake. Pastor Dean really didn't know teens if he thought a large body of water and some scary trees would be enough to keep hormones in check.

The heavy scent of pine tickled my nose. As I kept my eyes out for Paul's red shirt, I stumbled upon a yellow shirt, a multicolored scarf, what sounded like five or so kids having a small party deeper in the woods, and two counselors buried so deep in each other's faces, they didn't notice me. So much for night patrol and protecting the virtue of innocent Christian children.

I finally made it to the red shirt, where Paul leaned against the trunk of his tree, all out in the open, as if he didn't have a care in the world.

"Run for it if I get caught? Who exactly is supposed to be looking for me?" I asked. "It's like the whole damn camp is out in these woods."

Paul laughed. "I forgot it's always like this the first night. Pastor Dean thinks everyone is so high on his opening ceremony, and not yet bold enough to test the rules, he doesn't set out as many counselors on rat patrol as he should."

"Rat patrol?"

"It's part of the counselor's job to patrol for people at night, and then rat them out."

"Cute name. They should get a brand logo and matching shirts."

"That's part of what I wanted to talk to you about tonight."

I raised an eyebrow. "Branding the rat patrol?"

"No, about this place in general. But first, a story." He took my hand and led me through a tangle of overgrown roots and dense clusters of bushes until we reached a small clearing with a blanket laid out and a couple of cans of Coke. He'd drawn four cats in the dirt with a stick.

"Again with the cats." I sat down and crossed my legs, leaning back on my hands so I could stare up at the sliver of sky that cut through the canopy of pine needles. "Stories are only for the hideout."

"We're away from home, so I had to improvise."

"Are you sure no one else will try to claim this prime spot?"

"The forest is full of prime spots. They'll see my T-shirt and keep a hundred-yard radius away from here. No one wants to stumble upon something they'd feel obligated to report."

"Like a girl conspiring with her best friend to fake being a Christian to win her born-again ex back?"

Paul handed me a Coke and clinked his can with mine. "Exactly."

"Tell me about these cats." I swirled my finger in the dirt, drawing tiny stars above their heads. "Are they part of the lonely boy's troop?"

"No, these are different and infinitely more precious." He lay on his back with his hands laced under his head. "There once was a girl who trusted a terrible beast with her heart."

"Seems like a mistake on the girl's part."

"It was, but it's not her fault. The girl had been looking for someone to hold her heart for a long time. The beast had the ability to shift, and presented himself to the girl as a nice boy. One the girl thought she could trust."

"A tale as old as time."

"As expected, the beast was careless with the girl's heart. His hands were too small and he wasn't fit to hold it, and so he dropped her heart, shattering it into four pieces. But those

80

four pieces didn't turn to dust; they became alley cats with four distinct traits."

"I'm getting you a cat for Christmas."

He shushed me and continued on. "The first cat was angry, hissing at anyone who would pass. The second, feisty and full of fun. The third cried constantly, and the fourth had been injured, but suffered quietly as it stumbled on a broken paw. The cats tried to come together, but were too different and fought all the time, until the day they met a lonely boy."

"I wondered when he'd show up." I smiled over my Coke can. "He's my favorite."

"The lonely boy thought they fought all the time because they were hungry. So he took them back to his house, at great personal risk of having his neighbors call *Pet Hoarders*, since he already had twelve cats."

"The lonely boy is too good for this earth," I said.

"Eventually the feisty cat and the angry cat became one, and the boy found a cheetah in their place. It was then the girl came to collect the pieces of her heart, but she thought the cheetah was better and stronger, so she took only that and left her other two pieces behind. But the cheetah made the girl fast and prone to rash decisions. To the boy, all the cats were valuable, and the girl's heart wouldn't be right without them."

I used the stick to draw a frowning face in the dirt.

"It gets better," he said. "Because after a series of bad choices, the girl came to realize the parts of herself she rejected made her who she was, and so she comforted the crier and bandaged the cat with too much pride. They became whole with the others, and she gave a mighty roar as her heart transformed once again. For she'd always had the heart of a lioness; she just had to put the broken pieces back together."

"You were right." I rested my hand on his cheek. "It did get better. The girl might not be whole yet, but she's finding her way."

"I have no doubt she will."

"Did you still want to cover camp activities?" I yawned as the end of the day zapped the last of my energy. "What's this devotions thing we have first thing in the morning, and can we skip it?"

"It's church. As I recall, you're pretty comfortable sleeping there." He smirked.

"Ha." I shot him a dirty look. "What else should I expect tomorrow?"

"We'll get the workshop schedules at breakfast. Some of them are split up by gender."

"Gross. What if you're non-binary?"

Paul gave me a pointed look. "I think you know the answer to that."

"I think I hate this place."

"I think it's your fault we're here."

"I think you should shut up now." I gave him a light shove. "And I suppose I shouldn't talk during these workshops?"

"There's not a lot of talking involved. It's more like a lecture. Just keep in mind these are Christian lectures, and they might say some things you don't agree with."

"That's fine. Sounds like another opportunity to sleep." I waved away a mosquito that buzzed past my ear. "They'd probably kick me out if they knew I lied about all my churchy knowledge on my application."

"They won't kick you out for not knowing as much Scripture as they do." Paul nudged my arm. "But they might try to baptize you."

"Joke's on them. I took care of that before we came."

"You? Got baptized?" Paul raised his eyes to the heavens and whispered a prayer to a God he didn't believe in. "Where did this take place?"

"You have to promise not to laugh in my face."

Paul held out his pinkie. "Swear."

I hooked my pinkie through his. "Okay, so you know that guy who hangs out on Wilson and East? The one with the long beard who wears a THE END IS NEAR sandwich board?"

"I think I can see where this is going." Paul's lips twitched, and I gave him a stern look.

"Turns out he's an ordained minister."

"You don't say?" His dark eyes sparkled in the dim moonlight.

"You promised." I shook my finger at him. "Anyway, I filled up a cup of tap water at the gas station across the street and paid him five bucks to bless it and dump it on my head."

Paul held up his hand. "I'll be right back."

He walked around to the other side of a pine tree and laughed so hard, he shook a hawk out of the branches. It took off into the night with a shriek. After a good five minutes of losing it at my expense, he sat back down, his eyes still glistening with tears.

I crossed my arms. "You pinkie swore."

"I swore I wouldn't laugh in your face." He wiped his cheeks with the sleeve of his shirt. "On a more serious note, Gas Station Holy Water would be a great band name."

"This is why I didn't tell you," I muttered.

"Come on." He chuckled under his breath but, catching the look on my face, quickly straightened his features. "Do you want to know about the treasure hunt?"

"Yes, tell me everything." I sat up, happy to have a distraction from the ridiculous lengths I'd gone to for a religion I had no intention of actually joining.

"The teams are split up by school year, and they assign pairs by random draw."

"Gasp." I put my hand over my heart. "You mean boys and girls are actually allowed to be alone with each other? How scandalous."

"The whole camp participates. I wouldn't call that 'alone.' Each team has to find an object related to a Bible passage. Once they find it, they share with their partner what that passage means to them. It's supposed to help campers get to know each other."

"Snooze." And here I thought I'd get to do one activity where I didn't have to pretend to know Scripture. "Does everything have to be about the Bible?"

"It's Jesus camp. Were you expecting beer pong?"

"No, but it would've been cool if they'd just done a regular old treasure hunt."

"The treasure is supposed to be finding meaning in Christ's teachings."

"I'd rather have a handful of colored beads and some of those plastic gold coins." I yawned again. "Thanks for filling me in."

"It's going to be an early morning. Let's go." He helped me to my feet and grabbed his blanket and empty Coke cans.

We stepped out of the clearing, and the two counselors who'd gotten distracted appeared to be back on patrol. Paul grabbed me and tucked us behind a wide tree trunk as the crackle of their walkie-talkies passed. He put his finger to his lips, then pointed toward my cabin and took off running in the opposite direction, making enough noise to send the counselors crashing through the bushes after him. Which left the way clear for me.

As far as fake boyfriends went, I could've done a hell of a lot worse.

Chapter 8

I was the last one out of my cabin at ten to seven. It had been a weird night. I kept waking up with a start after a series of dreams that would've made my cabinmates blush. I couldn't recall most of the details, but Paul was there, and the feeling stuck with me when I woke. My REM cycle must not have gotten the message that our dating was just for show.

Outside, the rising sun burned low in the sky, casting the camp in a hazy orange glow. A robin swooped low over my head before disappearing into the woods. Morning dew clung to the grass along the trail, wetting my ankles as I made my way to the chapel.

Paul met me outside the doors. His freshly showered hair dripped onto his shoulders. "How did you sleep?"

"Fine." My cheeks grew hot as the sensations from my dreams flooded into me again. "Other than not getting enough. Did you get away last night?"

"Please. I'm offended you'd even ask."

We headed inside. The chapel smelled like pine cleaner and old people, and we took a seat in the back. Most of the camp had already arrived. Mandy and Ethan sat up front, where the light shone on their angelic heads like something out of a Michelangelo painting.

I pointed to a large portrait at the front of the chapel. "Who's that supposed to be?"

"You're kidding me, right?" Paul looked at me like I had a wad of spinach stuck in my teeth. "How have you never seen a picture of Jesus before?"

"I've seen plenty of pictures of Jesus, thanks. That is not Jesus." This portrait had dark blond hair and blue eyes, which was just wrong, and the kind of five-o'clock shadow that belonged in an eighties music video. "I think that guy used to do our landscaping."

Back when we had a garden and a lot more debt. My mom tried to keep it alive, but she got bored once she found out how much work it took to maintain.

Paul tilted his head. "I think my mom dated him before she met Brad."

"Probably because she thought he looked like Jesus."

A younger girl in the pew three rows ahead of us turned around and gave us a dirty look. I wiped the smile off my face and tried to appear as pious as one could at seven in the morning. Paul leaned back with his hands behind his head. Somehow we'd become the burnouts at the back of the class, the kind who'd carve skulls into their desks.

Pastor Dean took the podium to charm the true believers with all his Godly wisdom. Ten minutes in, my eyes started to droop, but I did manage to catch pieces of him trying to relate ancient passages to the life of a modern teenager. Not in a way that made sense to me. Paul told me if anyone asked my thoughts, to just pick a random sin and ponder what Jesus would do.

Paul tapped me on the forehead. "You're snoring."

"I wasn't even sleeping, just resting my eyes," I whispered.

Pastor Dean mentioned Paul, which got my attention. I nudged him. "He just said your name. Are you supposed to go up there?"

He gave me a funny look. "He's talking about Paul the Apostle."

"Sorry." I stifled a yawn. "I didn't know there was a dude named Paul in the Bible."

"Where do you think my parents got my name?"

"I don't know. I thought your mom was from the Midwest or something."

He snorted, and I elbowed him in the ribs.

Judging from the abundance of empty space, Pastor Dean didn't command the head count he probably needed to keep him rolling in hair gel and strobe lights. At the end of the sermon we all shuffled out, standing around in groups while we waited to be called in for breakfast. Apparently we were supposed to chat about what we took away from the sermon. My main takeaway had been to get more sleep if I had to suffer through that every morning.

"What did you think, CeCe?" Astrid gave me an encouraging smile. "I'm always fascinated with how new people interpret Pastor Dean's take on backsliding."

"Um . . ." I glanced at Paul. "Like take cocaine dealers, for example. What would Jesus do about the dealers? I think he would minister them, put them on the righteous path, and without the dealers, it's easier for the addicts not to backslide into a life of drugs and stuff."

The group stared at me in stunned silence. Ethan jerked his chin at Jerome, as if the two shared a joke and I was the punch line. Paul had his hand over his mouth, like he was trying to keep from laughing. Not exactly the response I'd hoped for, but I doubted any of them would've performed better under pressure.

"Sure." Astrid's baby-doll face puckered. "That's certainly one way to look at it."

"Can I talk to you for a second?" Paul took my arm and led

me to the other side of the chapel, checking to make sure we were alone. "Coke dealers?"

"You told me to pick a random sin and ponder." I crossed my arms. "You know I can't stand to be put on the spot."

"When I said pick a random sin, I had something a little tamer in mind. Rock music, R-rated movies, things like that."

I twirled my wrist. "Then you should've clarified."

"I swear, this little experiment of yours is going to kill me." He ran his hands through his hair. "If you want to fix this, mention the sermon at breakfast. Say something about how the type of media we consume can influence the decisions we make on a daily basis, and you think Pastor Dean has the right idea about garbage in and garbage out."

"And what idea is that?" Might as well be fully prepared. Who knew what would be sprung on me next?

"If you take garbage in—music with sexual messages, or violent video games—you'll regurgitate those messages in your thoughts and speech. Garbage out."

"That's the dumbest thing I've ever heard. That's like saying people aren't capable of independent thought. And isn't there a shit ton of sex and violence in the Bible?"

A smile quirked his lips. "Why are you arguing this with me? I'm not telling you what *I* believe; I'm telling you what *they* believe."

"Right." I put my hand on his arm. "When you talk like that, in this place, it's hard for me to remember you're not one of them."

"That's not comforting."

"I know. I'm sorry." When Paul's father left his family, I didn't think it would be possible to hate him more, but every time I saw what his leaving did to Paul, the way it wrecked everything he used to believe with his whole heart, I hated the man tenfold.

We headed into the dining hall and grabbed our trays like we had for dinner, but breakfast looked way more appealing. I got pancakes with a side of bacon, and another huge wedge of Colby cheese. It was worth it to come here for the cheese alone.

We went back to our table, where the counselors had already dropped off a stack of schedules. The workshops we could attend had titles like "Waiting for Marriage" (what a joke), "Carrying the Message" (probably for people who knew what the message was supposed to be), and "Building an Effective Youth Group", with Astrid leading.

I waved the paper in front of her. "You're teaching a workshop? That's so cool."

She beamed with pride. "I'm the youngest in camp history to be invited to teach."

"She's going to be the best teacher too." Mandy gave her a side squeeze. "She built her own church's youth group from ten kids in a basement to an entire movement in her town. She's an example to us all."

"I'm so going to that one." I turned to Paul. "What do you think?"

"I don't know." He rubbed his jaw. "Waiting for Marriage sounds pretty appealing."

"Ha. Ha." I laid my head on his shoulder. "That's not what you said last night."

Across the table, Peter's eyes popped out as he looked between the two of us. "Did you guys, you know? When you snuck out last night?"

Paul shook his head. "Sorry, my man. A gentleman never kisses and tells."

"There's a gentleman here?" I looked around. "Where?"

Paul put his arm around my waist and pulled me closer. "You're looking at him, sweetie bonbon."

"Oh, honeycomb caramel bear, how could I have forsaken you? Of course you're the gentleman caller I've dreamed of my whole life."

He took a spot of whipped cream from his hot chocolate and dabbed it on my nose. "It's okay, candy cane gummy tart. I still love you."

I swiped the rest of the whipped cream off his drink and rubbed it into his cheek. "I don't deserve you, peanut brittle sugar lump."

"There is something seriously wrong with you two," Jerome said.

Paul grabbed a napkin and cleaned up his cheek. "You're going to pay for that one later."

I wrinkled my nose at him. "The whipped cream or the sugar lump nickname?"

"Both."

Ethan cleared his throat, his face twisted in a scowl. "You two could probably use the Waiting for Marriage workshop for real."

I narrowed my eyes. "Why don't you lead the way?"

Mandy giggled, but not her usual bell-like giggle. This one was more nervous and strangled. "Why don't we all go to Astrid's workshop? It's a great way to support her, and we already know we should wait for marriage."

"I think that's a great idea," I said. "All in favor of supporting Astrid, raise your hand."

Everyone at the table, including Astrid, raised their hand. I'd expected Peter to just pick whatever workshop didn't include Jerome, but his hero worship for Paul far outweighed his fear of his camp bullies.

After helping the staff clean up the dining room, ticking another half hour off my community service, we followed Astrid like the Pied Piper to one of the log circles out by the lake. Ethan and Mandy shared a log, overlapping their pinkies, and it didn't even bother me. Which I'd keep telling myself until I believed it. I had to figure out how to deal, and denial seemed like a good place to start. In another life, I could've even seen myself as friends with Mandy. She saw the positive in everything, and I could've used more positive thinking.

I waited for Ethan to turn his gaze in our direction, then laid my head on Paul's shoulder. Playing the part of the good fake boyfriend, Paul put his arm around my waist and let his fingers skim my side, just under the hem of my T-shirt. I gasped as little goose bumps shivered along my skin and the sensations from my dreams last night came flooding back. Paul gave me a smug smile. I'd gotten so distracted, I'd forgotten to check Ethan's reaction. All this fake-dating was confusing my subconscious, but I was still in control and I needed to stay on task. I scooted an inch away from Paul and he put his arm back at his side.

Astrid shared her story, how she and a couple of friends would go to the mall and look for kids hanging out by themselves. The ones who looked lost. And she'd give them a place to call home, even if they didn't think of themselves as Christians to begin with.

I tilted my head toward Paul. "Is she calling the people she recruited sheep?"

"No, she's talking about the good shepherd, how he left his flock to search for the one lost lamb, how that lamb mattered as much to him as the rest."

"Oh." I knotted my fingers together. "So she is calling them sheep."

"It's a parable. When Jesus took a bunch of shit from religious leaders for dining with sinners, it's how he told them to shove it."

"No way." I leaned back on my hands in the grass. "That Jesus was one cool dude."

"Yes, he was."

I raised my eyebrows at Paul.

"Don't give me that look. I can respect Jesus and still not buy into the whole Son of God thing. If only he could see what some have done in his name."

"Not Astrid, though." I nodded to her. "She dines with sinners."

"Yeah. She's pretty cool too."

We listened to the rest of Astrid's workshop in silence. While I didn't really agree with the way she picked kids off who were lonely and in need of something—it felt too much like recruiting for a cult—she invited them without demanding they call themselves Christians first. She let them find their faith or not find it. At the end of the day, she welcomed everyone.

While the rest of the group headed off to get ready for the treasure hunt, I hung back and pulled Astrid aside. "That was really amazing."

"Thank you." She blushed. "I was so nervous. Could you tell?"

"Not at all. You're a total pro at this." I lowered my voice. "Between you and me, your workshop was the first thing here that didn't put me in a coma."

She laughed. "You're a trip, you know that, right?"

"What do you mean?" I might've revealed a bit too much. Thoughts of being exposed made my stomach churn—Pastor Dean would make me leave, Ethan would know I hadn't really come here to get closer to the Lord. The humiliation would be more than I could handle.

"Look, I know you're not as up on this stuff as the rest of us, and that's okay. I've seen a lot of girls like you come through my youth group."

I crossed my arms. "What do you mean by girls like me?"

"Girls who are looking for something. Girls who are wandering and haven't found their place yet." She put her arm around my shoulders. "Maybe you're grappling with the idea of faith, or maybe you have something else going on, but you obviously came here for a reason. I think we have a responsibility to help you find what you lost."

I very much doubted she'd agree if she knew what I'd come to retrieve. "You're not going to say anything to Pastor Dean, are you? About me maybe having fudged how devout I was to get a spot here this summer?"

"That's between you and Jesus."

Was that a guilt trip? It felt like one of those guilt trips Paul talked about. Not that it would work on me, but if I didn't already think Jesus could strike me down for a million other infractions, I might've been miffed.

"I'm not saying that in a backhanded way." Her soothing tone reminded me of warm honey over biscuits. "No judgment here. Your mind may plant your steps, but the Lord will lead your way. That's Proverbs 16:9."

"You sound like Paul."

"He's a good egg." She gave me the kind of smile that held all the secrets she'd take to her grave. No wonder she'd been able to build her youth group from the ground up. She had a way of gaining trust without being manipulative.

We walked to the center of camp, where Pastor Dean stood on an outdoor stage, his helmet hair glistening in the afternoon sun. Four glass jars sat on a table before him, one for each school year, filled with the names of all the campers. The freshman and sophomore jars held a lot more scraps of paper than the junior and senior ones.

After Pastor Dean pulled two names, he'd hand the pair a piece of paper and motion them to follow the others up to the woods. After going through the younger years, only eight of us seniors remained. He pulled Paul's name first, and I held my breath. A quick stab of disappointment followed when he got paired up with Peter. Who was supposed to help me cheat my way through finding the meaning in Christ's teachings now?

Pastor Dean called Ethan's name, and reached into the jar once more. "Francine Wells. Come on up and get your clue."

Chapter 9

I'd been so preoccupied with getting paired up with Paul, I'd totally forgotten about Ethan. My entire reason for being here. He gave me a shy smile, the kind he'd given me that day I helped him up in the hall, and my heart stuttered.

I took the clue, written on plain paper dipped in tea to make it look old, and unrolled it. We had to find a rock shaped like a heart. Great. I didn't have a clue how to relate that to the Bible. Too bad we didn't get a clue that required us to find two animals, because Noah's Ark was the only story I knew enough about to fake my way through.

We joined the others waiting, and Paul came over. "What did you get?"

"A heart-shaped rock." I held my paper out to him. "What am I supposed to do?"

"That's an easy one. Matthew 6:21: 'For where your treasure is, there will your heart be also.'" When I shook my head, he continued on. "It means if you make God your treasure, your heart will lead you to Heaven."

"I think I can fumble my way through that. Thanks."

I joined Ethan at our starting point near the edge of the woods, and Pastor Dean blew his whistle. Everyone spread out, crashing through the brush and over trails, looking for the item on their list. These kids took "finding meaning in Christ's teachings" pretty seriously.

Ethan led the way into the woods. Today he wore a Camp Three SixTeen T-shirt, which was sadly the best shirt in his wardrobe, but he also wore black socks with sandals. It's like he couldn't help but find the worst combination of clothes to string together.

"How are you fitting in here?" he asked.

"Fine. Astrid's workshop was pretty amazing."

"I didn't care for it." He picked up a lumpy rock and turned it over, rejecting it for not being heart-shaped enough, I guess. "She's a little too progressive for my taste."

"What's wrong with that?" How could he not like Astrid's workshop but stay awake through the snoozefest sermon this morning? I didn't get how his brain was wired.

"You probably wouldn't understand, since you're more the progressive type too." He made it sound like an insult, which immediately put my back up.

"She lets anyone join her youth group, and she doesn't judge them or turn them away if they aren't perfect Christians. If you think that's too progressive, I've got some really bad news for you about your man Jesus."

"My man Jesus, but not yours?" He raised an eyebrow.

"You know what I mean." I dug my nails into my palm and turned away from him. I had to be a little more careful with my words.

We walked farther into the woods, kicking over leaves and picking up various rocks, but none shaped like a heart. And Paul said this was an easy one. A bee landed on Ethan's arm and he freaked out. Like full-on-flailing, high-pitched-scream freak-out.

"You okay?" I tried not to let the secondhand embarrassment show on my face.

"I hate bees." He shuddered.

"I got that."

Awkward silence.

This was so uncomfortable. I didn't even know how to talk to him anymore. We'd had tons of meaningful conversations when we dated. He talked about church a lot, and I nodded and showed my support in the right places. None of my friends talked with their boyfriends about big-picture stuff like religion and God and life. But now that I was trying to make his stuff my stuff too, I had no idea what to say about it all.

"I bet Jesus loves bees," I said. "Without them, we'd all starve."

"Why do you do that?" The annoyance in his tone made me look around for someone else, even though we'd wandered away from the main group.

"Do what?"

"You have to be sarcastic about everything. And you wonder why things didn't work out between us." He picked up a heart-shaped rock and slapped it into my palm. "I'll pray for you, but I think we should stay away from each other."

"Hold on." I grabbed the back of his shirt. "You don't get to dump something like that on me and walk away. I wasn't being sarcastic. Bees flower most of the food we eat."

Was I really arguing about bees?

"That's not the point." He threw his hands in the air. "I don't care about the stupid bees."

"It sure looked like you cared when that one landed on you." He was making less sense than the night he'd tried to explain the born-again thing to me. "And what do you mean by 'you wonder why things didn't work out between us'?"

Pity filled his eyes, and I had to look away. I wanted him to see we could work, not to make him feel sorry for me. I didn't want his sorrys. I'd gotten enough of those the night he ended things.

"You told me you broke up with me so Jesus could restore your virginal heart." I handed the rock back to him. I didn't need this stone heart when I already had one of my own.

"I did." The pity in his tone turned to regret, but it felt faker than my devotion to the Lord. "But you have to admit, we probably would've broken up anyway."

A black cloud of dread hovered over me. "What are you talking about?"

"You must've known too." He rested a hand on my shoulder, then quickly pulled it away as if I'd burned him. "I belong with someone like Mandy."

I didn't know we'd break up. If I'd known from the start we never would've worked, I would've saved myself for someone else. Someone who gave a damn.

"Why did you have sex with me then?" If I had more to give, I might've started crying, but he'd taken it all, leaving me to wring out my leftover emotions like a dry sponge.

"I was enamored with you." Who even talked like that? "None of the girls I wanted to date would give me the time of day, but then you came along, fun and full of life."

And I'd felt all those things when I'd been with him. I could've spent hours watching him watch me, just to see the person I didn't believe I could be reflected back. "What changed? When did you stop seeing me that way?"

"I still see you that way." He smiled, but it didn't touch his eyes. I couldn't see myself there anymore, no matter how bad I wanted to. "But every time I talked about a sermon that got me really excited, I could tell you were bored."

"I'm here now. Doing this Jesus thing." Though I wasn't sure if it was for him or how he'd made me feel, or where the line between those two points existed. "Did you love me?"

His nostrils twitched. "That's a big question."

"No. It's a simple question. Either you did"—I held out one hand—"or you didn't." I held out the other hand and weighed them up and down. "Which one is it?"

"Don't do this. Don't make me the bad guy."

"How are you not the bad guy?" I shouted. "You told me you loved me, and now it's pretty obvious you don't want to say you lied. You took my virginity, knowing full well you had no intention of trying to make our relationship work for the long term. If you're not the bad guy, then who are you? Because I sure as shit don't know."

We had a lot of differences. Like, a lot. But I'd been willing to see past them, to be who he wanted, but he hadn't been willing to meet me halfway. He hadn't even been willing to stop wearing black socks with sandals.

"I'm done here. You're being irrational." He turned around and walked away.

"Fine. Go." All my hurt transformed, became something else. Something mean and angry. "But guess what? You're not a virgin, born-again or otherwise."

He glanced back at me.

"That's right. I said it. Jesus can't restore your virginity, because he's not the one who took it. I am. And I'm keeping it in a box with your dead dog Scout and your father's approval and all those other things you're never going to get back."

He shook his head, like I was the sad and desperate girl I'd tried so hard to hide. As he disappeared between a thick tangle of trees, I plopped down on a nearby log and rubbed my numb cheeks. I'd not only let the cat out of the bag, I'd flung the bag around before I opened it, releasing all the claws and teeth. This hadn't been why I'd come here, but all my reasons made less and less sense when I couldn't find the girl I wanted to be in Ethan. Without that, all I was left with was him, and I found that thought oddly depressing.

Leaves whipped together as Jerome cut through a cluster of small trees. He tripped over a root and sprawled out on the ground in front of me. Probably because he hadn't been able to see his tiny legs under his muscular upper body. He rose to his feet, his face red as he swept dirt and pine needles off his shirt.

"Are you okay?" I asked, not really caring.

"Yeah." He scratched his head, like he wasn't sure how

he'd gotten here. "Where's Ethan? I thought you two were partnered up?"

"He ditched me. Not that it matters to you."

"You don't like me. Why?" Jerome took a seat on the log, and I scooted away from him.

"Because you were shitty to Paul on the first day, and you're bros with Ethan."

His face screwed up, like he'd expected me to deny it. He clearly didn't know me very well. "That's a reason, but just so you know, I apologized to Paul, and Ethan isn't my bro."

"Sure he's not." I checked my nails for old polish I could scrape off. I wasn't in the mood to make nice. "That's why you two are always hanging out."

"I'm just trying to hang out with Sarina, and he's trying to hang out with Mandy, and those two are always together. We're cool, but we're not tight. Not like the girls."

"This has been fun, but I should get back, since my partner ditched me and all." I stood and brushed chips of old log off my shorts.

"I'm sorry he ditched you, and for whatever he did to you back home."

I spun around. "Did he say something to you?"

"No, but I get the feeling you two weren't really friends." He stuck out his hand, and I regarded him with caution.

"I made a bad impression when we first met, but I hope we can start over. Sarina speaks highly of you, and her opinion means a lot to me."

"I guess we can start over." I took his hand. "I'm CeCe. Nice to meet you."

"I'm Jerome. Nice to meet you too."

Pastor Dean's whistle blew in the distance, calling us back, and Jerome walked with me out of the woods. Ethan and I hadn't completed the task in the way it was meant, but we'd certainly revealed a lot more about each other than we ever had before. As soon as we hit the camp grounds again, I joined Peter and Paul near the stage.

"How did it go?" Paul asked. "Did you use the Matthew passage?"

"We didn't get around to it. I sort of yelled at him and he left mad."

Paul laughed. "I'm going to need to hear this story."

"It's not a very good one. I have to get to the nurse's station for my community service hours. I'll catch you later."

Ethan slung his arm around Mandy as he laughed with Sarina and Jerome. He caught my eye, and his expression turned somber. Whatever I'd been hoping to find when I came to camp didn't match my reality. The Ethan I knew—the one who questioned his upbringing and didn't want to be as emotionally detached as his father—had been replaced by this cold imposter.

But the real him must've been in there somewhere. He had to be.

Sarina set four brushes in front of me on our bathroom sink, and it felt very much like trying to guess which fork to use in a fancy restaurant. "Every eye shadow needs a good base."

Astrid sat on the edge of the bathtub, pen in hand. She'd dubbed herself the official record keeper, and promised to take notes on each step, so I'd be able to reference them at a later date. Learning how to do eye makeup had become a very complex endeavor.

Sarina smeared a creamy liquid over my eyelids. Her own eye shadow was a little simpler than the mermaids', but still stunning. The inside of her lid started as a shimmery white, and slowly blended to a sparkly navy on the outside.

She got out a neutral palette with shades ranging from cream to dark brown. "This is for everyday wear. Cover your whole lid with the lightest shade first."

"Did you get that?" I asked Astrid.

"Yep. Full lid, lightest color."

Sarina took the next thickest brush and dipped it in the next darkest color. "You want to draw a C, to about the halfway point." She moved the brush between my crease and back down to my lower lid, swooping it back again, like drawing a letter C on my eye. "The trick is making your eyes look bigger by having the darker colors on the outside."

"Write that down," I told Astrid.

"I'm writing everything down. You don't have to keep reminding me."

Sarina took the smallest brush and dabbed it in the darkest brown. "Draw another C over the last one, but smaller." She flicked it around the outside corner of my eye. "It should be half the size of the first C. Now blend." She took a Q-tip and rubbed it around on the C. "What do you think?"

I turned my head all different angles to see it properly. I'd always considered my brown eyes to be plain, but she'd made them come alive. They'd somehow become deeper, and the color sparkled with a hint of copper. "You're a miracle worker."

I'd never had nice eye shadow in my life. Turned out you couldn't just mash the nearest color to your face and expect decent results. Sarina had a soft, light voice and had made the explanations so simple. No wonder she had such a huge YouTube following.

"What's the last brush for?" I asked.

"Shimmer, if you want it." She took out a small single palette with the lightest of pink powders and dipped the last brush in. She pushed it into the corner of my inner eyelid and blended it outward, adding just a touch of light to my eyes.

She also taught me how to use my eyeliner to help make my eyes look bigger, and how to use a bristled brush to add definition to my eyebrows. It had been so long since I'd had a fun, chill-out-with-the-girls day. This was what I needed.

"Okay, everyone out." Sarina waved her hands to shoo us toward the door. "I had the broccoli salad for lunch, and it's finally catching up to me."

Sometimes they were a little too honest around here.

Astrid ripped out the notebook paper with all my eye makeup instructions and put her notebook back on her shelf. "This is why she should've taken the bed by the bathroom."

"Are you running another workshop tomorrow?" I asked.

"Yep. My high school requires twenty hours of community service to graduate too, and leading workshops is way better than some of the jobs they hand out around here."

"Tell me about it." I practically had to force Motrin on a girl at the nurse's station when she swore up and down her menstrual cramps were punishment for lustful thoughts. "I'm going to get some air."

I went outside to find Mandy on the front steps, twirling a stem of Queen Anne's lace between her fingers. It grew all over the boys' side of the lake.

"Nice flower." I took a seat beside her on the steps.

She gave me a faint smile. "Ethan gave it to me."

The knot around my heart tightened. As I spent more time on Ethan's ground, the less I knew which version of him was true. Maybe he'd been an ass all along, dormant while he was an outsider at school. Or maybe this environment brought out the worst in him. I used to think he was a good boyfriend, a romantic, because he picked me flowers and held my hand in public, but now that he was doing all those things for someone else, I didn't feel so special anymore.

"You don't seem happy." When her head shot up, I nodded to the Queen Anne's lace. "With the flower, I mean."

"No, it's a nice gesture." She sighed and set it to the side. "I don't know. He's felt different these past few days."

"How so?" I didn't really want to know, but on the other hand, I really did.

"Last summer we were on the same page about everything. Life, family, our faith, but lately . . . I don't know."

"Does it feel like he's a different person?" Because it certainly felt that way to me.

"Yeah. He's meaner and more jaded, about life in general. Maybe public school changed him?"

"Is he mean to you?" Something protective rose up inside me for Mandy, this girl I shouldn't care one iota about. I'd come here to steal her boyfriend, for crying out loud. But still. I felt a certain amount of loyalty toward her. The kind of kinship that came from really, truly understanding how someone else felt.

"Nothing like that. He's just so condescending. I don't even think he realizes he does it, but he acts like he's going to save me from my simple, homeschooled life. Without considering that I like my life. I love my family." When her bright eyes dimmed, I wanted to punch Ethan, not just for her or me, but for every girl who'd ever been made to feel like she was less than some guy.

"Doesn't he know you already have a savior?" I pointed to the sky.

She smiled and bumped my shoulder. "I'm glad you're here."

"I'm glad I'm here too." And for the first time, I actually meant it. "For what it's worth, guys are good at crafting personas if they want something, but trust your gut. You're a lot smarter than he gives you credit for."

"Thanks, sweetie bonbon."

I groaned. "I'm never going to live that down, am I?"

"Nope. Sorry." She patted my knee. "You lucked out and got one of the good ones."

Once she closed the door behind me, I whispered, "If only you knew how wrong you are."

Chapter 10

Four days into camp, and I still hadn't found my rhythm. The people were friendly enough—I actually enjoyed hanging out with my cabin—but this wasn't my world. I missed my other friends and my parents. If I tried to go home, though, my parents would be furious. They used to count the grapes left in my lunch box and deduct the value from my allowance to teach me to not be wasteful. They'd budgeted my absence down to the penny, and the nonrefundable check had already cleared.

Plus, I had my very limited supply of pride to consider. Finding the Ethan I knew was proving more difficult than I'd expected. He'd barely made eye contact with me since our blowup in the woods, and he made it a point to pick workshops I wouldn't be in, but I still cared. I hated that part of myself. I wanted to have fun, make harmless mistakes, and flirt with Christian boys. I wanted to feel something other than the persistent ache that buried itself in my heart and throbbed whenever I thought about Ethan.

After putting in my time at the nurse's station, I finally had a free afternoon to do whatever I wanted. Sarina had lifeguard duty, and I told her I'd stop down at the lake to save her from perpetual boredom. Mandy had built up the Blob so much on the ride over, I was eager to get a crack at it. Maybe some fun in the sun could chase away my gloom.

Halfway down the path to the lake, a snub-nosed college-aged counselor with blunt bangs stopped me. "What do you think you're doing?"

"Going swimming?" Was that not allowed? Everyone else was down at the lake.

"Not in that you're not." She motioned to my yellow-and-teal polka-dot bikini. "No two-piece swimsuits allowed at camp."

"Seriously?" I might've skimmed over that portion of the handbook. "Why not?"

"We dress modestly here, and if you'll remember your Scripture, I might direct you to Matthew 5:28."

I didn't need to look it up to know it probably had something to do with girls being the sole ones to blame for all the sinful boners of the world. "I didn't bring anything else."

"Come with me. We have something more appropriate in our extras pile." As I followed her in the opposite direction of the lake, she turned back to me. "Wrap that towel around yourself.

We don't need any of the boys running into you like that."

I'd lost my virginity in the back of a pickup truck to a guy who blamed me for his detour off the path of righteousness, and in a handful of words, this counselor had made me feel more ashamed of my body than I had when Ethan told me why we had to break up. Clutching my towel in a tight knot, I held it to my chest. My fingernails dug into my soft skin. In her eyes, it wasn't the sex that made me dirty; it was me. Like my very existence in a female form had to be covered up, hidden away. One of several reasons I could add to the growing pile of why I'd never be a Christian.

Paul crossed the path in front of us and stopped short. He had his towel around his neck, and his board shorts hung off his narrow hips. He'd gotten a couple of chest hairs since last summer, and the thought made me want to laugh. Or cry. Or cry-laugh.

"What's going on?" He must've seen something in my expression because his brows drew together in concern. "Are you okay?"

"Oh, you know." I kept my tone light, but I couldn't fool Paul. "Can't wear a two-piece to Jesus camp, because I guess the sight of a girl's stomach turns all the boys into horny werewolves. But guys can walk around shirtless with their nipples on full display."

The counselor grunted her disapproval. I'm sure she was

just itching to report this interaction to Pastor Dean. Not that I actually gave a crap anymore.

Paul looked between me and the counselor, and though he didn't say it out loud, I could practically hear him in my head saying, *See? This is what they're like. This is why I don't affiliate myself with them.* Instead he said, "I'll come with you."

"You most certainly will not." The counselor stood between us.

"Not to watch her change—sheesh, get your mind out of the gutter," Paul said, and satisfaction fluttered briefly inside me as the counselor's face turned red. "I'll wait outside until you're ready and we'll go down to the lake together."

"I suppose that's fine," the counselor said, as if she'd already tried and failed to think of an excuse for why that wouldn't be fine at all.

"It should be fine," I said. "He's seen me in less than this."

I dropped the towel to my feet. Paul swallowed hard as a soft light touched his eyes. We were in full-on fake relationship mode, and pretending with Paul while pissing off this counselor was the only thing that had made me feel good since my blowup with Ethan in the woods.

"Pick that towel back up," the counselor said as her gaze kept darting to the front of Paul's shorts. "Pastor Dean is going to hear about this."

"But this is my boyfriend." I stepped up to Paul and ran my hands down his chest. "I'm sure he doesn't mind what I wear to the lake. Do you, sugar lump?"

Paul wrapped an arm around the small of my back and pulled me roughly against him, where the line between real and pretend started to blur. "I think you look perfect."

There was a hard edge to his voice, like he was trying, and failing, to cage a wild animal. It tickled something inside me. Something that wanted to push it further. To take the ruse as far as it could go. I stood on my tiptoes and nipped his earlobe with my teeth. His chest rumbled as his thumbs brushed up my side, right where the strings of my bikini top gave way to more fabric. The counselor yanked my upper arm, pulling me away from Paul, who rubbed his hands over his face as he let out a deep breath.

The counselor wrapped my towel so tight around me, it almost choked off my air. "One more display like that, and I'm marching you both to Pastor Dean's office."

"You coming or not?" I glanced at Paul.

He shook the dazed look off his face. "Coming."

The three of us wound our way behind the girls' cabins until we came to a small wooden structure that looked like a windblown shack. The counselor motioned me inside and shut the door in Paul's face. The inside smelled like an old lady's garden shed. She clicked on a small light, revealing boxes of junk and old clothes.

"How many bodies do you think are buried beneath this floor?" I asked.

She did not find me nearly as amusing as I found myself. She grabbed what looked like a black bag from one of the boxes and flung it at me, slamming the door on her way out. The light above my head flickered. I pulled the—I guess it was a swimsuit—on over my bikini. No way would I let this thing touch my naked body. Not after it had most likely been rotting in a box for a decade. It had sleeves that went down to my elbows, leggings that ended just past my knees, and a giant dress-like structure covering me from head to toe. This was a disaster. They'd worn more revealing bathing suits during the Victorian era.

I stepped out of the shed with my arms crossed tightly over my chest. I would've been more comfortable if I'd been forced to cover my stomach with a scarlet *A*. Paul started laughing so hard, the counselor jumped. After giving me a once-over, she nodded and left us on our own. Probably because she knew no one would even think about having sex with me while I wore this monstrosity.

"Shut up." I punched Paul on the arm. "You could've warned me."

He backed away with his hands up. "Hey, I didn't read the handbook either."

"You've been here before."

"And you expected me to remember all the details?"

"I figured girls in swimsuits would've been a pretty clear memory for you. Who cares if anyone sees my stomach? It's not sexy or anything."

He gave me a wolfish grin. "Well, you do have a perversely small belly button."

"What?" I looked down at my covered stomach. "It's not perverse. It's dainty."

He slung an arm around my shoulders. "You over this yet?"

"I've been over this."

"Do you want to go home? We can call my mom and have her come pick us up. She'll be bummed camp didn't save our souls, but I think she'll understand."

"My parents would kill me, or ground me until I turned eighteen. They already paid, and you know how the Wellses' budget plan goes." I couldn't tell him I was also still holding on to the smallest bit of hope for Ethan. I wasn't in the mood for any more judgment this afternoon. "Two and a half more weeks. Then we can chill the rest of the summer."

"Let me know if you change your mind." He kissed my hand the way Ethan had kissed Mandy's, and I knew it was a joke, but I glanced down at the place where his lips had touched my skin. All the nerves underneath tingled.

"No one is around. You don't have to pretend to be my boyfriend."

"I know." He dropped my hand. "Race you to the lake?"

He took off before I could even get a start. "No fair—your legs are longer than mine and you're not wearing a muumuu."

My flip-flops smacked against the rocky path as I fought to catch up with him. He had a good hundred yards on me before the tree line opened up and the lake stretched out before us. I hunched over, trying to catch my breath before we joined the rest of the camp.

Paul jogged back to check on me. "That was pathetic. You used to be able to keep at least twenty yards between us."

I shoved him hard and he fell over in the grass. "Now you're on."

Before he could get back up, I dashed toward the lake. The soft, imported sand sank between my toes, and the first rush of the lake numbed my feet. Water splashed around me as Paul picked me up from my waist and spun me around.

"You cheater."

"I totally won." I hooked my leg around his, bringing us both crashing into the water. We surfaced, half choking, half laughing. "You're just mad because you didn't think of it first."

"That's the last freebie you get." He splashed me again before helping me up.

I held his arm and looked around for the first time at everyone else. Girls played chicken with boys in the deep end. A small girl went flying into the water as someone else jumped onto the opposite side of the Blob. Girls lay out on towels in the sun. All of them wearing very normal, very modern one-piece swimsuits. I was the only one who looked like the cover model for *Amish Illustrated*.

"I don't think I want to swim anymore," I said.

"Is everything okay?" He walked with me out of the water, stopping at the edge. "Don't feel embarrassed. I'm sure you're not the first who's had to wear the swimsuit of shame."

"No, I'm fine. I'm going to go change and read for a little while before dinner."

I left Paul at the lake, waving to Sarina as I headed back to our cabin. She didn't give my swimsuit a second look, and I had to give her credit for keeping a straight face. Or maybe she'd seen plenty of them over her years at camp.

After hanging up both my bikini and the borrowed suit, I lay down and grabbed one of my books, but I couldn't get into it. Too many thoughts buzzed around my mind: about Ethan and all the judgment, not knowing how to act, and second-guessing every word that came out of my mouth.

At least my cabinmates were cool. I owed Sarina a debt of gratitude for the eye makeup tutorial alone. Astrid was pretty awesome, even with all her Jesus talk. Mandy never treated me like I didn't belong, even though I clearly didn't.

And then there was Paul. God, if word got out back home we'd fake-dated, I'd be fielding questions for weeks. A lot of people assumed we'd couple up eventually, but I was the type who'd study all week for an exam, complete with color-coded index cards and a rewards system, while Paul slept with his books under his pillow and hoped for the best. He was too flippant and I was too determined once I set my mind to something. We'd be a disaster together.

Though pushing the boundaries of our fake relationship in front of the counselor had been fun. Paul would probably make a joke of it later on.

Maybe I'd have a clearer idea of what I wanted after the testimonial bonfire. Astrid talked about it like it was the highlight of the summer. Paul seemed a little more wary, but he was wary of everything around here. At least it promised to be entertaining. Whenever someone brought it up, they did so with a kind of buzz.

Like a wasp's nest waiting to be broken open.

Chapter 11

Paul came around the corner after his kitchen duty shift, and I sat up a little straighter. He had on an obscure band shirt rolled up to the sleeves, plaid shorts, and red Converse. The closer he got, the more my heart sped up. So weird. I wiped my damp palms on my shorts.

"Ready for lunch?" he asked. "I'm starving, and I have it on good authority they have Muenster cheese on the block today."

"Seriously?" I jumped to my feet. "That's almost as orgasmic as Brie."

He shook his head. "You really need to get out more."

We walked along the path toward the dining hall, waving to a group of juniors we recognized who were hanging out on a grassy hill while a guy who must've been the coolest dude at Jesus camp strummed his guitar and sang some song I'd never heard before. Another group of girls made flower crowns from Queen Anne's lace. Everyone looked so relaxed.

"Do you think they're happy?" I asked. "Like, genuinely happy, not hopped-up on Pastor Dean's Purplesaurus Rex."

"Maybe?" Paul walked on for a bit. "I used to think I was happy."

"Isn't thinking you're happy and being happy the same thing? Isn't it just a feeling? If you think you are, then you must be."

"Slow down. Aristotle Camp is five miles down the road."

"There's an Aristotle Camp?"

"Yep. It's right next to Camp Gullible."

"You are hilarious." We entered the dining hall and grabbed our trays. "What made you think you weren't really happy? After the fact, I mean."

"Because none of this is real. It's all carefully crafted and staged for maximum emotion." A sign above the apples said to take one. He grabbed one and put another on my tray so he could have two. "Take the testimony bonfire, for example. It's dark, people are hearing all these wild stories, and they think it's safe for them to expose themselves. But anything they share will be used against them."

"How so? Like a weapon?"

"Peter told me he shared his testimonial last year about being addicted to pornographic images. Not even real porn, just half-naked girls. A few days later they searched his room and found that motorcycle girl picture under his bed."

"That's entrapment," I said.

"They said it was for the well-being and safety of the other campers. And while I find his constant hogging of the bathroom to jack off annoying, who is he hurting? No one."

"That is way more information than I needed to know, thanks."

"Vanilla pudding?" the lunch helper asked, and I gagged.

Paul took it and dipped his finger in, making a big show of licking it off.

"You're disgusting," I said.

We took our trays to the table, where only Jerome and Sarina sat. Sarina reached for the salt, bumping Jerome's arm and then quickly pulling it away again. The two of them muttered apologies to each other and went back to eating in silence. I motioned at them as I looked at Paul, who shrugged and stuffed half his sub into his mouth.

"So," I said between bites of the best Muenster cheese ever, "what's going on with you two? You're being extra strange and polite around each other."

"Nothing," Sarina said, but she wouldn't meet my eyes.

Jerome picked up his tray. "I'm going to eat outside. Nice day and all."

Once he left, I turned back to Sarina. "Okay, what's really going on?"

She looked at Paul and then back at me, shaking her head. He stopped mid-bite and stood with his food. "I'm, uh, going to eat outside too. Nice day."

She watched Paul walk out of the hall and then she leaned forward, keeping her voice to a whisper. "We snuck out last night, me and Mandy, and met up with the boys."

"That's not a secret. Get to the good part."

"Ethan and Mandy went off on their own, like we knew they would, and I thought maybe it would be a good time to pick up where Jerome and I left off last summer."

I took another bite of cheese. "This is still not the good part."

"We start kissing and stuff, and I'm thinking that's all we're going to do, but then he grabs my hand and he moves it you-know-where."

"I don't." My eyes widened, the picture of innocence. "Tell me."

"His . . ." She nodded her head toward her lap. "His you know. His penis."

"His what?" I held a hand to my ear. "I didn't catch that."

"Penis!" she shouted, drawing the attention of the next table. As I tightened my lips to hold back the laugh, she turned to me, her face bright red. "You did that on purpose."

"Absolutely." I reached my hand across the table to grab hers. "But if you can't even say it, then you probably shouldn't be touching it."

"Right?" She breathed out a deep sigh, like I'd gotten her on some fundamental level. "I'd never touched one or even seen one. I panicked."

Now we'd gotten to the good part. "What did you do?"

"I pulled it. Really hard. I thought it was supposed to be like milking a cow, like that's what you had to do to force the stuff to come out."

"Oh no." Tears pricked the corners of my eyes from the force of trying to keep my face straight. "What happened after that?"

"He doubled over, fell on his knees, and I think he was crying. I'm not sure. I got scared. So I left him in the woods, with his pants around his ankles, holding his you-know-what."

"Hold on. I need a minute." I turned around so she wouldn't see me bite down on my fist to keep from losing it. When I faced her again, I hoped I looked somewhat serious. "And he's still talking to you? That's a good sign, right?"

"I guess." She buried her face in her hands. "But every time I see him, all I can think about is the way he screamed after I pulled on his you-know-what."

"Do you want to try it again with him, or no?"

"I don't think he'd let me near that area again, but if he did, maybe? I'm not sure if I really want to touch it again, or if I just want to try it again to show him I can without hurting him. Like a do-over."

"Now that, I understand." I still wondered if I'd been terrible at sex. I sort of froze up during the whole thing, and didn't really like it, but when it was done, I still wanted to try it again to see if I could erase the previous experience.

I'd never said any of that out loud though, not past the very brief non-details I gave Paul. People here were so honest, so open about the things they feared and when they screwed up. It was a refreshing break from normal life, where everyone tried to act like they had their shit together while hoping no one would see what a mess they were inside.

Sarina and I finished our lunches and helped with cleanup duty before going to the next workshop. A girls-only workshop. Astrid and Mandy met us at the door, and I chatted with Astrid about how her follow-up workshops had been going. Her baby-doll face came alive as she talked about the plans other people had shared to expand their own youth groups. In her mind, she'd done good by Jesus, and maybe she had. At least she'd helped a few more Christians realize what they could accomplish if they actually practiced what they preached.

"Settle down, girls." The counselor with the blunt bangs who'd made me change my swimsuit stood at the front of the room. "For those who don't know me, my name is Priscilla, and this is my fourth year as a counselor here at Camp Three SixTeen."

The group clapped, but I kept my hands in my lap. She

hadn't made a great impression the first time we met, and I shuddered to think of what she'd do in a girls-only workshop.

"In this workshop, we're going to talk about personal responsibility," Priscilla said.

After all the crap guys had put me through, that did not sit well with me.

"As girls, we have a responsibility to honor God in all things we do. This includes who we date, what media we consume, and what we choose to wear." Priscilla looked directly at me and my face flamed.

Mandy tugged on her shorts, as if she could stretch them down to her knees. "She's looking at me."

"No, she's looking at me," I said. "We had a run-in yesterday."

"Have you ever heard the phrase 'dress for the job you want to have'?" Priscilla paused and looked around the room, giving all the girls a chance to nod along. "The same applies to dating. Dress like you want to be seduced, and you will attract the kind of guy who will only try to seduce you, who won't value your heart or your mind."

Several of the girls around me got out their notebooks and jotted that down, and all the blood inside me boiled. How dare she? These girls were so open and receptive. They took everything to heart and didn't deserve to internalize this nonsense just because Christians couldn't bother to keep their asshole boys in line. Paul told me I shouldn't speak up at these things, but I couldn't just sit there and do nothing.

"Excuse me." I stood and every head in the room swiveled in my direction. The lights suddenly burned ten times brighter. "Hi. Hello there. Are you saying *girls* are to blame for the terrible way boys treat them? If this workshop is really about personal responsibility, where is the responsibility for the boys not to be douchebags?"

Sarina gasped beside me, while Astrid gave one of her secretive smiles. I was sure she found this whole thing fascinating. Mandy tugged on my hand, trying to get me to sit back down, but it was too late.

"The boys have their own workshop going right now." Priscilla peered down at me, even though I had three inches on her and I was at the back of the room.

"Pastor Dean gave a sermon about garbage in and garbage out, right? Well, I'm calling this workshop garbage." No one met my eyes, except Astrid. "Girls aren't seduced for what they wear. How do you explain sexual harassment? Or child molesters? Or rape?"

One of the younger girls in the front row covered her ears. Priscilla rubbed her shoulder and glared at me. "Actually, the Bible says—"

"Don't even think about it." I bared my teeth. "If you apologize for rapists or even breathe a word about what girls wear or how much they have to drink, so help me God, I will make you shut your mouth."

"CeCe, no." Mandy grabbed my hand harder. "No threats."

"It's fine," Priscilla said to Mandy. "I'm not feeling threatened. I realize this is a sensitive topic and not everyone is ready for these lessons. I'll apologize."

"That's not an apology," Astrid said. Now it was my turn to gape. "You basically said CeCe wasn't evolved enough in the Bible's teachings to comprehend, which is not only offensive, but your lesson is wrong. And I have Scripture to back me up."

"I'm well versed in Scripture." Priscilla smirked. "Timothy 2:9—"

"What does Timothy say about wearing pearls?" asked Astrid. I had no clue what Timothy thought about pearls, but from the look on Priscilla's face, it couldn't be good. Point, set, match. "I'm not saying girls should run around naked, but calling this workshop Personal Responsibility is in poor taste."

"Okay. This is a good conversation. One better saved for another time." Priscilla clutched her necklace with white fingers. "I'll apologize again. Let me change the subject. Let's instead address flirting. How suggestive glances and unnecessary touches on the arms or shoulders of boys can lead them to think you want more. While it might feel good in the moment—"

"This isn't a different subject," I said. "It's the exact same bullshit message."

Priscilla wrung her hands.

"That's all the confirmation I need." I picked up my notebook. "I'm out."

"I'm out too." Astrid grabbed her things and followed me to the door.

"Wait for me." Sarina jumped up and turned around, motioning to Mandy.

Mandy chewed on her lip as she looked between us and Priscilla. I doubted she'd ever put a foot out of line in her entire life, but I couldn't wait all day. After a few seconds I pushed open the door and walked into the bright sunlight.

"We just walked out of a workshop. Oh my God. Sorry, God." Sarina fisted her hands under her chin. "We're going to be punished. They'll call our parents."

"It's fine." Astrid put a hand on her shoulder and leveled her gaze. "The workshops are voluntary. If we miss devotions, that's another story."

"Okay." Sarina took several deep breaths. "I'm okay."

"I'm here." Mandy burst out of the building, the sun streaming through her golden hair.

"Took you long enough," Astrid said.

"It's not that I didn't want to go." Mandy's full bottom lip stuck out. "I've never bailed on a workshop before, even the really boring ones. CeCe, you were so brave. I knew what she said felt wrong, but wow. I had no idea how to vocalize it."

I blushed, something I'd been doing a lot lately. Maybe I was becoming more of a Christian girl than I thought. "The win should go to Astrid for her excellent use of Scripture to beat back the hypocrites."

She took a bow as we all gave her a round of classy golf clapping.

"Looks like we have the rest of the afternoon off before dinner," Sarina said. "What should we do? Go to the lake?"

"No, thanks." I wouldn't be going back to the lake for the rest of my time here. Not if I had to wear the slut-shaming bathing suit. "Why don't we grab some chips from the kitchen, go back to our cabin, and you can tell Astrid and Mandy about how you tried to milk Jerome?"

Sarina moaned. "I'd rather go back to Priscilla's awful workshop."

"Not a chance." Astrid hooked her arm through Sarina's. "I'm going to need to hear this."

"Me too," said Mandy. "How does one go about milking a guy? Did you grab his nipples and squeeze them?"

"Not his nipples," Sarina said in a small voice.

"Then what did you—oh." Mandy's face froze. "Oh no."

"Sarina!" Astrid laughed so loud, it echoed across the quiet camp.

"I didn't know what to do with it. It's not like they come with an instruction manual."

I snorted until I couldn't hold it in anymore. Beside me, Mandy laughed until she doubled over, holding her stomach, while Sarina watched us all with her hands on her hips.

"I'm glad my misery is bringing you all so much amusement." She sniffed before cracking a smile. "I guess it's kind of funny."

"Kind of?" My cheeks hurt from laughing so hard. "You know what would be a lot more useful than Priscilla's workshop on victim blaming? Sex Ed 101. This camp is clearly in some need of good, old-fashioned 'what goes where and how.'"

"Amen." Sarina slapped a hand over her mouth and glanced at the sky.

"Come on." Mandy skipped ahead of us. "The chips are waiting, and I'm going to need details. Who knows? I could've easily made the same mistake as you."

That would've been a true blessing.

Chapter 12

After we'd stuffed our faces with pilfered chips and discussed what we'd come to call Milk-Gate, Sarina gave us a live demonstration of one of her YouTube videos by transforming her eyes into blue butterfly wings. When I got home, I'd watch every one of her videos. She helped me with something a little less dramatic, but the gold sparkle still made me feel like a princess. We dressed in our best sundresses. My best happened to be a pink one with gold threading I'd brought to remind Ethan of our first date. But I loved the dress, even though I was confused about my feelings for the boy.

Paul took my hand on the way to dinner, and I tried not to notice my heartbeat thumping against his palm. "You look gorgeous. Missed you during free hour."

"Thanks." So. Much. Blushing. This was my best friend, not some cute guy who smiled at me in the hall, and we were only pretending. "I hung out with the girls in my cabin. There was an incident with Sarina and Jerome we had to discuss in lengthy detail."

"Does it have to do with why he tried to ice his dick the other night?"

"No! What is wrong with him?"

"He's sheltered." Paul shook his head. "I felt bad enough for the guy to stop him before it got ugly, but it would've been amusing if he'd gone through with it."

"They should talk more about sex here. How many untold injuries could've been prevented with a little education? It'd be way better than having girl-blaming lectures."

"So that's why you caused a ruckus during Priscilla's workshop." Paul put his hand on my waist and pulled me closer. "Would it be weird if I said I find that incredibly attractive?"

"No," I squeaked. "I'm not making it weird. You're the one making it weird. How did you hear about that anyway?" I waved a hand. "Never mind. I'm sure everyone heard about it. I'm surprised Pastor Dean didn't call us in for a meeting."

"He might yet." He let go of my waist and went back to holding my hand. Nice, easy hand-holding. "Try to lie low for the next few days."

After dinner Pastor Dean announced the talent show would be the last night of camp and reminded us all about the bonfire testimonials on Sunday. A hush had gone over the crowd, and once again I wondered what kind of shenanigans went on there. I couldn't imagine Astrid, Sarina, or Mandy having anything messy enough to share, and I couldn't have cared less about the boys, minus Paul. I already knew they were disgusting.

"Want to sneak out to the woods tonight?" Paul asked. "I have another story."

"You're full of them lately." I poked him in the stomach. "What's this one about?"

"A mean troll who lives under a bridge and makes all the girls who pass wear iron underwear in the name of protecting their virtue. But then it rains and they all get tetanus. It's a sad story, full of heroics and heartbreak."

"Iron Underwear would be a great band name." I turned my head. In the shadows Ethan held Mandy tight against him. The quick punch to my gut took me by surprise. I'd started to think I was used to seeing Ethan with someone who wasn't me, and then nope. Still hurt. Maybe it always would. "Same tree?"

"Yep, same red shirt." He left with Peter to go to the other side of the lake.

I went back to the cabin with Astrid and Sarina, and a few minutes later Mandy came in and collapsed on her bed. "Boys are exhausting."

Understatement of the year. I put a pillow over my face. "Did you and Ethan fight?"

"I tried to end things."

"You did?" I threw my pillow on the ground and sat straight up. "What happened?"

"He swore he would change, he said he would stop being so pushy. I told him I'd give him one more chance, but I don't know if I even want to. He's not the same guy I texted with during the school year."

"You two texted?" My voice sounded like it came from the opposite end of a long tunnel. My throat tightened as everything inside me shriveled up and died. Here lies CeCe, a girl with a paper husk where her heart used to be. "The whole school year?"

"Well, yeah." She looked at me as if I'd just asked if two plus two equaled five.

"Weren't you both seeing other people?" Like me. I'd regulated myself to one of the nameless and faceless Other People. A walk-on player in their epic love story.

"It's not like I cheated on the guys I dated. I stayed friends with Ethan after the summer ended, but it wasn't realistic for us to date. We live a hundred miles apart."

"Did he want to date you? Despite the mileage?"

"He wanted to see me when he got his truck, but I told him no." She picked at the rosebuds on her comforter. "I wasn't ready for anything that serious. I'm still not. I just wanted to have fun this summer."

"But he did. He wanted something serious." I followed this guy to Jesus camp, and I wasn't even his first crush, his first love, his first kiss, the first girl he pictured in his future. Mandy came before me in all the ways that counted. I'd just been the first girl who'd let him go all the way. The thing I thought mattered most only mattered to me. "Excuse me. Lady problems."

I got up, walked across the room like normal, closed the bathroom door behind me like normal, and slid to the floor. I held my chest and let the pain pulse against my open palm. The empty place inside me, the one Ethan had carved out the night he told me we couldn't see each other anymore, ached with regret. For how much of myself I'd given, and how little I'd gotten in return. Even if I'd completely reshaped myself into the person I thought he wanted me to be, he wouldn't have come back.

Because he'd never really been mine to begin with.

After a small eternity of letting my heart bleed on the dingy tile floor, Astrid tapped on the door. "CeCe? You okay in there? Do you want me to bring you to the nurse's station?"

"No, I'm fine." I peeled myself away from the wall, the newly dried paint tacky against my tank top, and peeked into the cabin. "What time is it?"

"Almost time for lights-out."

I waited until all the cabins went dark before I left,

keeping my eyes peeled for any counselors. Two of them sat on the lake dock, dipping their toes in the water, but no one would be stupid enough to sneak out on the water at night. It was too open. That didn't mean I was in the clear though. With every snapping twig or rustling bush, I'd whip my head around, prepared to make a run for it.

Paul had the same blanket and more cans of Coke set out. This time he'd drawn a stick figure with sharp teeth and blunt bangs, with a few stick figures who had padlocks drawn around their waists. This would be one of his better stories.

I took a long swallow of Coke and set my can to the side. "I know you've got a story planned, but I finally figured out Ethan is a liar and a cheat and he probably just used me, so go ahead and tell me you told me so and chastise me for dragging you up here for nothing."

"As much as I enjoy telling you I told you so, I get the feeling this might be a bad time." Paul scooted in closer to me. "What happened?"

"I'm a mess." I lay down on the blanket and flung an arm over my head. "Turns out, he texted with Mandy the whole time we were together because he always wanted to be with her, he never wanted me, and I hate this. I hate feeling like I'm not enough all the time. I wish I could just forget he ever existed."

"First off, you're always enough. Sometimes too much." Paul sprawled out next to me, propping his head up with his arm. "Why did you love him? He's a straightlaced Bible-thumper whose mother dresses him funny, and you're not any of those things."

"That's why I asked him out. I thought he'd be kind because he was straightlaced and talked about Jesus." Even if we weren't in the real hideout, I couldn't hide myself from Paul.

"There are plenty of guys who are kind and not into Jesus. Some of them are even kinder than the ones who twist Scripture in selfish ways."

"I know, but he was so different. The night he picked me up for our first date, I came downstairs in my spaghetti strap sundress, the one I wore tonight. He sucked his breath in through his teeth, as if he'd never seen anyone more beautiful. That's why I fell for him. Because he made me feel beautiful and it was empowering to think he felt lucky to be with me."

And there was the truth I hadn't been able to acknowledge, staring me right in the face. I'd needed him to need me. Not because I liked going to his boring family dinners and bowling with his youth group friends every weekend, but because he looked at me like I held his world in my hands. Being so openly, unapologetically wanted had been intoxicating.

"He *was* lucky to be with you," Paul said quietly.

"But he rejected me the moment we had sex, so what does that say about me?" All my worst fears surfaced. Up until we had sex, he'd been a caring and attentive boyfriend. "I think I did it wrong."

"Not possible." Paul sat up. "Did he tell you that? Because I will go kick his ass right now. I'm not even kidding."

"No, he didn't say that." I rested my hand on his knee. "But he didn't really have to, you know? He kept asking me and asking me, and when I finally gave in, he broke up with me two days later. I can connect the dots."

"Did he pressure you?" All the tendons in Paul's lean frame tightened.

"It's not like that." I held his hand, stroking the top with my thumb to soothe us both. "He didn't take advantage of me, or just plow his way in. He asked me, and I said yes."

"How many times did you say no first?"

This conversation had gone someplace I didn't want it to go. My stomach twisted in knots with all the guilt and frustration and hurt I'd taken on in the last month. I couldn't stand the way Paul looked at me, like he had to defend my honor or something.

Ethan wasn't the first guy to put the pressure on. If I wanted to, I could've told him to stop bugging me. I said yes because every time I said no, I disappeared when he looked at me.

Because I thought sex would bring back the girl who made him suck in his breath between his teeth. Because I thought he'd cherish me and hold me, and I'd feel loved. Maybe that wasn't a good or right reason, but it was my reason and my choice.

"CeCe." Paul's voice was strained. "Did you say no before you said yes?"

A couple of campers howled in the distance, impossible to see through the thick tangle of branches. If I'd let Paul tell his story about the troll instead of getting into all the ways Ethan continued to hurt me, I could've been having a good time too. I rolled my can between my hands. "I know what you're asking, and I'm begging you not to do this. Please."

"Jesus Christ." He rubbed his eyes. "What am I supposed to say to that?"

"He didn't rape me. I could've kept saying no, like I did the other times, and he would've eventually stopped asking." Tears pooled in my eyes. I felt raw and scratchy, like I'd been sunburned on the inside. "I said yes. I fully consented."

"The way he treated you isn't okay. You know that, right?" He kneeled in front of me with so much concern, I had to look away. "My mom has been hammering this into me since the day I tried to kiss you without asking and got a well-deserved right hook to my jaw. Consent is more than just saying yes once."

"I don't understand." Ethan had many faults, but he couldn't be expected to read minds. I didn't like the sex, but I didn't speak up to say so. That was on me.

"I can see your wheels spinning, and I have no idea what you're thinking, but consent should be an ongoing conversation. Did he check in with you? Did he make sure you were comfortable, that you were still enjoying things?"

Was that something guys were supposed to do? I'd had sex and still didn't know anything about it, other than it had made me feel empty. I thought being loved, winning him back, would fill me up again. My stomach rolled, and I crawled over to the nearest bush.

"Goddamn it." Paul held my hair as I puked. "I fucking hate that guy."

"I shouldn't have done it." I spit the last of the sickness out of my mouth. "It's my fault. I let him use me. What's wrong with me? Why am I like this?"

"It's not your fault." Paul gathered me in his arms and rubbed my back. "There is absolutely nothing wrong with you. You fell in love with someone who told you he loved you. You weren't wrong to believe him."

"I'm sorry I got sick." I rested my head on Paul's chest.

"Don't be." He stroked my hair. "You got hit with a lot of shit all at once."

Sonia Hartl

We stayed there in the dark for a long time, with no words or stories, just me and him and the comfortable silence. Paul knew all my worst parts. The girl I was and the girl I pretended to be. And through it all, he still treated me like the girl I wanted to be.

"You never liked Ethan, did you?" I asked. "Even when we were dating."

"He's pretty much everything I can't stand about Christians. Arrogant, hypocritical, uses the Bible as a weapon to justify all his shittier qualities."

"There are good ones too. Like your mom and stepdad. And you."

"I'm not a Christian."

"You used to be." Paul could be arrogant and hypocritical sometimes, but he never used the Bible as a weapon. Not like Ethan did. "The way you quote Scripture isn't the same as the way I memorized the order of US presidents. You make the words have meaning."

"They're just words."

"Fine, but if you're not a Christian, then what do you believe?"

"I could ask you the same question, and you know my baggage."

"All right." I cracked my knuckles. "I'll take a stab at it. When we die, I think our consciousness becomes part of the black matter that's stretching galaxies in this plane of existence away from each other as our sense of self takes shape in another dimension."

Amusement danced in his eyes. "Where do you come up with this stuff?"

"The Internet. And I also think time is circular, so we're always existing. The concept of death keeps us from going mad because we experience time as linear, and so we think there must be a beginning and an end, when it's actually happening at the same time."

"So that means you're living through this poorly thought out nightmare of a plan to win back Ethan, all the time, for all eternity? Damn. I kind of feel bad for you now."

I stuck my tongue out at him. "Since you put it that way, maybe I'll ditch that theory and stick to the one about the other dimensions."

"Look at you, changing your core beliefs to suit your needs. It's like you're becoming a certified Christian." He wiped a fake tear from his cheek. "I'm so proud."

"Speaking of which, I'm still going to ride out these next few weeks to get my community service done, and to avoid that whole grounded-for-life scenario."

"It's up to you." Paul rubbed his neck. "It's kind of fun pretending to be your summer boyfriend. Especially when you do that earlobe thing."

"I'm a girl of many talents." I stretched my arms. Devotions would come early, and I wanted to stay awake for at least one of them. "Though we could start acting like this is a regular camp, and forget about pretending to worship the guy who used to date your mom."

"Why does he have to be the guy who dated my mom? Why can't he be the guy who used to mow your grass?"

"Because it's funnier that way."

He groaned and buried his face in my hair.

Later we headed out of the clearing, and at the tree where his red shirt was hanging, he gave me a long, lingering hug. The kind that made me feel safe and warm. My head went a little dizzy. I'd probably stayed up too late, but it had been worth every minute, even if that meant I'd be sleeping through devotions. Again.

Chapter 13

After a long week of waiting for the event of the summer, the night of the bonfire testimony arrived. Most of the camp headed down to the giant fire pit by the lake while the senior leaders got stuck with dinner cleanup. The sky pulsed with light and the air shimmered with anticipation as a cool breeze kicked up off the water. I rubbed my arms against the chill. Paul unzipped his hoodie and draped it over me. It smelled of soap and sandalwood and hung down to my knees.

"Listen, before this gets going, I need to warn you again." He pulled me aside by one of the workshop buildings. "Don't feel compelled to share your testimony."

"Why do you keep thinking I'd do that? I don't even know what a testimony is."

"'Knowledge speaks, but wisdom listens.'"

I was perfectly capable of listening. I just chose not to most of the time. "Look at you, whipping out Bible quotes with an air of judgment. How Christian of you."

"Not a Bible verse. That one is courtesy of Jimi Hendrix."
He glanced at a group of younger campers laughing in their
tight group. "I just want you to be prepared for tonight. Ethan
might share. Don't let it get in your head."

"You're scaring me."

"Good. I hope it scares you out of speaking."

We scored a log-for-two closest to the fire. And by scored,
I meant we got shuffled there as part of the older group.
Apparently the oldest kids had the juiciest stories to share, so
they did the most talking. The freshmen stayed back to observe
what the horrors of the real world did to those supposedly
purest of heart.

Pastor Dean stood in front of the fire, slightly resembling
a mad, helmet-haired goblin, but I probably shouldn't have
made sharp judgments on him. The guy who used to date
Paul's mom was watching, after all. After more droning on,
where the listening part would've come in handy, he passed
the microphone to a junior girl who copped to stealing her
sister's clothes until she had a dream where Jesus made her go
to school naked. Yawn.

"I thought you said this was scandalous," I said to Paul.

"Wait for it," he said.

Next, a boy, who introduced himself as a rising sophomore,

confessed to being cursed with ear pimples for masturbating. He even managed to find a passage from Job to support how that had led him to give it up once he found Christ's love. They'd raid his cabin for sure. Still, pretty tame stuff compared to the peanut butter guy from Paul's first year. Although anything would seem tame compared to that.

The twitchy sophomore then handed off the mic to none other than my devious ex.

"Thank you, everyone, for being here for me tonight," Ethan said.

"Don't speak," Paul whispered beside me.

"I heard you the first thousand times," I hissed back. I sat on one of my hands, a physical reminder that even if Ethan confessed to not being a virgin, I had to stay quiet.

"I'd like to share with you all how I lost my way this past year, fell into temptation of the wickedest sort, and how Jesus's love called me back from the brink."

My stomach turned. This sounded awfully familiar. The night he'd broken up with me, he called me a temptation. I'd been so deep in my hurt and confusion, I hadn't realized how skillfully he'd snatched away my agency and reduced me to a problem he had to overcome. I thought he'd meant it as a compliment. In reality, it had been an insinuation.

"Go on, son." Pastor Dean laid a hand on his shoulder.

"I was deceived by a temptress, who promised me a better life outside the Lord. She seduced me into her bed, for which I'm not proud, but I know now this was Satan at work. He used this girl to steal my innocence and drag me down into a life of unforgivable sin."

I seduced *him*? On what planet?

"The next day I had a long conversation with my pastor back home. He recalled Timothy 2:22, encouraging me to flee the evil desires of youth and cut ties with this girl. He said if I came to Jesus with a pure heart, he would restore my virtue. I put in the work and had many conversations with God. I did as I was asked, and the Lord restored my virgin soul, where it will remain until I'm ready to give myself to one woman."

He smiled at Mandy, who looked as if everything she had believed to be true had just blown up in her face. The same look Paul had worn the day his father had left. She glanced at me, all pale cheeks and wide eyes, and I wanted to crawl under a log and burn. This couldn't have gotten any worse.

"But Jesus needed to test me, to make sure I remained true to my promise. He allowed temptation to follow me to camp." Oh my God. He wasn't done yet. "Though she claims she's here on her own journey, I have my doubts, given her history. But Jesus has blessed me with a forgiving heart, and I'm willing to hear how she has found her own purpose."

He stared right at me as he spoke, and I became a boiling pot ready to steam and hiss. He had no right. This was his kingdom. He could've been honest, and he would've still had the support of the camp. Aside from Paul, I was completely alone here. Forget crawling under a log. I wanted to shove his face in the fire.

I had no idea what I'd say, but I had to say something. All the shame of being used and discarded didn't compare to this public roasting. If I hadn't snuck out to meet Paul last night, I might've taken all this in and found a way to blame myself.

I wasn't confused anymore. I was one hundred percent certain I fucking hated Ethan.

"Don't," Paul whispered as he squeezed my free hand.

I yanked it away. I'd stayed quiet for Ethan's sake once before. I wouldn't do it again. It had cost me more in heartache than I'd been able to handle, and I deserved better.

"Yes. Why don't we start with the truth?" I stood and snatched the microphone out of Ethan's grasp. "Since we're all here sharing our personal shame or whatever, let me introduce myself. My name isn't Satan. It's actually Francine, but I hate that name, so just call me CeCe."

A few of the younger kids laughed nervously.

"See, my mom wanted to name me Fancy after her favorite Reba McEntire song, but that song is really about a poor mom selling her daughter into prostitution before she dies, so not really an appropriate name for a baby girl, you know what I mean? So she went with something respectful, but she could still call me Fancy as a nickname."

"This is very illuminating, Miss Wells, but your testimony? That's what tonight is really about," Pastor Dean said.

"Sorry. I'm getting to that." Beside me, Paul had his face in his hands, like he couldn't stand to watch the train wreck. "Tonight my ex-boyfriend tried to blame me for his descent into temptation, but I will have you know, he's the one who pressured me, okay? Let's just get that part straight. And it wasn't even good, so it's not like I'd actually want to do it with him again. I guess that's all. Just wanted to clarify my position." I pointed at myself. "Not the temptress here. I'm not the Whore of Babylon you're all looking for. Although, in hindsight, I suppose opening with the whole Fancy story wasn't the best idea. Thank you."

I handed the microphone back to Pastor Dean and let the stunned silence wash over me. A hundred pairs of eyes regarded me as if I'd grown an extra head. Even Pastor Dean, the man with all the words, didn't have anything to say. I didn't care. Ethan had dragged me through the mud, and I'd be damned if I let him get away with one more lie.

I glanced at Mandy, but she'd turned away, her hair

covering her face like a barrier between us. I had no idea what she thought or felt. Maybe I didn't really want to know.

Paul stood and stuck out his hand for the microphone. He tilted my chin with his fingertips and mouthed *I'm sorry* to me, though I didn't know if he meant he was sorry for what he was about to say, or sorry that I'd spoken up. Either way, this had taken a strange turn. I'd gotten the impression the "Don't speak" thing went for him as well.

"You've got a tough act to follow." Pastor Dean regarded him over the fire. "Forgive me for wondering if you really want to share your testimony, or if you're just going to stir the pot."

Paul's grip on the microphone tightened until his knuckles turned white under the shallow glow of the fire. "'There will be more rejoicing in Heaven over one sinner who repents than over ninety-nine righteous persons who do not need to repent.'"

"Luke 15:7," Astrid muttered behind me.

Pastor Dean nodded, a light smile touching his lips. "Go on, son."

"Before you judge CeCe, and I'm sure you are, think of your Scripture. James 3:14: 'But if you have bitter jealousy and selfish ambition in your heart, do not be arrogant and so lie against the truth.'"

Ethan jumped to his feet. "You're the last person who

should be picking apart my testimony. If we're going to quote Scripture, what about John 2:22: 'Who is the liar but the one who denies that Jesus is the Christ?'?"

I ping-ponged between the two of them. They might as well have been speaking in tongues for all I understood, but it sounded like Paul had called Ethan a liar, and Ethan had acted like he couldn't lie because of Jesus. Or something.

"CeCe can't interrupt to defend herself when you spread lies about her, but you're allowed to interrupt when I'm speaking the truth? Have a seat." Paul shoved him back onto his log. "I've got the mic now."

Jerome stood up. "Man, this is supposed to be a night of sharing our love for Jesus, and the two of you are out here swinging your dicks around."

A couple of boys in back burst out laughing. Pastor Dean tried to run a hand through his tightly gelled hair, but his fingers got stuck, which made a few of the counselors nudge each other. If this were a movie, an asteroid would strike at any moment, ending this whole bizarre evening in a fiery blaze.

"That's enough." Pastor Dean took the microphone back. "The three of you, back to your cabins. Now. We'll meet in the morning to discuss your future at this camp."

Priscilla took her role as guard dog pretty seriously. She grabbed my arm and hauled me away from the blessed souls who were in danger of being tainted by my mere presence. Michael, not Mike, led Paul and Ethan toward the other side of the lake, but he didn't attempt to manhandle them. I shook off Priscilla and stomped between a cluster of terrified girls. They cowered against each other, as if they feared coming in contact with the girl who had Satan working through her to ruin Christian boys.

I checked behind me for Mandy, though I had no idea what I'd say. Her log sat empty, along with Sarina's and Astrid's, and I assumed they'd be off comforting her while in their minds I became everything Ethan said.

The idea of leaving without my community service hours and getting grounded until I turned eighteen didn't seem so bad anymore.

As I slunk along behind Priscilla, I watched the boys until a row of cabins blocked my view. The bonfire crackled and popped in the distance. Testimonies carried on, though they became more muffled the closer we got to the woods. The tiny speakers set up by the lake were no competition for nature.

Priscilla deposited me in front of cabin eight. "I'll be out front for a while, so don't think about going anywhere."

"You're loving this, aren't you?"

"Let's just say, I'm not surprised."

"Cool. Glad we had this talk." I marched up the stairs and slammed the door.

The girls had turned out the lights, but the little jump from Sarina's bed and the lack of snores from Astrid's let me know they weren't actually sleeping. A Mandy-shaped mass, covered completely, gently shook on her bed. Her quiet sobs barely rose above the crickets chirping outdoors. I could wait until morning to find out exactly how much she hated me.

Chances were, I'd be going home anyway.

Chapter 14

Priscilla came to collect me before the rest of the girls woke up in the morning. Pastor Dean wanted to meet early, before devotions. Probably so he could usher us off the property before anyone saw us, and then act like we'd never been there at all.

Paul trekked around the trail by the lake. The sun had barely begun to light the sky, and a hazy twinkling of stars could still be seen hovering above the trees. I had no idea how he'd been able to share a cabin with Ethan after everything that had gone down. When he got close enough, I checked him over for any signs of a brawl, but he just looked a little sleep rumpled.

"What happened after the bonfire?" I grabbed his face, turning it from side to side to make sure he was okay. "You don't look like you fought."

"I didn't fight." He took my hands and held them. "They put Ethan in another cabin."

"I'm not sorry I spoke up."

"I told you it would be a disaster." He put his arm around me and pulled me to his side. "But you had a right to speak. I figured Ethan would mention his born-again vow, but I should've anticipated his total lack of responsibility. How did your night go?"

"They all pretended to be sleeping so they wouldn't have to talk to me." I swallowed the thick lump in my throat. I'd woken before everyone else, and might be sent packing while they were at devotions. Leaving things unresolved felt worse than being ignored. As much as facing Mandy terrified me, I owed it to her to let me have it. "Anyway, I'm sick of talking about it. Where's Ethan so we can get this over with?"

"I think Pastor Dean wants to meet with us first."

"Is that good?" I glanced at the chapel door. "Or bad?"

Paul shrugged. "This might be the end of the road."

"Yeah." I bumped him with my elbow. "Before I get grounded for the rest of the summer, I want you to know there isn't anyone else I'd rather fake-date while being a fake Christian."

"Same."

Before I had time to stress about it further, Pastor Dean poked his head out of the chapel and looked around. Like he really paid the counselors enough to stand guard over two almost grown teenagers at the butt crack of dawn. Frowning, he motioned us inside and shut the door. He had a mess of papers spread over his desk, and the chairs he directed us to sit in were so low to the ground, our heads barely rose above the desk. My dad would've called that a power move.

Pastor Dean steepled his fingers, the fresh coat of gel in his hair still slick from the initial application. He wore a tie shaped like an electric guitar, though I would've been willing to bet he was as much a rocker as I was a Christian. "I invited you here this morning to give you a chance to explain yourselves."

"I'm not sure what you want us to explain," I said. "I hope you can understand why I had to speak up last night."

"Believe it or not, Miss Wells, I do." He took off his hipster reading glasses and rubbed the bridge of his nose. "I'll be speaking to Mr. Jones later, but I hope you can understand my position as well."

"What is your position?" Paul asked.

"When your mother said you'd be coming to camp this summer, I was thrilled." Pastor Dean put his glasses back on and looked over the rims at Paul. "Your brothers were exemplary campers. But I'm not convinced you're here because you intended to return to your faith."

"I didn't abandon my faith." Paul peered over the desk, and his eyes scanned the papers spread around. "I cleared out the clutter."

"I see." Pastor Dean pulled all the papers together on his desk and stacked them off to the side. "I didn't call you both here to punish you. I want this camp to be a fun and safe place, but I have to think of the kids who came here because they've opened their hearts to the Lord and are eager to gain a better understanding of His word."

"And we want that too," I said. "We like the workshops and devotions and all that stuff. And okay, I'm not as well-versed in the Bible as everyone else, but I'm trying."

And by trying, I meant I'd been trying to win back my awful ex who wasn't worth the trouble, and now that I'd rather roll around in a patch of poison ivy than spend another second in his company, I'd try to avoid my parents' wrath if I got sent home early. But Pastor Dean didn't need to know that.

"Was disrupting Priscilla Wayland's workshop part of your effort?"

"No." I glanced down at my hands. "We don't get along."

"Here's what I'm going to do." Pastor Dean stood and walked around his desk. "I'm going to give you two another chance, but only one. No more staging workshop walkouts or starting public confrontations."

"Yes, sir," we said at the same time.

"Step one toe out of line, and you're done."

"I understand." I stood and shook his hand. "Thank you."

"I'm all about second chances, but don't make me regret it."

Astrid burst through the door, her curls flying in a million directions, a light sheen of sweat glistening her face. "You can't throw out CeCe. She's the best thing that ever happened to this camp, and if she's gone, I'm gone too."

Oh my God. Astrid was here. Standing up for *me*? My stomach started doing funny things, like the first time I'd gone to a school dance and swayed with Will Durham to an outdated love song. I could've hugged her, but I also wanted to shove her out the door so she wouldn't get in trouble.

"Me too." Sarina came in behind Astrid, her voice barely above a whisper. "But it would be great if you didn't kick her out, because my mom would be so mad if I left camp early."

I tried to get their attention, motioning to my neck for them to cut it out. As much as I loved them for coming to my defense, Astrid had worked so hard to get her workshop off the ground, and Sarina still needed to find the courage to tell her mom she wanted to keep her YouTube channel. They didn't deserve to lose everything they'd built over me.

Pastor Dean rubbed his temples. "No one is getting thrown out today."

"Oh." Astrid looked between us. "Right. Of course not. But if you want to throw Ethan out, we wouldn't be all that upset."

"Mr. Jones deserves a place here as much as anyone. 'Ask,

and it will be given to you; seek, and you will find; knock, and it will be opened to you.'"

"Matthew 7:7," Astrid said. She couldn't help herself.

Pastor Dean led us outside, where Ethan paced in front of the door, his face a light shade of green. Served him right. Astrid and Sarina flanked my sides, pushing Paul away.

"I'll catch up with you at devotions," Paul said.

I turned to Astrid and Sarina. "You guys are the best. But seriously, don't put yourselves out there like that for me. If I go home, it's not a big deal."

"It's a big deal to us," Astrid said.

I let that warm my heart for a moment, until we got back to the cabin, where Mandy sat on the steps, twirling the dried-up Queen Anne's lace between her fingers. I took a cautious step toward her, unsure if she wanted to hit me, less sure if I'd block her. She hadn't shown up at Pastor Dean's office, and I couldn't blame her for that. In fact, I wouldn't blame her if she never wanted to speak to me again.

"I ended things with Ethan," she said.

"Are you okay?" I couldn't read her expression. I didn't know her well enough yet. Which, oddly, made me feel worse.

She lifted her chin. "I will be."

"Why don't you two go inside?" Astrid nudged Sarina, who nodded in response. "Let us know if you need anything.

We'll be right on the front steps."

I wanted to stay outside too, with the two people who'd put themselves at risk to have my back, even if I didn't deserve it. But that would've been cowardly. The opposite of what Astrid and Sarina had done for me. So I ground my teeth and headed into the cabin.

Mandy sat cross-legged on the floor, picking at some loose threads on the rug as she refused to meet my eyes. I wanted to defend myself, but that didn't feel like the right course of action. Anything I could've said would've sounded like an excuse. I had to let her lead the way.

"I couldn't stay with him," she said.

A week ago, hearing those words would've meant everything to me. Now it just made me feel hollow. "I'm not after him, if that's what you think."

She jerked her head to the side, taking violent pains not to look at me. "Why did you come here? Because it's pretty obvious you're not a Christian. If it wasn't to get him back, what did you have to gain?"

Here it was. My truth. My testimony. And I'd be sharing it with the only person whose forgiveness I cared about. "It started that way. Wanting him back."

She sucked in a breath and I hated myself, but I had to put it out there.

"That all changed though, pretty fast, too," I said. "Ethan isn't the guy I wanted him to be. And to be completely honest, I don't think he ever was."

"Yeah," Mandy said. "He's not who I wanted him to be either."

Her bedside clock ticked off the seconds until they became minutes. The air buzzed thicker than the cloud of mosquitoes that hovered around our front porch at night. I closed my eyes and asked God, the guy who used to date Paul's mom, and the black matter of space to give me the strength to tell the whole story. I owed her that much.

"Once upon a time, I met someone who made me feel loved and wanted. When he looked at me, I felt important, like I was his world. Until I started saying no to sex. The more I said no, the more that important and wanted girl began to disappear." I squeezed my hands together until they went numb. "That's why I said yes."

Mandy drew her knees up to her chest.

"After I said yes, he broke up with me. He said he needed to get right with Jesus to be born-again, and I came to camp because I thought if I could act like I'd gotten right with Jesus too, I'd be wanted again. I tried so hard to be that girl, I'd forgotten who I was."

"Why didn't you tell me? I don't expect better from Ethan,

not anymore, but we're friends. Friends should always be truthful with each other, even when it hurts."

"At first I just wanted to win him back. I didn't care about anything else. Then I started to care, about you, Sarina, and Astrid. I felt like I fit in here, when I've never really fit anywhere. Then, when I didn't want him anymore, I thought the issue would disappear." I looked down at my knotted fingers. "Do you still consider me a friend?"

"I should hate you." Mandy went back to picking at the rug. "Ethan said he wanted a future with me, he said we'd give each other everything on our wedding night, but you got there first. And there is nothing that can change that."

"The only part of him I ever got was the most unremarkable thing. In the stuff that matters, where it all counts, you came first. Every time."

"You didn't let me finish." She wiped her tears away with the back of her hand. "He said what he wanted, but I never got to say what I wanted. That's one of many reasons why we wouldn't have worked out. I *should* hate you, but I don't. Not even a little bit."

All the tears she'd swept away somehow found their way to me. And I was the ugliest of criers. "I can't believe you still consider me a friend. I lied to you."

"But you won't do it again, right?"

"Never." I rubbed my cheeks. "How can you forgive me, just like that? If I were you, I'd put LEGOs in my bed and swap out my brush with someone who had lice."

"I didn't know if I would last night, but I stayed up late thinking everything over. I know you're not a Christian, so you might not understand, but if Jesus can die for our sins, who are we not to forgive mistakes?"

"You're right. I don't understand." I laughed through my snot-filled, puffy-eyed breakdown. "Can I hug you?"

"You better." She wrapped her arms around me, surrounding me with a light scent of peaches and clean cotton I'd never noticed on her before, and in them I found something that felt a lot like home.

"I'm so sorry I came here and messed up your relationship," I said.

"Don't be. I'm so sorry for what he did to you." She stroked my back. "I could never be with a guy who treated someone I care about like that."

"How can you even stand to be around me? I'm the interloper here."

"You're not." She pulled back and held my face in her hands. "He's the one who screwed up. And really, you looked so shocked when we got here, when you saw the two of us. Maybe part of me knew then, but I didn't want to admit it."

Mandy was so open to self-examination in ways I envied. It never occurred to me that she could've had the same blind spots as me when it came to Ethan, but I supposed even the most honest people could lie to themselves.

"I was so lost when he broke up with me," I said. "But I should've seen past his lies, or at least known better than to come here. I'm too impulsive. Ask Paul. He'll tell you I'm the worst."

"I doubt he'd say that." She smiled then, and even with tears and mascara drying on her cheeks, I'd never met someone more beautiful. "He really does love you."

"No, he doesn't. He's not my boyfriend, but we've been friends for a long time."

I didn't have a reason to fake it with Paul anymore. We could put an end to the ruse, he could find someone at camp to hook up with, and I could do whatever. Or maybe he'd be cool with keeping it going, just for laughs. The idea of going through another breakup right now, even a fake one, depressed the hell out of me.

"Is everything okay in here?" Astrid poked her head into the cabin.

"We're bonding over how much boys suck." Mandy motioned her inside. "I know you don't want to miss this."

"Oh good." Astrid pushed open the door. "Because we love

both of you and hate Ethan, and we'd have to bury him in the woods if he broke up our cabin."

"And then we'd go to Hell," Sarina whispered solemnly. "For murder."

"This just got really dark." I stood and dusted off my shorts. "Our cabin might get broken up anyway. Pastor Dean said if I put one more toe out of line, I'm finished here. I don't even know what the line is, so chances are, my toes are going to be all over it by the end of camp."

"It's not your fault Ethan sucks," Astrid said. "Pastor Dean let you stay because he saw right through Ethan's bogus testimony."

"We know Ethan only did that to shame you." Sarina glanced at the door as if Pastor Dean could hear her. "If it came down to it, we'd back you up again."

"No. You can't." They didn't need to get dragged down in my muck. "I'm not even a Christian. If I get sent home, life will go on."

"We don't care if you're not a Christian," Mandy said, taking a seat next to Astrid.

Astrid nodded. "You're one of us, and the girls of cabin eight stick together."

"Even if they call our parents"—Sarina gulped—"we're on your side."

"I don't deserve you all." I spread open my arms and motioned them to come closer. "I need a cabin eight group hug."

We stood there, holding each other together, while something inside me began to mend. When I'd first come here, I'd been looking for someone I thought I'd lost. I had no idea I should've been looking for myself. And these girls, who knew I didn't fit in, who believed completely different things than I did, cared enough to stand by me through it all.

Chapter 15

After devotions, we had some free time where none of us were on breakfast duty. Mandy lay on her bed with a cold washcloth over her eyes, while Astrid wrote in her journal. Sarina dug around in her makeup kit, tossing empty tubes of glitter into the wastebasket by her bed. She kept shooting me furtive glances, like she would burst if she didn't speak up, but she didn't know how to phrase whatever was on her mind.

"I'm curious about something." Sarina chewed on her thumb as she looked between me and Mandy. "I'm not sure if I should ask, though, because of everything that happened last night."

"Just spit it out," Astrid said.

"Okay." Sarina stood and paced back and forth, her hands tucked under her chin. "Okay. I'm just going to ask. You're not a virgin, CeCe?"

"I think that's been pretty well established," I said.

She clutched her flaming cheeks. "Whatwasitlike?"

"Huh?" She might as well have had marbles in her mouth. "I don't think I caught that."

"The sex," she whispered. "What was it like?"

Astrid snapped her journal shut, then opened it again, like she was poised to take notes. Mandy sat straight up, her washcloth falling onto her lap. Nothing like an early morning question about sex to get everyone's attention.

"Do you really want to know?" I asked.

"Yes," the three of them said in unison.

"All right, I guess you do." I laughed.

I didn't want to lay all the awful, embarrassing details out there, but I wished someone had talked about sex with me. Not the kind of conversation I'd had with my mom about the birds and the bees, where she threw a handful of condoms at me and told me to be safe, but the ugly stuff. The awkward stuff. The stuff no one talked about because they thought they were alone. The kind of conversations Paul's mom had with him.

"The truth is, it was . . . really bad," I said.

"How so?" Mandy asked.

"Should we be discussing this?" Talking about sex with my ex-boyfriend's even-more-recent ex-girlfriend felt all kinds of squicky. "It's not very Christian."

"Oh please." Astrid rolled her eyes. "It's a good thing

you're not a Christian then."

"Fine." This was normal. I could talk about this. "It hurt. A lot. And the second it started, I just wanted him to hurry up so it could be over."

"That sounds awful," Sarina said.

"It was, and sex is supposed to be great, right? Well, it wasn't like that for me. I didn't feel connected to him at all. I don't think he even looked at me. He sort of stared at my shoulder, while his face was all twisted up, like he was the one in pain."

"Just when I thought I couldn't hate him more," Astrid said.

Mandy stared at me with wide-eyed horror, as if she'd switched flights at the last minute and just heard the plane she was supposed to be on had crashed.

My worst insecurities bubbled to the surface. The stuff I couldn't even talk to Paul about. "The whole time, I analyzed. Was my butt too flat or was my stomach not flat enough? Did he notice the weird mole on the inside of my thigh? Did he think I smelled down there?"

"That is exactly what I'd do," Sarina said. "Like with Jerome, I was so hyper-focused on having no idea what to do, I freaked out."

"Exactly. And the worst part? When he finished and rolled off me, he just lay there. Didn't touch me or hug me or ask if I was okay. And I was left wondering if I'd been terrible at it, if maybe that was the real reason why he broke up with me."

"That's why you came here," Mandy said.

"What?" I shook my head. "No. I thought I loved him."

"Maybe," Mandy said quietly. "But maybe you also thought if you showed up here, crossing what he told you was the only bridge between you, then you'd know for sure. You'd walk away blaming yourself, and he'd get to walk away absolved of all responsibility."

My knees gave out, and I plopped down hard on my mattress. "Damn."

"I had no idea he could be so cruel." Mandy's eyes welled up again. "You didn't deserve to feel that way. How can he still call himself a Christian?"

"That settles it for me," Astrid said. "I'm never having sex."

"Me either," Sarina said.

"Wait, no." I held out my hands. "You guys, I didn't tell you this to scare you away from sex. I'm sure it can be nice, maybe even good. It just wasn't good for me."

"I think it sounds pretty accurate," Mandy said. "I mean . . . I don't know if I should say this. It might be too graphic."

I raised an eyebrow. "You're really going to hold back after what I just shared?"

"You're right." She blew out her breath. "I can't wear tampons. The one time I tried to put one in, it hurt so bad, I cried. And a . . . you-know-what has to be way bigger than a tampon."

"Depends," I muttered. "I guess you could try to milk one first, to see if you find one small enough."

Astrid scribbled furiously in her notebook. "How do you know if they're small enough?"

"That was a joke." I took the pen out of her hand.

"You're not pregnant, are you?" Sarina asked.

"God no. I mean, not that God." I pointed at the sky. "But no. We used protection. Which is a whole different can of worms."

"Tell us." Sarina leaned forward on her hands. "We need to know this stuff."

"He wanted me to help him put on the condom, but I didn't know how to do it. Looking back, he probably didn't either, but tried to pass it off like it would be sexy if I did it."

"That sounds like him," Mandy said.

"It took three attempts to get one of those suckers to stay on. I tried to expand the first one, because I thought you had to snap it on, but it slingshotted out of my hand and hit him in the eye. I have no idea how he stayed hard after that."

The girls laughed, but it had been a nightmare at the time. Especially because we were both naked. Being naked made everyday embarrassments ten times more mortifying, and hitting your boyfriend in the eye with a condom did *not* fall under everyday embarrassments.

"Here's the most important thing." I tossed Astrid her

pen. "Write this one down. Your partner should be checking in with you during sex. They should be making sure you're okay, and if you're not, it's okay to tell them to stop."

They nodded as if this were all new information, which made me feel infinitely better about my complete lack of knowledge in that department. This was the stuff they needed to teach in sex education. If I didn't know consent was a conversation, and these girls didn't know, I was willing to bet there were a whole lot of girls just like us. Girls who technically, legally consented because they said yes once and thought the emptiness they felt afterward was all their fault.

"You should be leading workshops. Not Priscilla," Astrid said.

I snorted. "I'm sure that would go over really well. The 'Truth About Sex 101.'"

"Why not?" Mandy clasped her hands. "You could totally teach this stuff. Imagine how many girls would benefit from being able to talk about this, free of judgment, where they could ask questions and get real answers."

"I'm one toe over the line away from being thrown out of here, remember? I highly doubt Pastor Dean would want me to regale his flock with the tragic truth about the night I lost my virginity."

"It's a shame." Astrid shut her journal and headed toward the bathroom. "Your story would probably do more for abstinence than all the teachings we've had about the subject combined."

"No. Again, no. I'm serious. That's not why I'm telling you all this."

Abstinence had not been my goal. Despite my horrible first experience, I wanted to do it again with someone I trusted. Especially now that I knew a guy should check in, that I could demand it, and I could stop if I didn't like it. Even after saying yes. Ethan had told me he loved me the night we'd had sex, but those weren't the three little words I'd needed to hear. "Are you okay?" would've gone a lot further. In fact, it would've made all the difference.

After our first workshop of the day, which Paul told me had been about Everyday Miracles, and which I might've spent the entire hour of staring at the wall and daydreaming about sexy pirates, we grabbed our lunch trays and sat outside under the big oak tree.

Priscilla walked by us and stopped short. Disbelief clouded her eyes, and I gave her a pageant wave. The Jesus camp version of the middle finger.

"She can't believe we're still here," I said to Paul. "Did the guy counselor stand guard outside your door last night too?"

"For a little bit, but he got called away by another emergency. A cabin full of freshmen boys were jumping on their beds and swinging their dicks around."

"They must've been putting out fires all over camp last night." And starting new ones. I ripped a corner off my wedge of Swiss cheese and dipped it in ranch dressing.

"At least they can't blame us for the dick swinging. That honor belongs to Jerome."

"Are you surprised we're still here?"

"Before our meeting with Pastor Dean, I would've said yes." Paul tapped his plastic fork against the rim of his plate. "Did you get a look at those papers on his desk?"

"No." Who cared about a bunch of bills and invoices? I got enough of that at home with my parents and their ridiculous spreadsheet.

"My mom's a benefactor of this place. A pretty generous one at that."

"That's probably how we got a spot here." The leadership program was supposed to be for seniors who'd attended previous years, and I'd assumed the recommendation letter had sealed the deal. "Does that bother you?"

"Not really. My brothers came here all four years. Aaron was a counselor for one year, but that's probably why Pastor Dean let us stay. This place can't run on the number of campers alone."

"Maybe if they'd let us wear two-piece suits and chilled out on all the workshops, this place would attract more campers." We had plenty of free time, but all the group activities centered on kids who'd grown up in the church, and knew all the teachings already. If they wanted to up attendance, they should do a little less pushing and a lot more accepting. "Pastor Dean should ask Astrid for tips on how to build an effective camp."

"That would be something to see." Paul took a bite of his sandwich. "I'm assuming the girls know I'm not really your boyfriend. Do you want to stage a breakup, or no?"

"Why? Is there someone you're interested in?" I tucked a lock of hair behind my ear, all casual. We hadn't really discussed the breakup portion of our arrangement, and for some reason the thought of it made me queasy. "Because it's cool if you are. I'll back off."

"Back off what?" He shoved a forkful of macaroni salad into his mouth, chewing while he contemplated. "I thought you'd be done with faking it."

"I guess." This breakup, fake-up, whatever, didn't feel right. But if he didn't want to pretend, I couldn't force him into a role he no longer wanted to play. "We don't need to stage anything; we can naturally go back to being friends."

"Naturally, huh?" He balled up his empty plate. "If that's what you want."

Everything had gotten twisted up. I had no idea what I wanted, but he sounded annoyed with the whole thing. Trying to figure out my feelings and his snappy tone was like walking barefoot and blindfolded through a desert.

Was I developing romantic feelings for Paul? I had a strong urge to dig a hole and bury myself in it. This was my best friend. The boy I'd grown up next door to my entire life. It had to be the fake-dating. I'd somehow manufactured feelings because I couldn't distinguish between real and not-real to save my life. I glanced at him and his expression floundered somewhere between irritated and confused. The same expression he'd worn when I'd complimented his cologne or that time I'd told him we should just go to junior prom together instead of stressing over finding and keeping dates.

My face flushed and I had to look away. God. What did that even mean? I couldn't have romantic feelings for Paul. Where would that leave me when he walked away? Would it hurt our friendship? The fact that I was asking these questions left me reeling.

Maybe I could dip my toe in the water and see if it was warm enough to wade in. "I told you I liked faking it with you, and I meant that."

"You also told me you didn't want to ride my bike when we were seven. But I distinctly recall you stealing it out of my garage while I was at church and bending the front wheel when you ran it into a ditch."

So much for testing the waters. "I'm so glad you're my best friend. Who else can I count on to hold a mistake over my head ten years after the fact?"

"More recently, you told me you didn't care about making junior prom court."

"I didn't."

He raised his eyebrows.

"Okay, fine. It was kind of cool." I threw a chunk of cheese at him. "Are you going to do this all afternoon? Trot out every lie I ever told and hold me to them all?"

"I don't know. Maybe."

"Good to know, because this mood sucks. Come find me when you've pulled your head out of your ass." I headed back to my cabin. Mandy and Astrid always acted like they knew something about Paul I didn't. Maybe they could sort out his shitty attitude.

"Wait. I'm sorry." He stood and jogged to catch up to me, tossing his plate into the garbage on the way. "I don't know why I'm being an ass."

"Forget it. But for the record"—I poked him in the chest—

"I felt really bad about your bike. I rolled pennies for a month to get it fixed."

"You never told me that." His expression turned too serious for broken bikes and rolled pennies. "I know everything about you. How do you still manage to surprise me?"

My toes tingled, putting me back on uneven ground. "A girl has to keep some secrets. But that was my last one, so way to ruin my mystique."

"I somehow doubt that's your last secret."

He tucked his hands into his pockets and strolled away, leaving me with a low level of frustration I'd attributed to my tingling toes and general cluelessness. Somewhere between the fake-dating and our non-breakup, we'd wandered into something different. Not platonic, but still friendly. I didn't know quite how to define it yet, but maybe, for once in my life, I didn't need to rush headlong into figuring it out. If I could learn how to swim in an ocean I'd created, I could learn how to bounce along and let the waves take me where I needed to go.

Chapter 16

Free hour was in full swing at camp. I gazed out at the lake, at all the kids flying in the air from the Blob, and had another stab of anger for Priscilla. Not getting to try that thing would be my biggest regret when I left this place.

I pushed open my cabin door and found a group of fifteen girls packed into our tiny room. Half the rising juniors and a few sophomores. They all eyed me with varying looks of curiosity and anticipation.

"Hello, everyone." I gave them an awkward wave.

"Excuse us." Astrid took my arm and led me outside.

I put my hands on my hips. "What's going on in there?"

"Don't be mad." She worried her heavy top lip between her teeth. "I did some thinking the other night, after all the stuff you told us, about how others could really benefit from hearing from you. The girls here . . . No one talks to them about sex."

"You want me to talk to a bunch of Christian girls about

sex?" Had she lost her mind? I was the furthest thing from a trained professional. "I can't do that. I'm already on super-thin ice, and if Pastor Dean gets word of this—"

"He won't." Astrid held my shoulders. "These girls are in need of information, and if someone doesn't tell them, it makes it easier for an Ethan to show them."

"I'm not sure what you want me to say." I hadn't considered losing my virginity to be some big secret, not at home anyway, but I didn't walk around with it written in black Sharpie on my forehead, either. "It's kind of personal. I didn't mind sharing with you and Mandy and Sarina, but I don't know anyone in there."

"You don't have to get as detailed as you did with us. But it would help them to know it wasn't all fun and games, you know? It could be like a sex workshop."

I was pretty sure a sex workshop fell under "putting a toe out of line." But if Astrid thought it was a good idea, maybe it wouldn't be so bad? If we didn't talk to each other, where could we go? They wouldn't talk to their parents or their pastors willingly, not if they were anything like me. I'd debated having surgical memory removal after my mom gave me the Talk.

"If I'm not comfortable with a question, I'm not going to answer it," I said.

"Absolutely."

"I'd rather not go through the whole story again. It would

be better if they just asked me stuff. That way they can decide what they want to know about."

"Great idea." Astrid nudged me forward. "You're a natural leader. They'll listen to you." She pushed the door open. "CeCe has agreed to answer any questions you might have, but please be respectful. If she says no, don't push it, or we'll end the discussion." She leaned against the wall beside me, giving everyone the stink-eye to let them know she meant business.

I cleared my throat. Public speaking, or any form of being put on the spot, usually had me searching in panic for the nearest exit, but I'd already told Astrid I'd do this. For reasons that escaped me at the moment. "Hi again. Most of you know me from the bonfire disaster. Since I've already been beyond humiliated in front of you all, what's a few invasive questions among strangers who may, or may not, think my eternal soul is up for damnation?"

A few of the girls in the back exchanged uneasy glances. This was going well. I turned to Astrid, who gave me an encouraging nod. I didn't know what she expected me to do. Maybe I knew how to give a hand job because Tyler Volk was a bossy asshole, and I knew what having sex exactly one time felt like, but that hardly made me fit to give a lecture on the subject. I thought maybe this was something we could talk about together, but Astrid clearly had other ideas. Ideas she hadn't bothered to discuss with me before she shoved me into this situation.

"I know you don't know me." A pretty Latina girl with eyelashes so long that they looked store-bought raised her hand. "I'm Autumn Ruiz, rising junior by the way, but we talked about what happened to you last night."

"And what did you decide?" I tried to keep the resentment out of my voice, but this wasn't how I'd planned to spend my free afternoon.

"We don't think you're going to Hell. Actually, we think it was awesome that you stood up for yourself." She glanced around at the other girls, who had apparently nominated Autumn to be their spokesperson. The girl sitting to her right whispered in her ear, face flaming.

"And we also think your boyfriend, Paul, is really cool," Autumn said. A few of the girls giggled.

"Paul is great, but he's not my boyfriend." Maybe I shouldn't have led with that. At the mention of Paul not being my boyfriend, two of the girls bent their heads together and started whispering. Which was unfortunate. Paul was not the good Christian boy they'd be able to bring home to Mom. "It's complicated. He's also had way more sex than me, so maybe he would be a better person for this Q and A."

"We can't talk to a guy about this stuff," said a blond sophomore I recognized from the dining hall. "They don't get it."

"No, I guess they don't," I said. "But if you're looking at me like I'm some kind of sexpert, you're going to be sorely disappointed. I've only done it the one time, with one guy. There are other partners, and not all sex is heterosexual."

Autumn averted her gaze. I hadn't missed the way her cheeks had darkened, but I didn't want to put her on the spot if she wasn't out yet or if I'd misjudged her blush. Astrid shifted her stance, and I glanced at her to back me up.

This was her idea, after all.

Astrid pushed off from the wall to stand closer to me, a subtle show of solidarity, and I wanted to hug her for it. "This is a safe place for us to talk honestly, and if you can't ensure your presence here is safe for everyone, you're welcome to leave."

A few of the girls looked around, as if they expected someone to walk out. No one did, much to my surprise, though Autumn put a lot of focus into picking at a hangnail on her thumb. At least we'd established some ground rules for this unexpected conversation.

After an uncomfortable beat, another girl raised her hand. "Does it hurt?"

"It hurt for me. A lot. Though I can't stress enough, this might not be the case for you, and if your partner doesn't care, it's going to hurt worse. Because they'll just go at it without bothering to see how you're holding up."

A few girls exchanged horrified glances, and I wanted to take the whole thing back. I kept letting my resentment for Ethan bite through my words.

"Look." I held out my hands. "It's not like I'll never have sex again. I just had a really bad experience, but I've talked to people who've done it a lot and they think it's great."

By people, I mainly meant Paul.

"Not everyone likes it though, right?" Astrid's nervous tone gave me pause. Astrid didn't get nervous, and I didn't want to give the impression that sex was some weird rite of passage.

I squeezed her shoulder. "Not everyone has to do it. I'm just talking about people who want to. They generally seem to think it's fun, or whatever."

"That's a lie the patriarchy tells us so boys can keep getting laid," said a short girl with a splash of freckles across her nose. Where did she get her information?

"The patriarchy desires girls while punishing them for being desirable. Your worth is measured by how well you squeeze between the lines. That's the lie." I did my best to keep the exasperation out of my voice, but from the way a few of the girls edged away from me, my best hadn't been good enough. "However, girls can, and do, enjoy sex. Haven't any of you ever masturbated? That felt good, right?"

Most of them shook their heads, some with more vigor

than others, which made me think they were lying. But I couldn't blame them. The one time I thought I'd give it a try, the idea of touching myself embarrassed me so much, I had to stop before I really started.

"Did you bleed?" a younger girl in back asked. "My cousin told me girls who have sex for the first time bleed worse than their periods, and it gets all over the guy."

"I bled a little, but it wasn't like anything out of a horror movie. Bleeding is going to be the least of your worries anyway. When you're naked in front of someone else, it's really hard not to pick yourself apart and focus on all your flaws."

The girl turned stark white, and I had to wonder if I was any better than her cousin, who had obviously tried to scare her into keeping her virginity. Every time I opened my mouth, it felt like I said the wrong thing. No matter how many times I told them sex could be good, it's like they didn't want to believe me. Or maybe they had no reason to. It's not like I had personal experience in good sex to back up my claim.

"I think I'm making a lot of mistakes here." I glanced back at Astrid, who had that secretive smile on her face again. "Can we take a break? I didn't expect to walk into this today."

"That's a good idea." Astrid took the lead in the room again. "Let's give this a rest, give CeCe a chance to be more prepared, and we'll pick another time to meet up."

After a few skeptical glances among the girls, they agreed. They probably thought of all the other times in their life they'd been promised a real discussion about sex, only to be told to wait. But I couldn't use them as an open forum for me to complain about all the ways one guy had let me down. That felt icky, and dishonest.

After the girls had filed out of our cabin, Astrid turned to me. "Sorry I sprung that on you."

"Yeah, what was that about?" I had a lot of annoyed energy buzzing around inside me, and I didn't have a place to direct it. This discussion Astrid promised had somehow turned into a lecture and a disaster. I wasn't mad at her, not really, but it felt like she'd led me into a tiger cage wearing a meat dress.

"Some of the younger girls came to me this afternoon with a lot of questions, and I didn't know how to answer them. I was serious when I said you should lead workshops."

"So you wanted me to scare them away from sex?"

"No. It's not like that at all. I want them to be prepared for what it's really like. None of us had any idea, and we're supposed to be the senior leaders here."

"That's the problem. I don't know what it's really like!" I exploded, and Astrid shrank back from me. "What I told you guys was really personal, and supposed to be just for us. I didn't know you were going to put me on display."

196

"I promise I didn't mean it like that." Astrid's baby-doll face scrunched up. "We learned so much from you, and I thought you could share your story, because I respect you."

"I know you're born into this life where you think every screwup is an opportunity for growth in other people, but that's not me. My embarrassing sex story is mine, and I choose who I share it with. Clearly, I made a mistake."

I walked away from her, slamming the door behind me.

Chapter 17

I marched up the path toward the big house, where I knew Paul would be on kitchen duty. I needed to see someone I trusted. With my eyes on my feet, I ran headfirst into him.

"Whoa. Hey." He held my shoulders to steady me. "Where are you going looking like someone just ran over your cat and now you're going to run over them?"

"I was looking for you," I said. "Can we go somewhere that isn't my cabin?"

"Hmm. Trouble in Christian paradise?"

"I think I traumatized, like, half the girls at camp."

Paul laughed. "Why does that not surprise me?"

"Forget hellfire and brimstone. If the powers that be really wanted to keep good Christian girls from having sex, they'd just tell them what it's really like."

"Ouch."

"Maybe that's an exaggeration. But still. I'm mad right

now, okay? Astrid invited a bunch of people to the cabin so she could put my awful sex life on display. Like I was a life lesson. 'Wait for sex, girls, or you'll end up like CeCe.'"

"I figured something like that would happen." His lips thinned. "Walk with me?"

We took the trail that led behind the chapel, one not as frequently used or as well maintained. The grass had grown over, and it brushed against my ankles. We walked past a building that had fallen out of use. The blue paint chipped from hard winters and clung to the old clapboard like silent tears. We found a flat rock up on a hill that overlooked the whole camp.

After a long beat of comfortable quiet, where we sat next to each other and stared at the lake, he turned to me. "Do you think Astrid set you up to be a fallen angel?"

"I don't know." I rubbed my burning cheeks. "She said she didn't mean it like that, and she always comes off as so genuine, but it felt like she wanted me to reinforce her stance on abstinence, and that's not what I'm about."

"Do you think it's possible they're just so starved for information, they'll take what they can get, even if it's not the greatest story?"

"I considered it." When I'd left my cabin, I'd figured they could Google anything they really wanted to know, but they lived different lives than me. I had no clue what kind of trouble they'd get into for a simple Google search if they got caught. Or what misinformation they'd stumble upon. The Internet was a wasteland.

"I'm not defending Astrid," Paul said. "Putting you on the spot like that wasn't a good idea, but she probably thinks highly of you if she trusts your advice. I don't think she intended to be malicious about it, or use you to scare Christian girls into waiting for marriage."

My jaw dropped. "You're giving her the benefit of the doubt?"

"Why so surprised? I like your cabin. They seem like cool girls."

"You don't like Christians."

"I don't like hypocrites." He ran a hand through his hair. "Growing up in the church, I met a lot of different types. A good majority used Christianity to further their own sense of superiority, to hold their faith and knowledge over others as a way to condemn them while lifting themselves up. But I also knew genuine people. Kind people."

"So what you're saying is, it's basically like the rest of the world? Because there are nice people and assholes in every walk of life."

"Yeah. I guess so." He frowned. "Though there is usually a higher concentration of assholes in Christian circles."

"Fair enough." I nudged him. "I just wish I had something

good to tell them about sex."

"Do you want to hear my opinion about it?"

"No, you'll just say sex is awesome. You've told me that enough, thanks."

He leaned back on his hands. "Did I ever tell you how scared I was the first time?"

"What?" I crossed my legs and faced him, my chin in my hands. "You were scared? Of sex? I don't believe it."

He looked around, like someone was hiding behind a tree, just waiting for him to confess his long-held fear. "This doesn't leave this rock."

I zipped my lips. "I swear on the guy who used to date your mom."

"The first time, I was terrified I'd be . . . well, I'd be like Ethan."

"You could never." My eyes widened. "But were you bad at it?"

"Probably." He laughed. "I could tell Lara wasn't enjoying it, so I asked her if she wanted to stop. She said she wanted to keep going, but I, uh, finished right then."

"Oh my God." That didn't match anything I'd heard about Paul in the locker room. He was the most experienced person I knew, and I used to be curious about the details, how it all worked, but he'd never said much beyond the basics.

"That night I couldn't sleep. I kept thinking I'd go to school the next day and she'd tell everyone I'd been a two-pump chump."

"Lara's not like that." She was my favorite of Paul's ex-girlfriends. She was one of the few who didn't act like I was a problem she had to get out of her way.

"I know." He stared off with a half smile on his face. "But that kind of stuff gets in your head. I hate saying this, but it didn't occur to me to help her finish, so she left frustrated and I left embarrassed, and the whole thing was kind of a mess."

"But it couldn't have been that bad. You guys did it again."

"Would you have done it with Ethan again? If he hadn't turned out to be a bag of dicks?"

"Yeah." I rested my weight on my elbows. "But not because I liked it. I thought I'd done a bad job, and I would've done it again to, I don't know, cancel out what happened before. I would've kept doing it until I felt like I'd done it right."

"That's fucking tragic."

"Tell me about it. Remember the summer I trained myself to dot every *i* with a heart? And then I went to school the first day and got in trouble and had to unlearn it all? It was kind of like that. I was trying to train myself into seeing little hearts when I had sex."

"Jesus." He swept a hand over his stricken face. "I wonder if it was like that for Lara. If she just kept doing it until it became tolerable."

"Maybe at first." When he paled, I hugged his arm. "But

she must've eventually enjoyed it, because she never said a bad word about you."

"I probably owe her an apology for all the bad sex."

"I think she's over it."

"I hope. We've both moved on, but damn, this conversation is bringing up my insecurities all over again."

I tapped a finger to my lips. "They say you never forget your first time, but I wonder if it's because the shame sticks with you forever and ever."

"I sure as hell hope not." He shuddered. "I definitely got better at it though. It's a small comfort, but I've got that, I guess."

"How did you get better? Does practice make perfect?"

"Um, it's not like dotting an *i* with a heart, if that's what you mean." His eyebrows drew together as he got lost in his thoughts. "After all the lectures from my mom about how to respect girls and what consent means, I learned how to listen."

"Listen to what? Are you saying you're a vagina whisperer?"

"Yes. Vaginas talk to me and tell me their secrets." He gave me a bland stare. "I mean, I listened to my girlfriends. Asked them what they wanted, if they liked something, and it became a lot more enjoyable for both of us."

"Girls talked about you. In the locker room. Like, all the time. It was annoying."

His chest puffed up, and I had to resist the urge to roll

my eyes. "What did they say? 'That dashing stud Paul, he's an amazing lover'? Or 'He's ruined me for all other guys'?"

"Pssh, please. No." I shoved him. "After you and Lara broke up, they all talked about how there was just something about you, and blah, blah, blah."

"I feel like you're leaving out the good stuff with the 'blah, blah, blah.'"

"Hardly." He really didn't need the encouragement. "And they constantly asked me if I'd be cool with them asking you out, like I was your keeper or something."

He tensed beside me. "What did you say?"

"I said I didn't care." I suddenly took a great amount of interest in the dandelions at my feet. A fruit fly landed on one of the petals and crawled inside. "What else would I say?"

"Nothing."

The silence stretched between us, and it felt like he was waiting for me to say something, but I didn't know what he wanted from me. I played with the string on the front of my hoodie. "Nothing?"

He took a deep breath but wouldn't meet my eyes. "I mean, I don't know why they'd ask. Everyone knew you were with Ethan."

Even from beyond the grave of my dead feelings, Ethan lingered like the worst kind of ghost. Not the kind with unfinished business, but the one who just refused to go away. "Ugh, I fucking hate that guy."

"Finally." Paul let out a deep, rumbling laugh.

"I'm serious."

"By all means, let it out. I'm here for this."

"God, it feels good to say that out loud. I hate his ugly shirts and how he'd wear black socks with sandals, and he'd take me to the same field to make out but didn't always bring a blanket. And I really hate how he picked his nose that one time, and wiped it under his truck seat like I couldn't see, but I totally saw it, and I almost broke up with him right then."

"Forget everything I said about coming to camp. This was worth it."

"Most of all, I hate how much I wanted my first time to be special, and how I made him special because of it." I'd been more honest in just over a week at camp than I'd been with myself in months, and it left me feeling drained and my heart sore. "How could you stand to be around me before I figured this out?"

He traced my jawline with his fingers and cupped my face with a gentle hand. "Because I always knew you'd come back, lioness."

I turned my head to hide my smile. We'd been touching each other in different and more intimate ways ever since we'd started fake-dating, which made the ruse more believable, but maybe it had started to become a bit too believable. Maybe that was why we hadn't had our official breakup yet. Though I still wasn't sure if my feelings were real, or if I'd created them. I liked being Paul's temporary girlfriend. I liked the way it made me feel. But was I really willing to risk our friendship over a few inconvenient butterflies?

Paul stood and stretched his arms over his head. "We should get back. We have another exciting round of workshops ahead of us before dinner."

I groaned. "Tell me again why I wanted to stay?"

"Because the Wells family budget requires you to be gone for three weeks. And I'm with you, even though I had looked forward to getting ripped working with my stepdad this summer."

"You'd be the worst buff guy ever. Your ego already needs a check, and you'd get bored with all the working out and try to hook up an Xbox to your treadmill."

"True story. Plus, I get my workouts in other ways." He wiggled his eyebrows.

"That's so charming." I gave him my sweetest smile. "And with all your good sex moves, it's a mystery as to why you're still single."

"Not really. That emotional investment you're so fond of just makes it easier for people to walk out on you." He shifted his stance and made quick work of changing the subject. "Are you going to bail on dinner to give more sex ed lessons?"

"I've had enough of sex today. I'd rather have cheese."

"You're in luck." He grabbed my hands to pull me to my feet, and I jumped off the rock, sticking the landing right beside him. "I helped out in the kitchen earlier, and I might've spied a giant block of Gouda."

I grabbed the front of his shirt. "Don't lie to me."

"Not kidding." He carefully removed my grip. "I almost stole it, because I know how much you hate to share, but I spent way too long just staring at it while I tried to figure out how to smuggle it under my shirt. The chef sort of caught on."

"Your efforts are noted." I laced my fingers and held them against my chest as I fluttered my lashes. "What would I do without you?"

"Eat less cheese, probably."

We came around the corner of the chapel, where Astrid, Sarina, and Mandy lingered outside the next workshop. They all had equal amounts of shame on their faces. I guess Astrid hadn't come up with the scheme on her own, but at least they knew they'd screwed up.

"Can we talk?" Astrid asked.

"I'll catch up with you at dinner," Paul said.

"Wait. Which workshop are you going to?" I asked.

"Waiting for Marriage." He stuck his tongue out and dashed off.

I turned back to Astrid, a laugh still on my face. "We can talk."

"We are so sorry," she said. Sarina and Mandy nodded next to her, even though they hadn't been there. "We never meant to put you in an uncomfortable position. We still think sex education is important and necessary, but we won't ask you to participate."

"We understand how that looked, and we can't apologize enough," Mandy said.

"We know a little bit," Astrid said. "Not a lot, but enough to keep the secret workshop going, we think. But we'll warn you when it's happening so you don't walk in to that again."

"I can cover"—Sarina's face flamed—"what to do when you touch you-know-what for the first time, and at least warn them that it is definitely *not* like milking a cow."

I looked them all over, finding nothing but sincerity. Astrid had irritated me by leading me into that situation without talking to me about it first, but she also put her entire camp experience on the line to defend me in Pastor Dean's office. She wouldn't have done that if she didn't actually care. Paul was right. These girls were the real deal.

"Thank you," I said. If Mandy could forgive me, who was I to hold a grudge? It's not like any of them had purposefully tried to steal my boyfriend. "Seriously. I love you guys."

"We love you too." Mandy brought us in for a group hug. "We've felt terrible all afternoon, and if you didn't forgive us, we'd understand, but it would've killed us."

"Cabin eight girls don't give up on each other so easily," I said. "I'm not comfortable talking about sex with strangers, but if any of you have questions when trying to do the workshop, I'll do my best to answer."

"No." Astrid shook her head. "You've already done enough. We'll cover it from here."

Mandy and Astrid headed inside, but Sarina hung back from the group, worrying her bottom lip between her teeth. She'd worn a similar expression right before she'd told me about Milk-Gate. Whatever she had on her mind, I hoped it didn't involve another injury.

"Can I talk to you for a second?" Sarina pulled me against her, like she didn't want anyone else to overhear.

"Sure." I walked with her around the side of the building. "What's going on?"

"Astrid said Autumn was at your sex workshop?"

"First of all, it wasn't *my* sex workshop—"

"Was she there?" Sarina continued to chew on her lip as she glanced around.

"Yeah." Okay, this had officially gotten weird. "Why?"

"Did she say anything about me?"

I figured Sarina knew Autumn the way everyone sort of knew each other at camp, but I'd never seen them hang out. "No. Am I missing something?"

Sarina glanced around again and lowered her voice. "You can't tell anyone. Not even Mandy and Astrid. No one knows."

"No one knows what?"

"We kissed last summer."

"Nice." I went to give her a fist bump, but she stared at me, stunned, like she couldn't believe she'd said those words out loud. "Come on, Autumn is sweet. At least she doesn't think I'm going to burn in Hell, so that's a plus. Do you like her?"

Sarina had a faraway look in her eyes. "Not anymore. I used to, but she seemed horrified afterward, and that's not exactly the response you want when you kiss someone. This place makes it hard to just exist, you know? There is all this pressure on us to be examples in our communities, examples for younger Christians, and they never make room for people who don't fit their mold. I can't really talk to anyone about it."

"You can talk to me. And I bet you could talk to Mandy and Astrid, too, but if you don't want to, I won't push it."

"Thanks." She walked with me back toward the workshop. "Sometimes I think it's easier for me, because I like guys, too, but it's really not. Pretending is never easy, is it?"

I gave her a lopsided grin. "Preaching to the choir, my friend."

We went inside the workshop, which I hadn't bothered to look up on the schedule. Astrid informed me it was another one on how to talk to non-Christians about Jesus, which meant it was the perfect time for me to catch another nap. They had a sprinkling of other topics, but a large number of workshops seemed to focus on converting other people. Maybe it had something to do with their dwindling resources, but if Pastor Dean really wanted to get more campers, he'd fashion it a lot less like a cult.

Chapter 18

After the workshop, aka my afternoon nap, and my rotation at the nurse's station, aka an hour of my life I'd never get back, I headed to my cabin. I pushed open the door to find Mandy, Sarina, and Astrid sitting on the braided rug with about a thousand condoms and three cucumbers. "Should I leave you alone with your . . . dates?"

Sarina yelped and threw her cucumber with a condom clinging to the end. It hit Astrid and fell to the ground. The condom got tangled in her hair. Astrid pulled it out of her curls, dropping it to the side with the other unwrapped ones.

"Where did you get all of these?" I picked up a box sitting on Astrid's bed. "Magnum, huh? You guys have really high expectations."

Mandy shifted her gaze, as if she expected a counselor to Kool-Aid-man it through the wall and bust her. "We raided Pastor Dean's storage cabinet."

"Ew." I did *not* want to think about why Pastor Dean had so many condoms on hand.

"They're not his." Astrid laughed. "It's all the condoms he's confiscated from room searches over the years. All Magnum. I don't think any of the guys who brought them actually thought they'd get to use them. They just wanted to say they needed the big ones."

"Boys are ridiculous." I picked up a cucumber. "But if you're trying to figure out how to roll on a condom, I wouldn't use these. You'll never meet this person. And if you do, run like hell, because wow."

"We thought bananas would be better, even if they're curved," Sarina said. "But one of the freshmen has a banana allergy, so there aren't any at camp."

"Even if they're curved?" I tossed the cucumber between my hands. "Surprise, sometimes people can be curved down there too."

"Was Ethan . . . ?" Mandy's face screwed up. "Nope. Forget it. I don't want to know."

"No, God, that's just a thing everyone knows," I said.

They all gave me blank stares. Okay. So maybe everyone didn't know. At least it wasn't a known thing at Jesus camp, but that wasn't really saying much.

"I mean, people like me," I said. "Who live in the real world."

"Are you saying we don't live in the real world?" The hard edge to Astrid's tone caught my attention. I'd never seen her mad like this before. Her eyes got brighter, but not a sparkly bright, more like a fire she could barely contain. It was equal parts terrifying and awesome.

"I mean, you know, social media and secular movies and things like that." I fumbled over my words as Astrid's gaze continued to cut into me. "I know you're on social media, but your interests are pretty tailored, and there's a bigger world out there."

"Oh yeah. Those things are all so real." Astrid crossed her arms. "Because people are their truest selves online and everything happens like it says in the movies, right?"

My cabinmates knew I wasn't a Christian. They accepted me anyway, without judgment or a hint of thinking of me as less than them, and I'd thrown it back in their faces, like I was somehow above them. I'd never been more annoyed with or ashamed of myself as I was in this moment. "You're right. I'm sorry—I screwed up. It won't happen again."

My conversation with Paul gnawed at me, where he said the girls at camp were starved for information. Hadn't I wanted the same thing? I knew enough to use condoms, but didn't know how to put one on. I knew romantic gestures felt nice, but didn't know they were just icing on a well-established cake. I knew saying yes meant consent. I didn't know pressure or fear of losing the guy negated the yes. I didn't know consent involved saying yes more than once, or that it was okay to take it back.

There was so much no one had ever talked to me about. And I had regular Internet access, unlike Mandy, and watched R-rated movies, unlike Astrid, and had a mom who held a pretty realistic worldview on teenage sex, unlike Sarina. I had the ability to get all the information I needed, but didn't bother to look up, because I assumed so much was common knowledge. Turned out, when it came to sex, knowledge wasn't all that common.

"Thank you for apologizing." Astrid's eyes cleared and she smiled, as if forgiveness came that easily to her. She patted the ground next to her, and I took a seat. "You weren't kidding about these things being slippery. I feel like I've dipped my fingers in motor oil."

"They put something on them to make them easier to slide in, I think." I blew one up and tied it into a balloon. "If you want to put a condom on something more realistic though, try starting out with a peanut."

"Nice burn," Sarina said. "But there aren't any peanuts at camp either."

I flicked the condom balloon in the air and Sarina and Mandy bounced it between them. "I could help you find something more

216

fitting and show you how they go on."

"Are you okay with that?" Astrid asked. "Because we're doing this for our secret workshop. We're trying to learn how, so we can teach it."

"I know. And I'm okay with that." I'd think of it as community service. The kind I wouldn't get credit for toward graduation. "I don't want to see any nice Christian boys lose an eyeball to a rogue slingshot incident."

"We should probably cancel our first meeting then," Mandy said. "Until we have something more appropriate to put the condoms on."

"When is the first meeting?" I asked.

"In an hour." Astrid gathered up the cucumbers and threw them in the trash.

"I've got this one," I said. "I don't think condoms are the right place to start anyway. There are other things worth talking about first."

"You want to lead?" Astrid asked, her eyebrows rising toward her hairline. "Don't get me wrong—I'd rather have you do this than me—but I don't want you to feel pressured or uncomfortable. I feel horrible about how things went last time."

"No, I want to. Not regularly, but I have a specific topic in mind for today." All the things I never knew overlapped with the things I knew now. If I could prevent even one girl from going through the same experience as me, it would all be worth it. "Someone needs to take notes, because we've got a lot of ground to cover."

Astrid grabbed her pen and notebook. "I'm on it."

Thirty girls gathered in a clearing in the woods, double the amount of the last impromptu meet-up. Word had spread. Everyone had blankets and comforters and had lain them over the pine needles and fallen leaves. Like a giant sleepover. Astrid brought along a canvas camp chair, so I'd be high enough for everyone to hear, and if everything went well, I'd even consider opening up a question-and-answer segment.

I sat crisscrossed and took a drink from a bottle of water. "I know a lot of you came here today expecting to learn how to put on a condom, but due to technical difficulties, we have to put that particular lesson on hold. I think we need to go back a little further than that anyway. Keep in mind that I'm straight and cis, and my experience is limited. I'm not the be-all and end-all of sexual knowledge. I'm in this with each of you, so it's going to be more of a discussion than the workshops you're used to. I'm hosting this first meeting on consent."

A girl in the front row rolled her eyes. "We know what consent is."

"Do you?" I motioned to her with the water bottle. "What is it then?"

She pulled on the ends of her dark curls, clearly not thinking I'd put her on the spot. "It's when you let a guy have sex with you."

"No." Did that sound harsh? I didn't mean for it to come out harsh, and I might've said the same thing a month ago, but I needed to be firm in this area. I glanced at Astrid, who gave me a thumbs-up. "Does anyone else have a better answer?"

Autumn raised her hand. "It's when you say it's okay."

"Still no." I took another drink. It felt like it was a hundred degrees in the shade.

A girl wearing braces who sat in the back row raised her hand. "It's when you say yes after being asked."

"Getting warmer, but still not there." I looked at the confused faces. They'd run out of answers, and still had no clue. I saw myself in every one of them. "This is why we're having this meeting. Because I used to think consent meant all those things too."

A girl leaned over to whisper in Autumn's ear and she raised her hand again. "We're having a little trouble understanding this. Are you saying consent isn't saying yes?"

"It's more than that," I said. "If you say no first, if you feel pressured, if you feel like you're going to make your partner angry, if they don't make it clear it's okay to say no, how much do you really mean that yes? *Yes* is just a word. You have to mean it for it to be consent."

The girls buzzed among themselves and Astrid raised her hand, probably to keep things moving along. "What happens if you say yes and change your mind?"

"It's okay for you to say no after you say yes," I said. "If you're uncomfortable, if you're having regrets, if you're bored, if you just plain don't feel like it, it doesn't matter the reason. You have a right to say no or stop whenever."

"Whoa." Autumn had a dazed look in her eyes. "I never thought about any of this."

"I know, right?" This meeting was way different from the last one. I didn't feel like an oddity on display. I had something important to say, and the girls looked at me like they were open to listening. "There's more. After you say yes, your partner should check in with you to make sure you're still okay. And it's okay to lay down those ground rules before you start. Have a conversation. Let them know what you want."

The girl who whispered to Autumn raised her hand. "I've never come close to having sex. I've never even kissed anyone before. What if I don't know what I want?"

I didn't really have an answer for her. This was where having a little more experience would've come in handy. The idea of telling a guy what I wanted scared the crap out of me, but I had to tell her something, or this meeting would fall apart.

"How do you know what kind of food you like to eat?" I asked.

"I don't know. I just try different things, and oh—" Her eyes lit up. "I see what you did there. Are you saying the key to finding what you want is trying different things?"

I nodded. That was exactly what I meant . . . after she'd provided the answer.

A girl with a narrow face, a camper I didn't recognize from the last meeting, raised her hand. "I'm not meaning to be disrespectful here, but isn't talking about wants and telling us to try different things just encouraging premarital sex?"

"Didn't you come here to learn how to put on a condom?" I asked.

She bit her lip. "Never mind."

I got out of my chair and kneeled in front of her. "If you're concerned about protecting your body, shouldn't you be equally concerned about protecting your heart?"

"That makes sense in my mind, but . . ." She tightly laced her fingers. "My whole life I've been told sex before marriage is a sin."

"Do you think I'm a sinner?"

"Yes." Her eyes filled as another girl pushed her in the back. "I'm not judging you, and I don't think Satan is working through you. I believe we're all sinners."

"Do you believe sinners should be punished?"

"No." She shook her head as her bottom lip trembled. "Nothing like that."

"Okay." I gave her a hug. "You're okay. If you want to wait for marriage, that is perfectly fine. The awesome thing about taking control of your body is that you get to make that choice. But once you're married, it's still important to know this stuff. Consent doesn't end when you say 'I do.'"

"Thanks," she whispered in my ear.

While I didn't agree with most of her beliefs, it wasn't my place to argue. I wanted everyone here to be honest, without feeling like they needed to defend themselves. Especially because I was still learning along with them.

I stood and paced in front of the group. "Here's the deal. I didn't know any of this before I had sex, and when it was over, I felt like I'd done something wrong. It's not supposed to be like that. You should be able to share the experience with someone you trust. If you can't trust someone to be considerate of your needs, how can you trust them at all?"

Sarina raised her hand. She quickly glanced at Autumn, and the two of them made the briefest of eye contact before looking away. "Are you afraid of having sex again?"

"No." I tapped a finger to my lips. "Maybe a little. But I'd like to think I'd make better choices now that I understand how it feels to make the wrong ones."

A junior girl with bright red cheeks, who sat on the opposite side of Autumn, raised her hand. "This might not be in line with the workshop, but is Paul really single?"

"I'm pleading the Fifth on that." Sure, Paul was single in the technical sense, but the idea of him dating other people made an angry snake coil in my belly. "Any other questions?"

A dozen hands shot into the air. I spent the rest of the afternoon fielding a million questions about every scenario imaginable. What if you had laryngitis and couldn't talk? What if the music was too loud and he couldn't hear you? What if he tripped when he had a hard-on and fell into you? I had to shake my head and pass on that one.

This hadn't been my intended purpose when I'd come to camp, but it filled that empty place inside me with something meaningful. My experiences mattered. What I had to say about them mattered. These girls were open and imaginative, they cared about everything almost as much as they cared about each other, and it made me damn proud to be part of this.

Chapter 19

Today marked the last day I'd have to help out in the nurse's station. Thank God. Half the kids at camp expected the healing hand of Heaven to cure their everyday ails. I wasn't good enough at science or the Bible to take on this job. I'd be rotated to the arts and crafts room, which I hadn't set foot in, but that suited me fine. I'd made awesome macaroni necklaces in elementary school.

Nurse Holland, a gray-haired lady with a wide smile, told me I'd be showing my replacement around for the next hour. Though there wasn't a whole lot to the cramped room with three chairs, a single cot, and a wall of metallic shelves packed with first-aid supplies. I'd have at least fifty-nine minutes of my shift left to spare.

"I'm going to take my lunch and watch my stories now." Nurse Holland had a mean *General Hospital* addiction. "Radio me if things get out of hand."

She left and Ethan walked in after her, wearing a lime-green shirt with a picture of a tractor on it. He took one look at me and turned a deep shade of red. I couldn't read his expression. My hand reached for the radio on instinct.

"Do you think I'm going to hurt you?" He took a step forward, and must've seen something on my face, because he stepped back again. "You actually think I'm going to hurt you. Wow. How did we get here?"

"I'm not comfortable being alone with you." It stung a little, saying that out loud and knowing it was true. "Either you can leave or I can. I don't really care which."

"I'll go. I'm sorry being around me bothers you." The troubled look in his eyes almost made me feel bad for him. Almost. He turned to go, and a young kid who must've been a freshman burst through the door holding his face as blood ran between his fingers.

My stomach went woozy. I couldn't stand the sight of blood. Just another reason why this job was the worst. "Sit him in the chair and get him a towel!" I yelled at Ethan.

Ethan shifted the weight between his feet. "I thought you wanted me to go."

"We're clearly not alone." I flung my arm toward the bleeding kid. "Help him."

Ethan guided the kid toward a chair and got a white towel

off the counter. He tilted the kid's head back and had him grab it while he got another to clean him up. Across the room, I bit my hand and tried not to throw up. Eventually the blood flow slowed to a trickle, and the kid switched to tissues. Ethan threw the bloody towels in a bag and took them out back.

"What's your name?" I asked the kid.

"Jonah Phan." He dabbed at his nose with a tissue. "I think I broke my nose."

"How? Where are your friends? Did anyone see you get hurt?"

He flinched as I fired questions at him. "No one saw me. I was messing around by the dock and tried to balance between two canoes. I fell and hit my face on one of them."

"Why on earth—never mind. Don't need to know." I poked at the bridge of his nose and it didn't wobble. "It might swell. I'll get you some ice and you can wait here for Nurse Holland to get back." She was going to be pissed at this kid for interrupting her stories.

I snapped on a pair of rubber gloves, picked up one of the tissues by the white corner, and brought it to the trash. Jonah threw his hand out. "Wait. Don't throw that away yet."

"Are you serious?" I held the tissue away from me and curled my lip. "Do you want to keep it as some kind of souvenir?"

"Can you pull it apart?" His eyes shone as he looked at the tissue. "My mom found an image of Jesus on my bandage after the first time I skinned my knee, and she told me it meant I was blessed. I just want to see if it's still true."

"If you were truly blessed, you wouldn't have fallen face-first into a canoe."

"I guess you're right." He kicked the chair leg.

"Okay, I'll do it, but just this once." The kid looked so downtrodden, it wouldn't hurt to let him have a go at the Christian Rorschach test. I used my index fingers and thumbs on the corners and pulled the tissue apart. "See anything?"

He tilted his head. "I don't know. It could be Jesus, or a butterfly."

"Maybe it's Jesus warning you not to fly too high. Keep those feet on the ground and off boats." I threw the tissue and the gloves in the trash and immediately pumped a gallon of hand sanitizer into my palm. "I'll radio the nurse to make sure nothing is broken."

Once Nurse Holland came back to fuss over Jonah, the boy who'd tried to walk on water, I stepped out into the sunlight. Warm rays washed over me, burning off the chill of the nurse's station. I turned the corner, and bumped into Ethan.

"Sorry." I spun around and went the other way.

"CeCe, wait." Ethan caught up to me. "Can we talk? Out

here in the open, since you're not okay being alone with me."

"I'm not really interested in anything you have to say, to be honest."

"Please." His deep brown eyes pleaded with me. "I've been waiting for a chance to say I'm sorry, and I can't seem to get you alone. I don't want to upset Mandy by going around her when she doesn't want to see me."

"Fine." I crossed my arms and tapped my foot against the gravel path. An apology was about the only thing I'd be willing to hear from him. "Make it quick."

"Are you afraid of me?" The anguish in his voice caught me off guard. I'd almost gotten accustomed to the cold and distant version of camp Ethan.

"I'm not afraid. I'd just rather not be anywhere near you. Especially not alone. Not after what you did to me at the bonfire."

"I feel terrible about that. I'm sorry. The bonfire got out of hand, but I still would've shared my testimony, even if you hadn't been here."

"Are you serious? That's your idea of an apology?" Not only did he have zero regrets about the bonfire, he still saw himself as the victim. "You lied about me to the whole camp. You referred to me as Satan in disguise."

"I didn't mean you were Satan." He stared at his feet. "I meant the act of sex."

"Sex isn't dirty or immoral, and it's certainly not Satan's doing." I didn't know why I even bothered. "If you really felt that way about sex, maybe you should've told me that before you put so much pressure on me to do it."

"That's how Satan works." He shook his head as if I were the one who didn't get it. "He influences your heart and makes you do things you wouldn't normally do."

"What a load of bullshit." I threw my hands into the air. "If you want to be sincere, try taking some responsibility for your actions."

"That's not what I believe, though."

"Isn't that convenient?" This whole conversation was pointless and a complete waste of my time. "Have you ever thought maybe your beliefs are screwed up?"

"Yes." He tilted his head back and rubbed his eyes. "I question everything I've been taught. All the time. I questioned it the most when we were together."

I looked for the guy I thought I knew, and couldn't even find the one I'd created in my head. "How did you become like this? That crap you pulled at the bonfire? You don't act like that at home; you don't talk like that. It's so fake."

"My pastor advised me to seek redemption. I went through some intense spiritual lessons with him, which forced me to confront how absorbed I'd gotten in mainstream culture once

230

I started public school."

"You're making it sound like you were brainwashed." Or maybe he'd always been like this. Maybe he'd tried to change himself to fit in at school. While I understood that particular problem more than I cared to admit, I didn't use people and throw them away on my path to finding myself. "Why didn't you talk to me? I would've listened."

"I got scared." He rubbed his eyes. "The day after we had sex, I had so many doubts. About what we'd done, and about who I was becoming."

Part of me felt bad for him. The part that was trained by society to think of my fears and needs and wants as lesser. The part that demanded I feel guilty for the shortcomings of others. The part quick to shoulder blame where I'd been hurt.

The part I refused to accommodate, because I knew all the ways it could break me.

"I was scared too," I said. The hopeful look on his face, like he had my empathy, turned my stomach. "But you left me to deal with it on my own."

"I didn't want to leave you." He reached for my hand, and I backed away. "But in order to strengthen my relationship with Jesus, I had to make sacrifices."

"What sacrifices have you made?"

"I lost you." He kicked a rock at his feet. "I lost Mandy."

"Because of your choices." I closed my eyes and counted to ten, taking deep breaths in between. We didn't think the same, so it was no surprise we couldn't communicate the same. "Sacrifice is something you do for the good of others. Not for the good of yourself."

His posture stiffened. The apologetic mask he wore slipped, revealing a haughty and proud boy who didn't like to be told no. The true form he hid under the nice guy veneer. "I don't expect you to get it, since you're not a real Christian."

"That's a weak argument. I may not know the Bible, but I'm familiar with another book called *Merriam-Webster*. And you better believe I know the definition of *sacrifice*."

I walked away, not even giving him a backward glance. The days of being manipulated by his sob stories and conflicted feelings about his faith were over. I had nothing left to give him. I'd taken it all back for myself, and I intended to keep it.

Chapter 20

Arts and crafts appealed to me way more than the nurse's station, even if the room was a little dead. Occasionally we'd get some freshmen girls in who wanted to make friendship bracelets, but most of the kids at camp were too old for finger painting and papier-mâché. I had no issue with it though. I got to put in my hour with Mandy, and we invented our own bizarre game of Pictionary using melting beads to pass the time.

"Are you guys almost done?" Sarina burst into the arts and crafts room, her skin still shimmering from her suntan lotion. "I'm in desperate need of help here."

Sarina and Jerome had apparently gotten over their awkward phase at the lake today, where they both had lifeguard duty. She planned to sneak out to meet him. That meant endless hours of agonizing over underwear he'd never see, and her choices ran between plain cotton, cotton with stripes, and cotton with flowers. At least she didn't have days-of-the-week panties. Not that it mattered.

"Almost." Mandy contemplated my collection of melting green beads. "Is it a mossy rock? Or is it supposed to be a shamrock?"

"It's clearly a turtle." I pointed to its head. "How can you not see it?"

"I don't know." Sarina peered over my shoulder. "Looks like a rock to me."

"This is a terrible game." I swept the beads back into the box. "We're free to go, but you'll have to have the great underwear debate without me. I'm on dinner prep."

"Boo," Sarina said.

They went back to the cabin while I put my time in at the kitchen. Paul hadn't been lying about the Gouda. They had waited a few days to bring it out, and I snuck a bite while cutting it up for the cheese board. After mixing the salad, I took off my apron and left. Hopefully I'd have time for a quick shower. I smelled like a vegetable garden.

Sarina still hadn't finalized her underwear choice by the time I'd finished getting ready, and I told her to worry about it after dinner. We walked down to the dining hall and met up with the boys. Ethan lagged behind them, no doubt wanting to avoid all of us. I hadn't seen him around camp all day, not even at lunch, and it surprised me how little I cared about him now.

So much had changed in such a short time. He gave Mandy a weak smile, which wasn't returned.

I hooked my arm through Mandy's. "Are you doing okay?"

"Yeah. Even knowing what I know about him, it still hurts. And I feel guilty for hurting, which hurts more. Is there something wrong with me?"

"No." I slowed our pace until we remained a little behind the group. "It's okay to hurt. If you need anything, we're here for you. Girls of cabin eight for life, right?"

"For life." She smiled.

In the dining hall, I got in line with my tray, next to Paul. "Tell me if you see anything you could put a condom on. Something long and hard enough."

"What the hell is going on in cabin eight?" he asked.

"Language, Mr. Romanowski."

After the success of the consent workshop, more girls had come to the next one, which Sarina had led on how not to give a hand job. I had to miss that one due to our conflicting schedules, but Astrid said she ran it like she runs her YouTube tutorials. With a soothing voice and clear, easy-to-understand directions. Sarina planned to lead a follow-up workshop, if tonight's meet-up with Jerome went well. Mandy offered to pitch in for one on masturbation, and steam practically poured out of her burning ears when she told us that, but she said she had to work up the nerve to do it before she could talk about it. Which left the much-anticipated condom one. And since we all agreed that one should be a group effort, we had to wait for our schedules to line up.

As I passed by the sandwiches, which didn't offer much in the sex ed department, Mandy approached with a long pretzel stick. "What do you think about this?"

"Too skinny," I said. "But frozen breadsticks might work."

"No, seriously," Paul said. "What the hell is going on in cabin eight?"

"It's not a big deal." I lowered my voice. "I'm trying to teach some of the girls here how to roll on a condom, and cucumbers aren't realistic."

"Says you." He smirked.

"Says every girl who's ever been with you."

That wiped the smile off his face.

I picked up a corn on the cob and put it on my plate. Not ideal, the kernels could pose a problem, and no one wanted to picture getting it on with a bumpy yellow penis. The Polish sausages might've been too on the nose, and floppy, but if they were frozen, maybe. I put one on the tray. Paul side-eyed my dinner selections but kept his mouth shut. The salad bar had much better options, but everything had been cut up. At the end of the line I put a cream roll on the tray. The bread would be way too flaky, but it would at least be able to offer a live demonstration of the endgame. And I grabbed a huge chunk of Gouda, just for me.

"That is the most Freudian dinner I've ever seen in my life," Paul said.

"Thank you." If I hadn't been holding my tray, I would've curtsied.

We got back to the table, where Sarina and Jerome sat next to each other, giggling. I'd gotten the wrong impression of Jerome when we'd first arrived at camp, but the way he treated Sarina, even after Milk-Gate, warmed my heart.

Peter eyed my tray, glancing at me with red cheeks. I winked at him, and I swear he almost passed out. Nothing got by that kid. Ethan had abandoned our table for a group of junior guys I didn't recognize. Which was for the best. The bonfire debacle still hadn't blown over, and my cabinmates were a fierce and protective pack.

"Do you think you can get some of these, frozen?" I cut my Polish sausage down the middle and stuck a fork in one half, holding it up for Astrid.

"I think I can do better." Astrid turned her salad bowl toward me. "Check it out. They've got zucchini. Those are way smaller than cucumbers."

"Perfect," I said.

"You girls." Jerome shook his head. "If Pastor Dean finds out about this, he's going to send you all packing."

"But he won't find out because you're not going to tell him," Astrid said.

"Tell him what?" Peter blurted out. The curiosity must've been killing him.

"Nothing you need to know, young whippersnapper," Jerome said.

"I'm the same age as the rest of you," Peter grumbled.

"I have no clue what's going on either," Paul said. Which made Peter sit up a little straighter. If Paul didn't know, he probably thought it wasn't worth knowing.

I ate my cheese and corn, leaving the sausage behind. It weirded me out the way Peter kept looking at it and my mouth, like he couldn't wait for me to take a bite. Tonight's activity included a dance, but we could go back to our cabins if we wanted. As soon as we cleared out the benches and the strobe lights went on, I knew this dance wouldn't be for me. I didn't recognize the music, and not in the way I didn't recognize Paul's music.

Paul walked with me toward my cabin after dinner. "I thought you didn't want any part of scaring Christian girls out of sex."

"I'm not scaring anyone. I told you the meeting I led went pretty well," I said. "Tomorrow I'm going to teach them how to put on a condom, which is a necessary life skill."

"How noble of you." He rolled a rock under his foot.

"I didn't think I'd want to get into it, but the girls were pretty respectful at my last meeting, and I know what Astrid's trying to do. Her heart is in the right place."

"It's probably more useful than the Waiting for Marriage workshop." He mimicked throwing up, and I laughed.

"You brought that on yourself." I bumped him with my elbow. "I just hate that I'm the only vocal example these girls have right now. They should explore their sexuality without terrible expectations. I want them to be prepared, not terrified."

"You know what you should do then?" He bent down to whisper in my ear, and his cheek brushed against mine. I shivered as he tucked back a lock of my hair. "Have good sex."

Dozens of goose bumps peppered my skin. I leaned closer to him, taking in the scent of soap and sandalwood, and an idea started to form in my head. One that left me breathless. I'd gotten so caught up in this epic game of pretend, teetering between my platonic and not-so-platonic feelings for Paul, it hadn't occurred to me that I had a third option. One where I could explore my feelings without consequences. Where his issues with commitment wouldn't matter. Without relationship statuses and formal dates and ugly breakups. We'd been through almost everything together. Our friendship could survive a little good sex.

But how did one casually mention the idea of having sex to their best friend? *Hey, you're single and I'm single?* Ew. No. That was what old people said to each other on a hookup cruise. *I'm interested in having sex that doesn't suck—would you be available for that this week?* Might as well be asking for an oil change at a full-service gas station.

He waved a hand in front of my face. "Are you still there?"

"Yeah. Just thinking. About nothing. Regular stuff." So smooth.

"Right . . ." He gave me one of his half smiles. "See you tomorrow?"

"You too," I managed to call after he'd gotten a good thirty yards away.

Mandy came up behind me, with Sarina on her other side. Tonight was the big night. Hand job attempt number two, and over dinner she'd decided on the flower panties Jerome wouldn't actually see.

Shortly after we got back to the cabin, Astrid burst through the door, lifted her shirt, and pulled four zucchinis out of the waist of her shorts. "The whole time I was walking out of the kitchen I thought one of these was going to fall out of my shorts, and I would've had no way to explain myself."

Sarina picked one of them up and wrapped her hand around it. "Should I, um, practice before I meet Jerome tonight?"

"Honey, no." I plucked the zucchini out of her hand. "That's like trying to squeeze blood from a stone. Just get a firm grip, not too firm, and move your hand up and down. You could spit on your hand if it feels too dry or you think you might be in danger of pulling. If you're not feeling sure, ask him what he wants. Communication, remember?"

"What if he wants to . . . reciprocate?"

I shrugged. "Go with it if it's something you want to do? I don't know. Again, I wasn't a fan, but maybe you will be."

The one time Ethan tried hand stimulation, he just shoved his finger in and out of me. It was worse than the sex. His nails had been dirty from helping his dad clean out their shed, and I didn't even want him to touch me, but he insisted. Like he was doing me a favor.

"Is there anything I should know?" Sarina knotted her fingers together. "Should I spray some perfume down there, just in case?"

"Absolutely not. That's a yeast infection waiting to happen." I grabbed her shoulders and looked her square in the eye. "If he makes a single offhand remark about how you smell, I will personally remove his balls."

"You're really scary right now," she said. "I kind of like it."

"Guys say things without realizing how bad it messes us up. Even if they don't mean it, or if they don't know better, it's no excuse for them to be shitheads."

"Ethan didn't say anything like that about you, did he?" Mandy asked quietly.

"No, he still has his balls intact, but it happened to another girl at my school, and it was the worst. Karma came back, though. The guy couldn't even get a date to prom. Every girl in school was terrified he'd do the same to them."

"Serves him right," Astrid said. "I hate the way guys can get away with saying whatever they want about us, but we can't ever win. If we even act like we know what sex is, we're sluts. If we aren't interested in sex, we're cold and emotionless."

"It's unfair," I said. "That's why we have to be vigilant and have each other's backs."

"Seriously," Mandy said. "If we don't look out for each other, no one else will."

"Guys who would do that kind of thing don't deserve us anyway," Sarina said.

"Hear, hear." Astrid pumped her fist in the air.

Sarina went to the bathroom to brush her short cap of hair one more time and apply some last minute berry-flavored lip gloss. She'd colored her eyebrows royal blue and drawn peacock feathers on her lids. When she came out of the bathroom, we oohed and aahed over how pretty she looked, and fussed over the cute summer dress she'd picked out to wear. And like proud parents sending their baby off to college, we crowded at the door and made sure she got to the woods without getting caught.

"Okay," I said once we got back inside. "Let's roll some condoms on these zucchinis."

After I showed them how to pinch the tip so air wouldn't get in, the girls quickly became skilled at outfitting their vegetables. It helped that they had something appropriately sized to work with. At the end of the night, Mandy filled a condom with water and put it on Sarina's pillow. A little you-suck-for-getting-action-while-we're-all-cooped-up-in-here present from us to her. Hopefully her night went so well, she wouldn't care all that much.

As my head hit my pillow, Paul's suggestion to have good sex lingered. If Sarina could work up the courage to try another hand job after Milk-Gate, I could ask Paul to have sex with me. It didn't need to be all emotional. Paul had sex all the time without emotion, and he was a lot better off than me. Time was ticking away at camp. I had to do it before we left, or I'd never get up the nerve to ask him again.

Chapter 21

The next morning, I woke to a tickling sensation on my nose. I reached up to scratch it, and got a face full of shaving cream. Sputtering, I rolled over and wiped my face on my pillow.

"Good morning." Sarina stood over me, laughing, a feather in her hand. "I really appreciated laying my head down last night and having a wet condom explode all over my pillow, so I'm just returning the favor."

"Why me? What about the other two?"

"They'll get theirs when they wake up." Sarina moved on to Astrid, who slept with her hand open and hanging off the bed.

We kind of had it coming.

"How did it go last night?" I asked once we'd all been woken up via shaving cream to the face. "Did you do the thing?"

Sarina got a dreamy look on her face as she hugged her comforter. "I did the thing. And he did the thing to me, and it was amazing."

"It was?" While I was happy for her, I felt like I'd spent months training for a marathon, only to get beaten by someone who'd never run a day in their life.

"Don't get me wrong—I'm still terrified of going that far—but I could do the manual stuff forever. You would've been so proud of me too. I was like a traffic-directing cop." She signaled with her hands. "Over here, too far to the right, now you're clear to go on through."

"Did it hurt when he put his fingers inside you?" Mandy had a look of horror on her face, no doubt recalling her one and only attempt at wearing tampons.

"He didn't put his fingers inside me, just, you know." Sarina twirled her wrist. "Worked on the outside. And it sort of built up, like I had to sneeze. Down there. All my muscles tightened up, and then I let go. My head and stomach felt weightless, but in a good way."

Sarina, who last week couldn't even say the word *penis* out loud, was now schooling me on how to have an orgasm. I'd officially entered the Twilight Zone.

"We should add this to the workshop." Astrid grabbed a notebook, all business, and started jotting things down. "Can you go into more detail? I don't understand what you mean by having to sneeze down there. Was the weightlessness similar to a roller coaster?"

246

"It's kind of hard to describe. You know something is happening to your body, and you want it to happen right away, but getting there feels good too." She blushed so hard, even her neck turned red. "I can't believe I'm saying all this out loud."

"I have to get in the shower now, but I'm so happy for you," I said.

And I meant it. I loved Sarina and I wanted nothing but the best for her, but it still stung. I'd made out with plenty of guys. I'd touched them and let them touch me, but I'd never felt what she described. My insecurities always took me out of the moment. Instead of letting go, I focused on all my faults and flaws. I had to wonder if I'd never experienced what she had because I was broken. Maybe the problem hadn't been Ethan. Maybe it really was me.

After I got out of the shower and got dressed, the girls were still going over every detail of Sarina's night. Now she was claiming she could hear angels' trumpets, and it was all too much. I threw my hair into a wet bun and headed to devotions.

Paul waited for me outside the chapel, and all the things I'd been feeling the night before came into sharp focus. He always told me sex wasn't a big deal, so what was I worried about? I just had to ask him. And not because Sarina had gotten to experience something I'd missed out on. Or mostly not because of that anyway. It would be fine. We'd be fine.

He lifted his hand in a casual wave as I approached. "How did it go with the zucchinis last night? Did you make men out of those boys?"

"Do you want to have sex with me?" I pushed the words out before I could think about the consequences of them, or think at all.

His expression froze before melting into amusement. "Right now?"

"Not right now. Tonight." I waited a beat for him to say something, without really giving him a chance to turn me down. "Never mind. It was a dumb joke."

"Hold up." He studied my face. "You're serious."

"No, I'm not." I stared at the cross hanging over the chapel door above his head. "Forget I said anything. Don't make this weird."

My face burned hotter than the rising sun. Why couldn't I have taken one second to think this through before opening my mouth? I should've stayed at the cabin with Astrid. She would've listened to me and talked me out of this nonsense.

"'Don't make this weird'? This whole summer has been weird." His voice had gotten lower with every word as his expression hardened. He glared at me, and I shriveled against the fire in his gaze. "You wanted to go to Jesus camp, even though I warned you it would be a disaster, and I said fine. Then

248

you wanted to play house to save face in front of Ethan, and I went along with it, but this is beyond fucked-up, even for you."

A few younger campers looked back at him and scurried into the chapel. I hadn't seen Paul this pissed at me since that time in seventh grade when I'd accidentally started a rumor he had a third nipple. In my defense, when we played Two Truths and a Lie at Isha Singh's sleepover, I didn't know everyone would pick the wrong "truth" and run with it.

"What's your problem?" My tone matched my temper. "You're the one who told me I should try having good sex."

"I didn't mean with me!"

"Why? What would be so terrible about having sex with me?"

Tears pooled under my lids, and I willed them back as all my fears rose to the surface. Humiliation staved off the edge of whatever temporary jealousy I'd felt toward Sarina. I'd actually started to believe Paul and I weren't just pretending. I should've known better though; I practically had a degree in one-sided feelings.

"I didn't mean it like that." His shoulders slumped. "But you just dropped this on me. How did you expect me to react?"

"Maybe how you usually act? You said yourself sex isn't a big deal."

He reeled back as if I'd slapped him. "Are you holding that against me?"

"Yes. No. Maybe. I don't know." I had too many feelings in too short a time, and they tumbled over each other, making it impossible for me to find what was true.

"And you threw out the idea of us having sex, because this is what I'm known for, so who the hell cares, right?" He curled his lip, like the very thought disgusted him. "Paul is good for an orgasm, so forget about ten years of friendship? Wow, CeCe. I knew you were impulsive, but I had no idea you could be so goddamned selfish."

"Do you think I don't care about our friendship? That it never once crossed my mind? I don't want to screw that up or ruin what we have, especially if I end up like Lara." Or Bree or Sydney or a dozen other girls.

"What does she have to do with anything?" He shoved his hands through his hair. "Lara and I are friends. You and Lara are friends."

I knew in my head Lara was irrelevant, but my heart kept pushing to hear things I didn't want to know like a jealous, irrational person. "She was pretty hurt when you broke up with her."

"She's with Matt now, and she knows we weren't a good fit." Paul started pacing and raised a fist to his mouth. "Did she tell you I hurt her? Why are we even talking about this?"

"Because you and I wouldn't be friends anymore, and you're so important to me. But I've also been having all these other feelings. I'm not sure if it's the fake-dating or what, and I thought sex could be an alternative to a messy breakup."

"Wait. Back up. What do you mean by 'breakup'?" He put his palms out, like I was the one who'd blown up in this argument and he had to approach me with caution. "Are you talking about a relationship here? Or are you talking about sex?"

I couldn't answer him. Not when he'd made it clear he had no interest in either.

"Don't worry about it." I tried to smile, to act like everything was okay, even though I was dying inside. "I was jealous of Sarina and wanted to make myself feel better. I'm sorry. I think our fake-dating got in my head."

"You asked me to have sex because you were feeling insecure?"

"Yep. That's all it was." If he wanted an out, I'd give him an out. "I didn't think you'd get so mad, or I never would've brought it up."

"Good to know." Clenching his fists, Paul walked away from me.

"Where are you going?" I ran after him, and grabbed his arm, pulling him to a stop. "I get you're irritated with me, but you can't skip devotions."

"Don't tell me what I'm feeling. You have no clue. None at all."

He whirled around, leaving me completely dumbfounded as he stormed away. He clearly didn't want to have sex, but taking the idea back had pissed him off even more. I couldn't say anything to make it right. He couldn't even stand to be around me. I hugged myself as I made my way into the chapel, horrified with the mess I'd created.

I could've dealt with him saying he didn't think of me that way. Maybe I could've even dealt with him laughing at me, but I couldn't deal with him shutting me out. He was my best friend. The person I cared about more than anyone in the world.

And I was losing him.

Chapter 22

I entered the chapel, numb and confused, and took a seat in the back pew I usually occupied with Paul. As much as I'd wanted to chase him down and fix us, I had no idea what to say. *Sorry I asked you to have sex?* Even thinking those words made me want to vomit.

Pastor Dean took the stage to give his sermon. "Today I'll be sharing the Apostle Paul's message of love. Turn to Corinthians 13:4: 'Love is patient, love is kind.'"

Welp. I picked a terrible day to stay awake for devotions. As Pastor Dean droned on, I couldn't sit still. I picked at my nails and shifted in my seat. I tapped my foot against the pew leg and pulled out a hymn book. The pages made a lot of noise as I flicked through them, and a few people turned around to look at me. I folded a loose piece of paper I'd found in the Bible holder into a paper airplane and threw it toward Astrid. It hit another kid in the back of the head.

Why had Paul gotten so mad at me? If he had asked me to have sex, I would've . . . felt like a convenience, an acceptable option. Like I meant nothing more than that.

Oh God.

I'd screwed up so bad, but I still didn't have a clue how to proceed, or what I wanted. After my last experience, I wasn't exactly eager to put myself out there again. Though Paul didn't make me feel bad about myself. With Ethan, I'd felt like I needed his approval, as if how *I* felt about me depended on how *he* felt about me. And I never measured up, was never good enough. It made me miserable.

Paul knew me, all my worst parts, which he had no trouble calling out, and all my best parts too. I didn't seek his approval, because I never needed it. I didn't have an arbitrary line to measure up to, because he never treated me as if I'd fallen short. I could just be me.

Things had changed between us this summer, even before I'd brought up sex, leaving me stuck in the middle of what was and what could be. I thought I might've started to manufacture feelings from the fake-dating. Or I didn't want to admit otherwise, in case he didn't feel the same way. And okay, I found him appealing, but was I actually in love with him? My heart sped up as I tested the weight of that word. Attraction was one thing, but love was something different. Something unexpected.

"I thought it would be simpler to just have sex," I whispered to myself. "Without all those other complicated feelings screwing up our friendship."

A kid in the row ahead of me turned around to give me the stink-eye. I recognized him as the ear-pimple sophomore from the bonfire, and really, he had no room to judge.

"Let us bow our heads to pray," Pastor Dean said.

If only I could go back in time and work through some of this stuff first. I should've gone to Paul honestly, before I asked him to have sex, the way he always came to me. I should've talked to him about all my warm and soft feelings, instead of letting my worst ones guide me. Insecurity would forever be my worst enemy. Because I couldn't deal with falling for my best friend. Because I was in love with my best friend.

"I'm in love with Paul." I let it out in a rush, like, if I didn't say it fast enough, I'd lose my nerve. Several people turned around to shush me, and I waved them off.

There. I said it. No going back. But what was I supposed to do now? He wasn't talking to me. Maybe he would if I told him the truth. At least he'd be understanding, even if he didn't return my feelings. I gulped. I wasn't the most well versed in the truth, all things considered, but if I wanted to make us right again, I had to come to Jesus.

So to speak.

After breakfast and the morning workshop, I took the overgrown path behind the chapel, somehow knowing I'd find him on the flat rock. He had his back to the camp, with his head bowed, and I wondered if he might've been praying. Not wanting to pry into his private moment, I stayed back until he raised his head and turned to me. There was a sadness that hadn't been there before, and it was all my fault. In order to fix this, I had to be cautious. Slow down. I'd already made a giant mess, and I wouldn't get another chance.

"I thought you'd get the hint when I didn't go to breakfast," he said.

"I owe you a huge apology." I sat next to him and laid my head against his shoulder. He tensed, but he didn't push me off him. I could do this. "I messed up, and I'm sorry."

"Yeah, you did." He scooted away from me and stood, and for a second I thought he was going to walk away from me. "How could you, of all people, try to use me for sex?"

"I thought if we did the no-strings-attached thing, we could keep feelings out of it. No one would get hurt."

"Be real, CeCe." His gaze went flat, like I was a stranger to him. "You meant you. You wouldn't get hurt. You didn't give a damn about my feelings."

"What feelings?" My voice sounded as small as I felt. "I'm the one who makes a big deal about everything, right? You're the one who doesn't commit."

"You know why. You know better than anyone what my father walking out did to me. If a pastor who swore in front of God to always be there couldn't even stay, what's to stop anyone else from . . ." His voice had gone thick. He sat again, but turned away from me. Not soon enough to hide the tears clinging to his lower lashes, threatening to spill over.

My stomach bottomed out as the gravity of what I'd done hit me full force. I'd been so caught up in my own emotions, I had no clue how bad I'd hurt my best friend. I'd always been jealous of Paul. The way he could go through relationships without seeming to care, while I felt everything with so much intensity, I thought it might kill me. In some ways, he had it worse. Sure, I got hurt, but at least I hadn't been afraid to try.

"I'm so sorry." I hugged his arm. "So incredibly sorry."

"I trusted you. I thought you were the only person who understood me." His frame shook as I wrapped my arms around him. The tears he'd tried so hard to hold back soaked into my T-shirt. He didn't need my sloppy declarations of love right now. He needed his best friend.

I held him tighter, until the shaking stopped and my shirt began to dry. "You can trust me. I'll never bring up sex again,

I promise. We can talk about cheese and make fun of Pastor Dean's stupid ties, and do a few pranks to give him hell while we're here."

"Is that what you want?" He moved back and looked at me with clear eyes. "For this to be that one time you asked me to have sex? Something we can laugh about years later?"

No. "Yes." I'd tell him whatever he needed to hear. "We're friends." Even if I'd go on wanting him so bad that every time he'd get a new girlfriend, a little piece of me would die inside. "I just want us to stay that way." No, I didn't. "Isn't that what you want?"

"I want to tell you a story."

"Now?" What the hell? I was not in the mood for a story. I wanted something real from him. No more second-guessing and tripping over my feelings and saying the wrong things.

"It starts a long time ago, with a boy who grew up in the church. He loved his father, who claimed he spoke the word of God. But one day the boy discovered his father was a deceiver, and because his father's word meant nothing, he also believed God's word meant nothing."

I took his hand and squeezed it. Paul had lost a lot more than his faith in God when his father walked out. The lonely boy too good for this earth deserved someone better. Someone who didn't have to learn how to swim, because she already knew how.

"He was angry with his father, but he also felt a hole in his heart where love used to be," Paul said. "So he attempted to fill that hole in other ways."

"Filling the hole? Way to knock that metaphor out of the park."

He cracked a smile, the first one I'd seen from him since our fight this morning. "You know what I mean. He looked for ways not to love."

"Is he still?" I swallowed hard. "Not interested in love?"

"The boy *tried* not to love, but he wasn't very successful. Because he'd known love since he was seven, when a girl stole his new bike and crashed it into a ditch, and he wasn't mad. This girl was fearless. She could do anything, and the boy couldn't help but fall in love."

My breath caught. Every feeling I'd ever had tumbled around inside me in a free fall, but for once I didn't speak. I didn't have the words.

"But he didn't think she returned his love, so he was content to be her friend and confidant. Because he loved her, he wanted her to be happy. Do you want me to keep going?"

"Yes." It came out as more of a harsh gasp than an actual word.

"One day the inevitable happened. The girl found what she thought was love, and it tore the boy in two, but he pretended to be supportive. And when the other boy broke her heart, it took everything in him not to tear that boy in two for being dumb enough to let the girl go."

"Paul." My heart ached. For him. For me. For all the years we'd been friends, with neither of us crossing that line. Until we went to camp, and I pushed him into pretending to be my boyfriend for superficial reasons.

"And when the girl, known for her impulsiveness, a quality the boy long admired, still wanted the one who'd broken her heart, the boy offered to help. Not because he wanted her to get the other back, but because he'd sworn he'd always be there."

"Even through the girl's many, many mistakes?"

"The girl had to make those mistakes to see the truth about the other," Paul said. "But it didn't make the boy happy like he thought it would. Because the other had to hurt the girl for her to see he was no good, and the boy hated seeing the girl hurt. Worse, she questioned herself, when the boy who had always loved her wished she could see what he's always seen."

All the signs had been there. His irrational—which turned out to be rational—hatred for Ethan. He'd volunteered to come to camp with me, even though it opened all his old wounds from his father. All the little ways we'd touched or flirted in our own weird way.

"Then one day the girl came to the boy and asked him to have sex with her, out of the blue. And almost immediately said it was a joke, but the boy loved the girl, and knew when the girl was lying to him."

"This story just got really awful," I said.

"The boy was angry with her request. Maybe a little flattered, because the boy has an ego, but mostly pissed. Because the boy thought the girl would never use him. Maybe it's the boy's fault too, for never telling the girl how he felt."

"I didn't know." I grabbed his hands. "I swear, if I'd known, this whole thing would've gone differently. I would've—"

"You would've what? Lied to me? Told me you loved me because you felt guilty?"

"That's not what I said. You're making assumptions."

"Based on what you told me." He stood. "I can't do this right now. I have to pack."

"What do you mean?" Panic clogged my throat. "Are you leaving?"

"I talked to Pastor Dean. This farce has gone on long enough. I'm calling my mom to come pick me up." He walked away from me, his long legs taking him halfway down the hill before I could process what had happened.

Chapter 23

Paul wasn't at lunch, but I didn't expect to find him in the dining hall. He needed a minute to cool off before I approached him again. No way would he leave without settling things with us. Even if he wasn't that far off on why I'd rushed to ask him to have sex. Ugh. The mortification of it all sat like a rock in my stomach.

Astrid set her tray next to me at our bench. "You look terrible."

I poked at my sandwich, not having the stomach to actually eat it. "Paul loves me."

"Wow. You're just now figuring that out?" Astrid shook her head. "You're supposed to be the most aware one among all of us."

"You knew?" I grabbed her arm. "Did he tell you? What did he say?"

"He didn't need to tell me." She patted my hand, loosening my death grip. "It's written all over his face every time he looks at you."

I must've become immune to it. He said he'd loved me since we were seven, but how was I supposed to know what love looked like? I thought that was just his regular face. "How does he look at me?"

"Like you look at cheese."

"Oh my God."

"I know. It's pretty intense." She cut into her chicken breast. "Paul is a great guy. A little lost, occasionally bordering on offensive with his blasphemy, and he can be full of himself sometimes, but overall great. And he'd do anything for you."

"Did everyone know this except me?"

"Oh yeah. We had bets on how long it'd be before you two hooked up."

"Aren't you all against gambling?"

"It's a figure of speech." Astrid rolled her eyes. "We didn't bet actual money."

"He's so pissed at me though. The whole thing got blown out of proportion. I never should've asked him to have sex with me."

Astrid's fork clattered to the floor. "That was fast."

"It was really bad, like I'm not sure if I can take it back." I chewed on my lip. "I was jealous of Sarina, because I had all this experience, but I never had an orgasm. And she gets one on her first try. I felt like I'd been left behind, or there was something wrong with me."

"That's fair. You got robbed in that department."

"I knew Paul had all kinds of experience, and the way girls had talked about him in the locker room . . . Let's just say, he knows what to do."

"Is that all you want from him?"

"No, but he wouldn't even let me explain." I buried my face in my hands.

"So you propositioned him under the guise of only being interested in sex, and it threw you for a loop when he didn't want to be used for that. From an outside perspective, I can see why he'd be upset. But it's really not that complicated."

"But what if I can't fix things?"

"I don't think that will be a problem. I'm pretty good at observation." Which was probably why she was such a good note taker.

The thing about Paul was he held me when I cried, told me stories where I triumphed, made me laugh until my sides hurt, and he never let anyone get away with hurting me, not even myself. All those were fine qualities in a best friend. Then there was the way he made my toes tingle, my skin shiver whenever he touched me, and my dreams stimulating. When it came to sex, I couldn't picture anyone but him.

"He wants to leave," I said. "He's already talked to Pastor Dean."

Astrid picked up her tray. "Then you'd better hurry."

"Wait." I grabbed her wrist before she could walk away. "He still thinks I only wanted to use him for sex. What am I supposed to do?"

"Tell him you love him. I promise, it'll work out okay." She squeezed my shoulder and went to help with the lunch cleanup.

I left the dining hall and ran around the lake to the boys' cabins. Technically, girls weren't allowed on the boys' side of the lake. But technically, I also didn't give a shit about camp rules. At least not when they got in the way of me talking to Paul.

When I knocked on the door to Paul's cabin, Jerome answered the door, shirtless, and immediately grabbed a sheet off his bed to cover himself. Like he didn't go shirtless on lifeguard duty every day. "Um. What are you doing here?"

"Is Paul here?" I asked. "I need to talk to him."

"Gone." He stifled a yawn.

I pushed him out of the way to see for myself, and he stumbled around on his tiny legs before falling back on his bed. "What do you mean he's gone? Where did he go?"

Peter came out of the bathroom. "CeCe? Are you allowed to be here?"

"What do you think?" My near hysterical bursting into their cabin wasn't doing me any favors in the getting-quick-answers department. "Where's Paul?"

"He packed up his stuff," Ethan said. "He's going to Pastor Dean's office now to call his mom to come get him. Wouldn't say why, though."

"Right now?" This couldn't be happening. He couldn't go yet. I was supposed to tell him how I felt and we were going to make up and everything was going to be okay.

"Uh, yeah." Ethan gave me a funny look. "I'm surprised he stayed this long. Considering neither one of you is a real Christian, I thought you'd both go together."

"No offense," said Jerome, "but you really shouldn't be in our cabin."

"I'm leaving." I had to catch Paul before he called his mom.

As I hustled out of the boys' cabin, I began formulating what I'd say. He had to hear me out before he left. If he really loved me, he'd give me the chance to explain. I didn't even hear Ethan until he caught up to me halfway around the lake.

"Do you want me to walk with you?" he asked.

"I'm not in the mood," I said. "Go back to your cabin."

He jogged beside me to keep up with my strides. "I was thinking about our conversation the other day. Actually, it's been haunting me, and I feel like I owe you a real apology."

"I'm not doing this again." The lake was so close. I could shove him and keep going. "What do you want? My forgiveness? Fine. I forgive you. Now go away."

"Thank you." Relief broke out on his face. "I really needed to hear that."

"I don't want your thanks. I said I've forgiven you, but I'll never forget. And you know what's sad about that? I'm pretty sure that makes me more of a real Christian than you." I left him standing by the water, though it had been so tempting to give him a little push.

As I made my way past the edge of the woods, Sarina waved me over and pointed up the path. "Astrid told me you were looking for Paul. I tried to stall him for you."

"Thanks." I ran in the direction she'd pointed. No way was Paul going to walk away from me for a third time today. Not without a fight. He was so close.

I cut through a cluster of trees near Pastor Dean's office. Mandy stood in front of the door doing some kind of weird shuffle-dance with Paul. He'd try to go around her, and she'd block him. He dodged the other way, and she threw her arm out to stop him. With her athletic skills, he didn't stand a chance. As soon as she caught my eye, she spun him around and sprinted away, buying me a few seconds to reach him in the confusion.

As soon as he saw me, he put his hand on the door.

"Paul, wait," I said.

He turned the knob.

"I swear on the guy who used to date your mom, if you meant one word of what you said earlier, you'll get your ass back here and talk to me."

He turned around and raised his eyebrows.

"You didn't even listen to my side of the story." I marched up to him and shoved him in the chest. "You just dropped that bomb and walked away, because that's what you do, right? And now you're just going to leave camp without talking to me first? Fuck that."

His shoulders sagged. "I really don't want to lose our friendship, but if you keep pushing this I'm-an-asshole-who-walks-away narrative, you just might."

"Then quit being an asshole who walks away." I took a deep breath. Picking another fight with him wouldn't accomplish anything. Time to go for all or nothing. "I hate that we're fighting, and I hate that you keep putting words in my mouth. And I really hate how you're assuming I don't love you. Because I do, more than you can possibly know."

"But . . . ?" His voice cracked.

"But you might not love me anymore once you hear the truth, and I'm okay with that. I owe you some honesty, because Lord knows I haven't been very honest lately."

"You don't owe me anything."

"Please." I grabbed his hand and led him toward a small wooded area with a dozen fallen logs. "Please sit. I need to say this."

He sighed, and his face screwed up with resignation. I'd almost let him go. Let him walk away from me. As much as it hurt to lay all my feelings out there and deal with whatever he had to say, I couldn't let him do that. He needed to hear the whole truth. He shifted his stance, but he eventually sat next to me.

"I'm not going to tell you a story, because this is real. I'm CeCe and you're Paul and we're us. No more pretend."

"Okay." His expression was guarded, but he stayed.

"I used to think love meant nice boys wrapped in ugly shirts. At first Ethan made me feel good about myself, because I wanted to be wanted, but even after he made me feel terrible, I still thought I loved him. Because I had a really messed-up notion of what love was supposed to be like."

"So you decided to use me because you were feeling shitty about Ethan." Paul shook his head. "No need to rehash all this. I was there, remember?"

I pursed my lips. "Are you ever going to let me finish talking? Because I'm pretty sure I didn't ask for commentary."

"Sorry. Go on."

Here were all the ugly parts of me laid bare. Paul had seen

270

me at my worst, treated me with respect at my worst, but even he didn't know the parts I'd kept from everyone, including myself. I had no idea what he'd think afterward.

"When Ethan left me, I thought the solution was to pretend to be someone else, someone he really wanted. I didn't know he lied about why we broke up—that he didn't cherish me the way I deserved— so I came up with a crackpot and impulsive idea to get him back. Because I'm known for such things."

Paul smiled, but it was half-hearted at best.

"And my best friend, the boy I loved most in the world, volunteered to come with me. Because he'd always been there for me. And me, being impulsive and selfish, boxed you in to pretending to be my boyfriend. Because I didn't want to look like a stalker to Ethan, whose opinion I never should've cared about in the first place."

"This is making you look really bad," Paul said.

"Oh, don't worry. It gets worse. Anyway, I really liked pretending to be your girlfriend. I liked it so much that even when it no longer became necessary to pretend, I couldn't bring myself to fake our breakup. Then I shared my terrible sex experience with my cabin, and the girls started to have experiences of their own. Experiences that weren't terrible. And it made me incredibly jealous, because let's remember that I am a selfish girl."

I paused to take a breath. Here was where it would all come out, and if he walked away now, all those shattered pieces of my heart wouldn't have the chance to transform. This wasn't a need to be wanted or a fake feeling from a fake relationship. This wasn't a story. I meant every word, and I put it all on the line.

"I wanted to feel good too," I said. "I'd been having strange, arousing dreams, and I propositioned you because I thought if anyone could make me orgasm, it was you and the reputation you worked really hard for. I thought if we just had sex, we could salvage our friendship when it ended."

"What makes you think it would end?" He spoke so softly, I had to lean closer.

"Because you're not known for long-term relationships, and I have a history of hating all my exes, which would be a sad thing for both of us. But that was before I understood how you felt. Which doesn't really matter, because I went ahead and fell in love with you anyway. I guess I have a terrible sense of self-preservation."

There it was. The whole truth. His emotional disconnect from relationships scared me, and I never wanted to mess up our friendship. But there also wasn't anyone else I wanted to mess up with more than him.

"I don't believe you." He stared off in the distance, refusing to meet my eyes, and I had no idea what was going on inside his head. "I want to, but you just decided you love me today? After our fight? That's not how it works."

"I didn't think it worked like that either, but then I consulted the wise oracle, Astrid, since I couldn't access Google in this strange new land."

"I wonder what makes the oracle such an expert."

"The oracle takes good notes and sees things people try to hide. She knew I loved you before I said anything. I've loved you for longer than I've been able to admit. Now I'm afraid."

"Why are you afraid?"

"I'm afraid because I want to have sex, but I'm worried it still won't be good. I'm afraid that once we do it, you won't care about me anymore. I'm afraid I'm broken."

"You're not broken—you're vulnerable." He turned to me and tilted my chin. "You're my best friend. I think you might be in over your head, but I love you. I've always loved you."

He leaned down, pausing for just a moment. I touched my lips to his and my world opened up. His kiss was soft and hesitant as much as mine was reserved and insecure. The feel of him touching me this way, kissing me this way, was like a long-held sob that had finally broken free. A good cry after a bout of silent sadness. He was patient, kissing me gently, letting me lead the way. Until I gained enough confidence to pull him closer. He tilted my head back and kissed me so deep, my entire body shuddered in response.

His fingers trailed down my collarbone, traced a line down my side, and rested on the small of my back, with the lightest of pressure. With his other hand, he cupped my face, running his thumb along my jaw as he backed away slightly from his kiss, and then went back in, with even more urgency than the last time. My body shuddered again. Everywhere he touched me burned; everywhere he hadn't touched me needed him to. This was what it felt like to want.

He pulled back, still holding me, staring at me in a sleepy way, like he was half dreaming. "Goddamn. CeCe. What the fuck?"

My eyes welled. I'd never been kissed like that in my life, but maybe I'd misinterpreted it. Maybe I wasn't any good. "Did I do it wrong?"

"No. God, no." He pulled me against his chest. "I felt like I was drowning, and I needed you more than I needed air. Fuck."

"Just so we're clear, that's a good thing, right?"

He laughed. "What did it feel like for you?"

"The same. But that doesn't mean you thought it was good. I mean, sure, I'm a warm body, and I'll bet that makes me perfectly adequate, but we still haven't had sex. Kissing is easy. It's basic. Anyone can kiss."

"Christ, I've never wanted to kick Ethan's ass more for doing this to you." He stood and paced in front of me. "Kissing is not basic. I've kissed a lot of girls; you've kissed a lot of boys. Have you ever experienced anything like that before?"

"No, but—"

"You're not just a warm body, and there is nothing 'adequate' about you. I could kiss like that forever, withering away while I lost myself in you, and I'd consider it a good life."

"Oh. Since you put it like that, I guess I did okay." Pushing my insecurity aside, I wrapped my arms around him and held him tight against me. "Would now be a better time to bring up sex? Because I'm still really interested in doing that."

He took a deep, ragged breath. "Let me go back to my cabin and grab a blanket."

"Not right now. Tonight. We still have to go to our workshops."

"Fuck the workshops. I'd rather spend the rest of the day and night buried inside you."

All my muscles turned to warm liquid. If I hadn't been holding on to him, my knees might've given out on me. "I need to talk to the girls before I do this, and change into better underwear." I'd finally get to wear my red lace. "If you don't have any condoms with you, I have, like, a billion in my cabin. All Magnum, though."

"I have condoms." He paused. "But bring the Magnums, just in case."

That scared me more than the possibility of not being good at sex. Even if I was into it, even if I wanted him, it would still probably hurt. But I trusted him. He'd take care of me, and maybe I'd be able to relax enough to enjoy it. That was the only first that mattered to me.

Chapter 24

For the rest of the morning, I could barely sit through the workshop. Astrid passed me a note asking what happened, and I replied with two words: *The truth.* She read my response and gave me a sour look, clearly not satisfied, but I didn't want any details written where someone else could see them. The camp had too many busybodies.

Sarina had to get down to lifeguard duty, but Astrid and Mandy cornered me as soon as we were dismissed. Not that I'd planned to keep anything from them.

"Are you and Paul a couple? A real one, I mean," Astrid said.

"I think so?" We hadn't actually made anything official, but we had plenty of time to hash out the details later. "We're going to have sex, though."

"I knew it." Mandy clapped her hands. "From that first day in the van, you could cut the sexual tension between you two with a knife. This is so exciting."

"I kissed him," I said. "Not just a regular kiss. My whole body responded to him. I was shaking and shuddering in his arms, and I'm still not sure what happened."

"Did you . . . ?" Mandy glanced around, looking for any counselors. "Did you orgasm from a kiss? Because that sounds a lot like what Sarina described."

"No. I didn't feel like I was flying and I didn't hear angel trumpets." Though, to be honest, if I had heard angel trumpets, I'd probably think they were there to smite me. "It wasn't something that built up in me; it was just . . . wanting. And it was consuming."

"Wow. That sounds amazing." Mandy got a faraway look in her eyes, like between me and Sarina we'd single-handedly changed her mind about wanting to have sex. Whatever guy won her heart had no idea how lucky he'd be.

"I need your opinions on my underwear." The anticipation of it all made my heart beat faster. "Keep in mind he's actually going to see it."

"What's he going to see?" Paul came up behind me, wrapping his arms around my waist and drawing me close. I snuggled against his chest.

"My underwear," I said.

Astrid and Mandy gasped, while Paul laughed. I was so accustomed to telling him everything, it didn't occur to me to be coy. I was just me and he was just him.

"Have I ever told you how much I love the way you say whatever you're thinking, without stopping to think about it at all?" he asked.

"Yes." I tapped a finger to my chin. "I believe you called me brash and tactless."

"That's right." He kissed my temple. "Of course you weren't talking about showing me your underwear at the time. Feel free to let all those thoughts out."

"Food?" I asked. "You're going to need all your energy for tonight."

"You talk a big game." He gave me a quick squeeze before letting go. "But you make a good point. I'll catch you inside."

Mandy and Astrid let go of a collective sigh as he walked away.

"So, underwear opinions after lunch?" I asked.

"You should skip afternoon workshops," Astrid said. "Because we'll want all the details, and there is no way we're staying up late enough to hear them."

"I can't skip. Paul can't either. I know you said they're voluntary, but they really aren't for us. Pastor Dean is chomping for a reason to toss us out of here."

"We'll cover for you," Mandy said. "Say you weren't feeling well. Women problems. They never question those. Besides, ever since the bonfire, the woods are crawling with counselors at night trying to catch kids out of bed."

"How did Sarina and Jerome get away with last night?"

"She took him to that shack, where Priscilla made you put on that horrible swimsuit, but Sarina said it smelled like her grandma's house in there and it almost killed the mood."

"You guys really want me to have sex." I looked over both of their eager faces. "What would Jesus do? Would he support this kind of debauchery?"

"Don't make me pull out all the Bible verses that support love," Astrid said. "Because I will, and I'll lecture you all afternoon and make you memorize them."

Point taken.

We went into the dining hall, where Paul had reached the end of the line with enough food to feed an entire football team. How much energy did he think he'd need? I tapped him on the shoulder and he turned around, his eyes softening as soon as he saw me.

"I'm ready now," I said.

"Now?" He turned around to set his tray down, picked it back up, set it back down, and grabbed my hand. "Forget the food. Let's go."

"We can eat first if you're hungry." I laughed.

"Nope. Do you have any idea how hard it was to sit through

a single workshop with that kiss playing over and over again in my mind?"

"Do you want to go to your cabin for a blanket and condoms?"

"No. Too far. Your cabin is closer."

"What about my underwear? I should change into something nicer."

"I don't care what you've got on; you won't be wearing it long anyway."

Oh my God. We were really going to do this. A thrill shivered up my spine.

He waited outside while I dashed into my cabin and grabbed my comforter and five condoms. Probably overreaching there, but it was better to have more than less.

We took the trail along the woods, quiet with everyone either down at the lake or in the dining room for lunch. Instead of stopping in the clearing we'd hung out in the first night of camp, Paul went deeper into the woods.

"I don't want us to get interrupted," he said.

"Do you know your way back?"

"Unfortunately, yes. But if you want to stay out here for the rest of the summer, I can build us a tree house, and I wouldn't be opposed to hunting and gathering."

"I think we'd need more than five condoms for the whole summer."

"We might need more than five condoms just today."

"Seriously?" My eyes bugged out. I thought I'd way overestimated.

"No." He laughed and took my hand. "But you thought I was, and that's all the boost to my ego I'm going to need going forward."

"Remind me again why I'm doing this with you?"

"Because no one else makes you feel like this." He kissed my neck, and just having his lips touch me made my entire body light up and draw closer to him. "And I've got great taste in music, and know all the things you love best, and you have the most fun with me."

He stopped in a small clearing surrounded by wild strawberry bushes, with just enough room to lay down my comforter. It was all fun and games when I could talk about being assertive in the secret workshops or talk about sex with Paul, but now that we were here, all my nerves surfaced again. I rubbed my elbows while he looked around, scratching his shoulder.

"How should we start this?" I took off my shirt. "Should we get naked first?"

"Maybe shirts first." He took off his. "We can let things progress from here."

"Are you nervous?" I wrapped my arms around my stomach, and he held his shirt to his chest, not letting it drop to the ground.

"I've never done this in the daylight before." He let his shirt go, and it puddled at his feet. "I like your bra. I'm glad you didn't change it."

I looked down at the plain white cotton with a pink rosebud in the center. "Thanks. I got it on clearance. I mean, not me, my mom did. When we went shopping."

"That's cool. I always like a good sale."

We looked at each other and laughed.

"This is so awkward," I said. "We should've just done it on the log when we were in the moment. Now I'm like, *What are you thinking? Is he disappointed?*"

"You could never disappoint me." He stepped closer. "You're so beautiful."

"Thanks, you too. Except handsome. Or strapping? Nice-looking. You look nice. Great. You look great." Argh. I could stop talking at any point now. "This is so dumb. I've seen you in your swim trunks every summer since we were kids."

He cracked a smile. "I'm going to assume you're tongue-tied because I'm so hot, you can't even form whole sentences."

"I want to say something sarcastic right now, but I feel this might not be the best time or place."

"That's too bad." He rested his hands on my hips, and I put my arms around the back of his neck. "Because I'm going to need you to do a lot of talking."

"I know." Knowing and doing were two different things, but I'd have to cross that bridge when I got there. "You need to do some talking too."

"Not a problem." His fingers skimmed my back and I shivered. "For me, I can read your body language some of the time, but I never want to assume. I'll always ask. When we do things that are new to you, I need to know what you like."

"What if I don't know what I like?"

"You'll know what you don't. Just tell me. I won't be offended."

"But what if you like it?"

"Don't worry about me. I like everything." He kissed my neck again. "If it feels good to you, that's all I need. That's what gets me off."

I nearly had my first orgasm from his words alone. No wonder the girls from the locker room called him a giver. I had no idea what that even meant. The concept was so far beyond my comprehension, but it made me infinitely more comfortable.

We kissed, with the same mind-blowing intensity we'd had earlier, lowering to our knees and eventually lying down, with him on his side next to me. A rock poked into my back, and I fidgeted, accidentally knocking my forehead into his.

"Sorry." I rubbed his head. "Rock. In my back."

"Here." He slid me over three feet. "Is that better?"

"Yeah." We kissed more, and I could feel him ready, pushed up against my thigh. "Should we get the condom on?"

"Not yet," he said. "What do you want me to do?"

"I don't know." His question left me panicking. I'd never been asked that before. I just went along with whatever and pretended to enjoy it. "Take my bra off and touch me."

He unhooked the back, and I instantly had the urge to cover myself. What if they were too small? Or my nipples were misshapen? As soon as he took my bra off and tossed it to the side, I rolled into him, mashing my chest against his so he couldn't look at me.

"Is this okay?" He ran his fingers between my breasts, under them, and back up the sides.

"I'm going to be honest here. I want to lie on my back, so my stomach doesn't roll up, but then it flattens my boobs, and I feel like I look weird naked."

"You definitely don't look weird. You are gorgeous." He kissed me from my collarbone down to my stomach. "I could look at you all day like this."

"That's really nice of you to say." I was the actual worst at pillow talk.

When he linked his fingers with mine, I took his hand and placed it between my legs. I almost lost my nerve. What if he pulled it away? But he looked at me with such openness, it made me more open to showing him what I wanted.

"Over the shorts or under?" he asked.

"Under," I squeaked.

"Over the underwear or under?"

"Are you going to ask me every time you do something?"

"Yes." He kissed me again.

"Fine." I could do this. I could talk to him while we did things. "Under."

"Why do you sound so mad about it?" He teased the waistband of my cotton underwear, and I mourned not changing into the red lace-and-satin panties I'd brought in my suitcase's secret compartment.

"I'm not mad. I'm just not good at all this naked conversation."

"I just had to make sure you wanted me to do this." He touched me between my legs, under the shorts, under the underwear, and my heart leapt into my throat.

"More," I choked out. "Like that."

He moved his fingers in a circle, and all the nerves in my body squeezed down to that one point. "Do you like this?"

"Yes," I said breathlessly. "Don't stop. I will fucking kill you if you stop."

"Wow, you just got really good at naked conversation." He laughed.

I lost the fine amount of control I had left as all of my nerves exploded. My legs trembled and my back arched off the ground. Spots of light clouded my vision, and a strangled cry trapped in the back of my throat broke free. Then, as quickly as it had hit me, it was over, and a warm glow spread through my entire body.

"What was that?" I asked.

He buried his head in my sweat-slicked shoulder. "Correct me if I'm wrong, but I believe you just had an orgasm."

"Oh my God. That's what it feels like?"

"Pretty awesome, huh?" He kissed my neck, right below my ear. "Though next time I could do without the death threats."

"Sorry." I snorted. "It got away from me. Do you want me to . . . ?" I reached for the zipper on his shorts and he drew my hand back.

"Better not. I'm only good for one go, and I really don't want to waste it."

"What if I'm only good for one too?"

"Then we stop." He kissed me. "I wasn't lying when I said I'm only interested in doing what feels good for you. If you're not enjoying it, there is no way I can."

"I'd really enjoy it if you took off my shorts, and took yours off too."

He stood and undid his shorts, his briefs showing his very clear erection.

"The underwear should go too." I turned my head while

he undressed, like I wanted to offer him some modesty, which was ridiculous.

He kneeled at my feet and pulled off my shorts. I nodded when he touched the waistband of my cotton underwear, the giant ones I wore on laundry days, because I couldn't manage sexy to save my life. If he noticed, he didn't comment. He put his hand on the small of my back and pulled me against him.

He definitely knew what he was doing. As his other hand roamed over me, touching new places and letting me respond to them, I finally worked up the nerve to touch him. At first I let my hands hang loosely over his shoulders, not really sure what to do or what felt good. But it turned out he responded to touch like I did, and it didn't take long to find out what he liked. Even though he said he liked everything.

"Condom. Now." Impossibly, that sensation of my nerves gathering started to build again, and this time I wanted all of him.

He rolled the condom on and laid me on my back. "I'm going to go slow."

Cradling my head under his arms, he entered me, and I gasped.

"Does it hurt?" he asked.

"It hurts a little. How far in are you?"

"About halfway." He pulled out again. "Do you want to stop? I won't be upset."

"No. I want to do it. Just keep going." I took him in my hand and guided him back inside me. "Slow."

He entered me again, sliding about halfway in and holding still while I got used to the feel of him. Then he went in all the way, and I bit down on my lip.

"Is this okay?" he asked.

"It doesn't really hurt right now. It's just a lot of pressure sitting right there. It's getting easier, though."

"I want to try something." He pulled out of me and lay on his back. "If you are on top, you can control the angle, the speed, how much you can take in."

"I don't know how to do that." I'd never been in control. The one time I did do it, I just lay there. "But I could try."

"Set the speed, and I'll match it." He put his hands on my hips and lowered me onto him.

He'd been right. I had much more control over what I could handle from here. At first I hovered above him on my knees, taking him in about halfway, until I got more comfortable. Then I went all the way down, and back up again. His fingers dug into the soft flesh around my hips, but not in a way that hurt. It grounded me and helped me hold on too.

I leaned down, placing my hand on either side as I rocked against him. He didn't look over my shoulder or even close his eyes. He looked directly at me, and it made me feel way more exposed than taking off my clothes. But I didn't look away. I matched his gaze, giving everything back as he told me how much he loved me and how I made him feel. I'd never been more connected to another human.

Every time I came down on top of him, I hit a spot inside me that wanted him more, with faster speed. He matched my pace until I clenched, like a fist had started to squeeze inside me. I cried out as he grabbed my hips and trembled, but I wasn't quite there. So close.

The sex was still phenomenal, so much more than I ever thought it could be, and I was certain I'd get there next time. I rolled over and lay with my arms out. All my muscles felt like jelly, and I never wanted to move again. I couldn't even focus on the weird mole inside my thigh, because I was too tired to give a damn.

Paul discarded the condom and gathered me against him, throwing my comforter over us. He kissed my head and my nose and my lips. "That was incredible."

"We should've had sex ages ago." My throat was desperately dry, but I'd never been more content in my entire life. "I didn't finish, but I got super-close, and I think I might be able to next time."

"Shit." He held me tighter. "I'm so sorry. I tried to hold out, but it's been a while. Do you want me to finish you the other way?"

"No, I'm exhausted. I just told you because I want to be honest. All the time. I still thought it was amazing, and you're amazing, and I can't believe this is happening."

"You can't? I'm terrified of letting you go. I'm afraid I'm going to wake up in my cabin and discover none of this really happened. My sheets would be a mess."

We both badly needed water and something to eat, but neither of us wanted to get up. The idea of letting Paul build us a tree house had some merit. I snuggled against him, closing my eyes and letting the warm feeling drift with me.

Chapter 25

I woke with a start, disoriented and sore. Darkness had settled over the woods. I had no idea what time it was thanks to the no phones rule. I nudged Paul, who dragged me against him, half asleep, but apparently ready for round two.

"Wake up," I said. "It's dark outside."

He sat up and rubbed his hands over his face. "How long have we been out?"

"I have no idea." An owl hooted in the distance, and we'd gone pretty far from camp. Other things, hungry things, could've been lurking in the trees. "Can you still find your way back in the dark, or should we wait for morning?"

"We'll get eaten alive if we stay out here." He slapped at a mosquito that had landed on his arm. "I can get us back to camp."

I'd just pulled my shirt over my head, when two flashlights cut between us. We both stumbled back as the light passed over our eyes. "There they are!" a male voice called out.

Priscilla and Michael, not Mike, broke through our clearing, followed by two more counselors. Fear pulsed in my ears, drowning out all other noise. This was bad. Really bad.

"Do you know we've been looking for the two of you for hours?" Priscilla stood with her hands on her hips. "Did you think hiding out here would be fun? That no one would come looking for you?"

"We came out here way earlier and fell asleep," I said. "We were just about to make our way back to camp. What time is it?"

"Eleven at night," Michael, not Mike, said. "Your parents have been called." He got on the walkie-talkie. "We found them out in the woods. We're bringing them in."

My mom must've been having a heart attack right now. "Why did you call our parents? You didn't think that could've waited until after you found us?"

"We have to notify the parents right away if their children go missing. You're still a minor according to the law. Let's move."

The walk back to camp took a million times longer. We'd gone really deep into the woods, but we were still on camp grounds and we were still campers, which meant we'd be subject to camp penalty. This meant the end.

I held on to Paul as we navigated overgrown roots and fallen branches in the dark. Each twig that snapped in the distance made me jump. "I'm scared."

"Don't worry. I'll handle it," he whispered.

"Handle it how?"

He didn't respond.

"Paul." At the sound of my voice, Priscilla sent us a sharp look. "Answer me."

His jaw remained set as we reached the edge of the woods.

Pastor Dean waited for us on the first path. "Priscilla, if you'd take Miss Wells back to her cabin, I'd like to speak with Mr. Romanowski tonight."

Whatever Paul was planning, he wouldn't share it with me. A sense of unease settled in my stomach. I had to talk to him before he said something he couldn't take back. I broke away from Priscilla and ran to where he walked beside Pastor Dean, but they weren't alone.

"Paul?" His mom ran forward and wrapped her arms around him. "Praise God. You had me so worried. What were you thinking, running away like that?"

I shrank back into the shadows. I had a serious amount of respect for Paul's mom; she had been like a second mom to me growing up. If she knew where we'd been and what we'd been doing, I'd never be able to look her in the face again.

"We have a lot to discuss," Pastor Dean said. "Let's move this to my office."

I had no way to reach Paul without going through his

mom, so I headed back to my cabin to wait for whatever came next. Priscilla tried to lecture me along the way, but I tuned her out. She wasn't the boss of me. She wasn't even the boss of camp. Once my porch light came into view, I rushed ahead of her and threw open the door.

Astrid, Mandy, and Sarina jumped up as soon as I ran inside. "What happened? Where have you been? We've been so worried." They pelted me with question after question until Priscilla walked in behind me.

"Lights-out," Priscilla said.

"I don't think so," I said. "I need to talk to my mom."

"Your mother has been informed you've been found; she'll be expecting your call in the morning." Priscilla opened a side storage closet and pulled out a cot and a ratty wool blanket. "I'm staying here tonight. This cabin has caused quite enough problems this summer."

"What are you talking about?" I crossed my arms. "Other than thinking your workshop sucked, we've been pretty well behaved. At least they've been, and I have been too, until tonight."

"There was a raid on our cabin after lunch," Sarina said.

"Oh shit." The condoms they'd stolen from Pastor Dean's storage. He had to have noticed them missing at one point. It hadn't even occurred to us to hide them.

"Language, Miss Wells," Priscilla said.

"Fuck off." Priscilla's presence in our cabin, where we all shared the most intimate parts of ourselves, made my skin crawl. She had no business being here. "I'm pretty sure I'm in a lot more trouble right now. Dropping a few curse words isn't going to matter much."

Mandy gasped. "Don't make it worse, CeCe. They haven't even had a chance to punish us yet because they got so caught up in finding you."

"What are they going to do?" I asked. "Throw us in a hole? Feed us nothing but bread and cheese? That's fine with me. I happen to love both of those things."

"They could kick us out of camp," Astrid said.

Getting kicked out of camp would be way worse for them than it would be for me. They had reputations within their community, certain family obligations, and résumés to Christian colleges to think about. None of that stuff mattered to me. My parents would probably ground me, but they wouldn't disown me. My future didn't depend on this place.

"They're not going to kick you out of camp," I said. "Because I stole the condoms."

Priscilla rolled her eyes. "We already knew that. I said lights-out. We'll deal with the condoms in the morning, after we call your mother and have you meet with Pastor Dean about your disappearing act."

"Hold on," Astrid said. "Why did you assume CeCe stole the condoms?"

"Because unlike her, the three of you have sterling records here at camp." Priscilla shook out her blanket. "She's also a known fornicator, and the only one with motive to steal them."

"Known Fornicator would be a great band name." They'd probably be the kind of band Paul listened to, so underground that they hadn't even heard of themselves.

"That's bigotry," Sarina said. "You're targeting her because you know she's not a Christian. And so what? That's her choice. Besides, I stole the condoms."

"No, she didn't." I loved Sarina, but her mom would kill her if she got kicked out of camp. "I stole the condoms, everyone knows, end of story."

"Neither of them stole the condoms, because I did," Mandy said. "I took them right out of the storage unit when Pastor Dean was in the dining hall."

"And why would you steal condoms?" Priscilla asked, probably expecting her not to have an answer, because only known fornicators knew what to do with condoms.

Mandy flipped her hair over her shoulder. "I used to date Ethan Jones."

"I know you and your family." Priscilla paled. "You wouldn't."

"I would. I planned on having all kinds of dirty sex with him. That's what the zucchinis were for." Mandy's face screwed up. "He's into that kind of thing."

Oh my God. I wanted to simultaneously hug her and cover her mouth to keep her from getting in trouble. If the situation weren't so serious, I would've doubled over with laughter. These girls never ceased to impress me.

"She's messing with you," Astrid said. "I stole the condoms. Ask any of the junior or sophomore girls. I led a series of secret workshops dealing with sex education."

What was she doing? Those workshops she led, the camp-approved ones, would get her into any Christian college she wanted to attend, and I had no doubt Astrid would run this world one day. "I led the workshops," I said. "Ask any of the girls. They'll tell you it started with me."

"I'm sure they would," Priscilla said. "Astrid, I know you preach abstinence in your youth group. I'm not buying your secret workshop story for a second."

"My youth group will be undergoing a change once I leave here." Astrid took my hand. "I'm not so arrogant in my faith that it can't evolve. I'm constantly learning."

"Your faith is being poisoned by toxic influences," Priscilla said.

"No." Astrid put her full might into that one word, and

Priscilla shrank back. "I plan to run a more open-minded group. Even if I'm not having sex, there are people in my group who might, and I won't abandon them or make them feel like they can't come to me for help."

"Is that for real?" I asked her. "That is so cool. You're going to rock that group."

Astrid squeezed my side. "I owe it all to you."

"I said lights-out!" Priscilla yelled, and flipped the switch, plunging us into darkness.

I'd set Mandy's little alarm to go off before the sun came up. As soon as I got out of bed, I threw on a pair of yoga pants and a Camp Three SixTeen T-shirt. Priscilla snored lightly on her borrowed cot, and because I was extra petty, it warmed my heart to see she'd probably have a kink in her neck from going without a pillow.

Priscilla sat up and rubbed her neck. "Time to call your mother."

She led me to Pastor Dean's office and left me there, presumably so she could go get more sleep. The sun peeked over the hill with the flat rock. I walked into the dark office and sat down in one of the low-to-the-ground chairs.

Pastor Dean folded his hands, his desk significantly cleaner. "Before we call your mother, there are some things we need to go over. Mr. Romanowski is no longer at camp."

I nodded at the ground, refusing to meet his gaze. "I guess I'll be following him."

"Not today. He told me he put the condoms in your cabin as a prank and led you out to the woods for another prank, but got lost." Pastor Dean took off his glasses and set them on his open Bible. "This is dangerous behavior, so I had no choice but to remove him."

"Wait. What?" That was what Paul had meant when he said he'd handle it. "You didn't even ask me if that was true. You just assumed and sent him home. Why? Because he's not the Christian you want him to be?"

"Mr. Romanowski is beyond our help, but we still have a place here for you."

"I don't want to be here anymore."

I tucked my legs underneath me so I could rise high enough in the chair to meet Pastor Dean's eyes. I wanted to make damn sure he knew I was beyond his kind of help as well. I wouldn't give him any part of me. Not after he'd made Paul leave without bothering to speak to me first, like what I had to say was irrelevant.

"Your mother wants you to stay. You're very close to

earning enough community service hours to meet your graduation requirement. With no more distractions, I think you can accomplish a great deal in your last week."

"Why do you want me here? I'm not a Christian, and don't plan on becoming one."

"We're all God's children." His hand rested on a stack of bills. "I see the way you influence the cabin eight girls. If you open your heart to Jesus, you can be a real example here."

"Is that Christian talk for your camp is going broke and you want me to be your poster child?" I crossed my arms. "Wouldn't that be a bit of genius advertising? Look, wealthy parents, see how I saved this godless heathen. Send your children here, and I'll fix them."

"No, and that's quite enough." A vein in his temple throbbed as he dialed my mom's cell with a shaking finger. He handed me the phone.

"Mom," I said as soon as she answered. "I'm so sorry you were worried."

"Fancy girl. I'm just glad you're okay. It gave me a scare, but I figured you'd gotten into your usual trouble with Paul." If she only knew. "You two have always been thick as thieves."

"He's home now. Have you seen him?"

"Not yet, no."

"Mom." I sucked in a breath. "I know the budget is

all-important to you, but I'm miserable here. I want to come home."

"Fancy, no. It's not about the budget. We don't care about that." She pulled the phone away from her ear and said something muffled to my dad. "Your father wants you to know we do care about the budget, but not at your expense."

"I can come home?" The hopeful note in my voice made Pastor Dean frown.

"No, but not because of the budget. You said yourself this is a great opportunity to . . . well, I don't remember your exact speech, but it was enough to convince me and your father. You've got those community service hours to think about. You can see Paul next week."

Next week felt like a lifetime, and I had no interest in perpetuating Pastor Dean's brand of conversion. I needed to leave. And if my mom wouldn't let me go home, I'd have to get kicked out. Not so easy when Pastor Dean seemed intent on saving my soul.

"I love you, Mom. See you soon." I handed the phone back to Pastor Dean and left his office without saying another word.

Chapter 26

Back at the cabin, Sarina had taken over the bathroom, but she left the door open so she could listen in. Mandy clipped her nails into a little trash can by her bed, and I sat crisscrossed on the braided rug next to Astrid while she brushed my knotted hair. I filled them in on the finer details of what me and Paul had done in the woods, how he'd gotten our whole cabin off the hook for the condoms, and my intentions to leave.

"Do you want us to create a diversion so you can sneak into Pastor Dean's office and call Paul?" Mandy asked. "It might make today easier if you could hear his voice."

"No, I'm working up something to get sent home sooner rather than later."

The ruse had run its course. I couldn't stay here anymore. Not without Paul. Even though I adored my cabinmates, we were more than this camp with its rigid rules and unrealistic expectations and false morality.

"What are you working up?" Astrid asked. "Can we help?"

"I haven't fully planned it yet, but I'll let you know once I do. Did you write down your numbers? I want to stay in touch after I leave here." I stared at my lap. "And maybe, if you're okay with it, I'd love to check out your youth group sometime."

"You'd be our guest of honor." Astrid wrote down everyone's numbers on a piece of notebook paper and then tucked it into my suitcase next to my eye shadow notes. "We should head down to devotions."

"Not going." I couldn't bear the idea of sitting in the back pew without Paul.

"You won't get kicked out for that," Mandy said. "Maybe before, but not now."

"I know, but I could sleep there, or I could sleep here. I choose here."

Sarina finished her makeup, a universe of sparkling stars with blue and purple space clouds, and came out of the bathroom. My heart dropped a little when I thought about waking up tomorrow and not seeing them in the beds next to mine. They'd become a family to me when I'd needed a shoulder to lean on, and I'd miss the hell out of them.

"Don't look so sad." Sarina touched my cheek. "It's not over yet."

"It's almost over," I said as they closed the door behind them.

I sat on Astrid's bed with my legs crossed and took out her notebook, giving them one last story before I left. After I said my goodbye in the best way I knew how, I got in the shower. I buffed and shaved, and took extra time exfoliating. I was still a little sore between my legs. It was hard to believe what I'd been doing less than a day ago.

I curled my hair, dipping into Sarina's makeup to do my eyes and paint my lips a bright cherry red. I looked pretty damn good. After I put on a button-down shirt and hosed myself with Vanilla Buttercream body spray, I stared at my reflection in the mirror and took a deep breath.

"Here's your one chance, Fancy. Don't let me down."

I gave myself a final once-over and prepared to head down to breakfast, when the girls all piled into the cabin after devotions. "You look amazing," Mandy said. "What's going on?"

"Something has to be going on for me to look amazing? Wow, thanks," I said.

Astrid leaned into me and sniffed. "You smell like birthday cake and bad decisions."

"It's my signature scent."

"Little Red Corvette is a good lip color." Sarina walked in a circle around me, tapping her chin. "Doesn't really go with that outfit, though."

"Seriously," Astrid said. "From the neck up, you look ready

to fight ten guys with a stiletto and a nail file. You already told us you're planning something, so what is it? And more important, why are you leaving us out of it?"

So much for keeping them out of trouble. The more questions I tried to dodge, the more they demanded answers. "I know how I'm going to get kicked out of camp, and I don't want you to get involved, so it would be cool if you avoided me for the rest of the morning."

"At least tell us what you're going to do." Mandy stuck out her bottom lip.

"Fine." I couldn't resist Mandy's pouty face. "But promise me you won't try to stop me or take part in this. This is between me and Pastor Dean and Priscilla."

I filled them in on what I wanted to do, though I could hardly call it a plan. It was a CeCe-style plan, and the best thing I could come up with in the moment. I wanted to make it very clear to Pastor Dean where I stood, while also letting everyone who stayed for Priscilla's workshop know how I felt about what she had to say.

"I can't believe you're going to do that," Sarina said.

"I can't believe you didn't do it sooner," Mandy said.

Astrid gave me an appraising look. "Do you think this is the best way to go about it?"

"Probably not." I shrugged. "But the girls at this camp are

amazing. They are so smart and caring and sure of themselves, and don't deserve to grow up hating their bodies because they are told they're dirty and sinful until they believe it."

"Agreed. We're with you." Astrid linked her arm through mine.

"Yep." Sarina linked her arm with Astrid's.

"Girls of cabin eight for life." Mandy grinned at me as she linked her arm with Sarina's.

I loved my cabin so much, it hurt. They almost made me want to forget my whole scheme and stay here with them forever, but it was time for me to go home. And they would support me, because that was what families did. We'd found something real in each other, and it didn't depend on what I pretended to believe or where I spent the rest of my summer.

By the time we'd made it down to breakfast, the boys were already at our table. Including Ethan, who thought he had a right to sit there now that Paul was gone, and didn't really give a crap about respecting the distance Mandy wanted. No surprises there.

I stood on top of the table, drawing the attention of the room. My heart beat steadily, a soft pulse against my chest. I'd never been more sure of myself. Pastor Dean had already gone back to his office, and I was disappointed he'd miss the show, but he'd hear about it soon enough. Priscilla narrowed her eyes, and I locked my gaze with hers. I wanted to make it perfectly clear who I was speaking to and where she could stick her "personal responsibility."

"Hey, everyone!" I shouted. "If you don't mind, I'd like to say something."

Forks clattered to trays and voices hushed to a low buzz as everyone prepared for what looked to be a certain train wreck. And I intended to deliver the goods. I undid my top button.

"She's going to strip," Peter said.

"No, she's not," said Ethan.

"Listen up, everyone." Mandy stood and Sarina joined her, digging her nails into her cheeks as she stood. No doubt thinking about how furious her mom would be. Astrid just wore a small smile as she took her place next to Sarina.

Together, the three of them ushered the kids away from the nearest tables and pushed them back in a line, forming a barricade between me and the counselors trying to get through the crowd. They bought me enough time to make my grand exit. Even if they didn't necessarily believe in what I was about to do, they had faith in me. It was all I needed.

Everything from head to toe tingled. The more buttons I undid, the bolder I became, like I could do anything. I undid another button. Then two more.

My sweat-slicked fingers slipped on the second-to-last

button, and all the muscles in my back clenched against my spine. It was one thing to think about stripping to get kicked out, and another thing entirely to do it in front of people.

I undid the last button and my entire shirt opened, revealing my yellow-and-teal polka-dot bikini. I twirled my shirt in the air, and flung it on top of Peter's head. The entire room burst into cheers and catcalls. The counselors tried to push through the crowd, but most of the boys had stood up to get a better view.

"Told you," said Peter, who balled up my shirt, his cheeks bright red.

"You've made your point," Priscilla called from behind a group of boys. "You can step down now."

"I've just begun to make my point." I undid my shorts and dropped them. "This bikini used to make me feel good. Until you told me I couldn't wear it. By trying to force me to be modest for the boys, you made me feel ashamed of being a girl."

But it was my body, and I'd decide how I felt about it from now on. There, in a room full of Christians, under the watchful eye of the guy who used to date Paul's mom, I took control of myself. I wasn't shameful or vulgar. I was a girl in a bathing suit who knew her own heart and mind. And I was fucking powerful.

I reached around the back to unhook the top, and a few of the girls in the crowd gasped.

Finally, Michael, not Mike, broke through my cabinmates' table barrier. Astrid tried to block him, and Sarina dove for his ankles, but he dodged them both. He grabbed me around the waist, hauling me off the table. Part of me was relieved. I hadn't really wanted to bring out my boobs, but I'd been willing to go as far as I'd needed to get out of here.

"Looks like we've got a handsy one here!" I called, and the male counselor released me, which sent a peel of laughter through the crowd.

After they failed to retrieve my shirt from Peter, they gave up and ushered me out of the dining hall in nothing but my bikini top and shorts. Priscilla shoved a Camp Three SixTeen shirt over my head. She marched me straight to Pastor Dean's office and pushed me through the door.

"What's going on here?" He peered over his reading glasses and sighed, like he hadn't really expected to see anyone else.

"Sir, this girl caused a commotion at breakfast, stripping on a table in front of all the boys," Priscilla said. "We barely got her out of there before she took it too far."

Taking it too far was my personal motto. "I want to go home. If you don't let me leave, I'm going to strip at every meal until you let me go, and next time my boobs are coming out."

Pastor Dean rubbed his temple as he picked up the phone. "Michael, bring the van around. We have a camper who needs a ride to the bus station." He hung up. "I'm disappointed in you, Miss Wells. You know this means you'll be giving up your community service."

"This isn't my community. I have no business serving it. Can I call my mom?"

He turned the phone around to me. Instead of dialing my mom's cell, I called Paul's grandpa. A number I had memorized by heart since he'd been our emergency contact for over a decade. He answered, and his warm voice chased out the chill in the room.

"Grandpa? It's CeCe."

"I'm afraid I don't know a grown CeCe. The only one I know is a little girl in pigtails with a smart mouth and a taste for blueberries." Grandpa liked his jokes.

"Are you still hiring pickers for the summer? Because I could really use a job."

"Sure thing. I've always got a spot on my farm for a girl who can sell individual berries for a dollar." His booming laugh sent a wave of relief through me.

"Thanks, I'll be in touch as soon as I'm home." I hung up and dialed my mom next, and she agreed to pick me up at the bus station. I couldn't tell if she was mad, or in the middle of the monthly bills. Her voice tended to sound the same during both.

Priscilla escorted me back to my cabin so I could pack,

and I shoved her onto the front porch and slammed the door in her face. She didn't belong in our cabin. After I put my things away, and double-checked to make sure I had the girls' numbers, I flipped open Astrid's notebook and left it faceup on her bed. Taking one last look around, I picked up my suitcase and headed out to meet Michael, not Mike, at the van to take me to the bus.

Sarina, Mandy, and Astrid,

Once upon a time there was a girl who thought she'd found a prince, so she followed him to his kingdom. But he didn't want her, and it turned out, the girl didn't want him either. She wanted a true prince. The girl floundered in this new land. She'd been told it was a dark place with no Wi-Fi, but soon she was greeted by three lights. One with a talented gift she shared with the girl, and so the girl knew friendship. Another with an amazing power to forgive, and so the girl knew compassion. And one more with the heart of a guiding leader, and so the girl knew wisdom.

See, the girl came to this land broken and unsure of herself, but the three new lights in her life reminded her of who she was, and who she could still yet be. While it hurt the girl to tell them goodbye, she knew she belonged in another land. But she'd carry their light with her on her travels, because, of all the lessons they had taught her, the most important one was love. They'd given it to her without condition, and she held it dear, because no matter how far apart life took them, they would always be the girls of cabin eight.

Be in touch soon.

Love, CeCe

Chapter 27

My mom picked me up at the bus station and folded me into her arms. Her light fruity perfume reminded me of Mandy. I wanted to be home, but I'd also miss doing makeup with Sarina, playing melting bead Pictionary with Mandy, and getting life lessons from Astrid. The girls of cabin eight would always be a part of me.

Mom held me by the shoulders and frowned. "You know you're grounded, right?"

"I figured as much. I'm sorry I didn't listen to you, but I couldn't stay there anymore."

Mom gave a long-winded sigh. "It's not just about camp. You quit PETA, the ski club, and said you won't be doing yearbook again next year. When we sent you there, we had hoped you'd be able to finish at least one thing you started, but you fell short of earning your community service hours."

I didn't finish camp in the traditional sense, but I'd found what I needed there anyway. The cabin eight girls might've called it God's grace. I called it learning from my mistakes. "This isn't like those other times I just gave up. I talked to Paul's grandpa, and he's going to let me work on his blueberry farm until I earn enough to pay you back for camp."

"Sounds like you've made some grown-up decisions." Mom hugged my side as she picked up my suitcase in her other hand. "Let me talk to your father about the budget; maybe we can give you a little leeway if you earn back those community service hours, too."

"I'm not doing this for the budget; I'm doing this for me. Let's just call it . . . personal responsibility." The true definition of Priscilla's horribly titled workshop. If I wanted to take genuine steps to correct my mistakes, I had to do more than say I was sorry. Sorry was a feeling. Making amends meant change.

"I guess we should've shipped you off to Christian camp ages ago." Mom ruffled the top of my head. "I'm really proud of you, Fancy girl."

On the way home, my mom turned up her favorite radio station, featuring the hits of yesterday and today. If they defined "today" as ten years ago. Mom had no shame when it came to belting out an off-key Mariah Carey song with the windows down, and I'd missed her so much, I didn't even mind. That much.

Mom pulled into our driveway and parked. An unfamiliar car hugged the curb in front of Paul's house. "Mom, I know I'm grounded, but can I go next door for a minute?"

"That's fine, but be back before your father gets home from work. We'll discuss your grounding as a family." She hauled my suitcase out of the trunk and went inside.

Normally, I would've burst into Paul's backyard and made myself at home on his porch under the misting umbrella, but I had no idea if he'd been grounded, and I certainly didn't want to tell his mom why I was home early too. Especially because she'd gone to bat for the both of us by writing those letters of recommendation.

As I stepped over the short hedge separating our property, Paul's back gate creaked open, except he wasn't the one who came out front. My heart skipped as I caught sight of a willowy redhead. I trusted Paul not to call his ex behind my back. But what was she doing here?

"Hey, Lara," I said.

She jumped like a cat under a backfiring car. "Hey. I thought you were at camp?"

"I'm back now." The air around me dropped to subzero. I'd always liked Lara, but that was before I'd caught her sneaking out of Paul's house the day after we'd had sex.

Confusion clouded her eyes for an instant before she

started laughing. "I know everyone says this, but I promise this isn't what it looks like."

"You're not here to see Paul?"

"I came here to see him, but only because he called me to apologize for reasons that still completely escape me." A bemused smile touched her lips. "He's an odd duck."

"Seriously?" I couldn't believe he'd actually done it. "He told me he owed you an apology for being terrible at sex the first time, but I thought he was being facetious."

"God, no. That's not . . ." Her eyes widened. "He told you about that?"

I kicked my heel against the cement walk. "He said it didn't last very long."

She snorted. "Losing your virginity sucks. Nobody knows what the hell they're doing. But no. That's not why he called. He somehow got it in his head that he hurt me, even though I've been with Matt, and happy, for the last six months."

"Huh." I avoided her gaze. "Wonder where he got an idea like that?"

"Probably from the girl who drives him batshit."

I glared at her.

"Lighten up. I'm joking." She nudged me. "I appreciate you sticking up for me on a girl level, but I'm not moping over my lost love."

"So, you weren't hurt when he broke up with you?" On one hand, I was enormously relieved, but on the other, how could she be happy without Paul? Yeah, couldn't relate.

"I was devastated. I cried for days and couldn't imagine feeling a worse pain in my life." She tilted her head in contemplation. "But even then, I knew we didn't belong together. I think I got too hung up on the virginity thing. I blame society."

"I blame society too." All the reasons why Lara was my favorite came into sharp focus. "I mean, seriously? Why all the pomp and circumstance around your first time?"

"Who knows? It's the worst." She shook her head. "Anyway, I should be going. I have a hot date with my hotter boyfriend. But we're okay, me and you. Even when I hated you for being everything I wasn't, I still liked you."

She ran back to her car, her fiery hair streaming behind her. Paul had apologized to Lara for their breakup. I'd never heard of him apologizing to anyone before. Maybe we'd both grown as people from that weird two weeks at Jesus camp. I debated going back home, to let it sink in, but that wouldn't have been me. After doing a quick check of the backyard to make sure Paul wasn't outside, I ran into my house and pulled every sheet out of our linen closet.

I kept a careful eye on Paul's bedroom window as I draped my old One Direction sheets over the trampoline. I grabbed a rock from the garden and threw it at his window, and then threw two more rocks because it took three attempts to hit the glass pane. As soon as his blinds rustled, I disappeared inside the hideout.

Paul's shadow fell on the other side of the sheets. "What are you doing home?"

I leaned up on my elbows. "What's the password?"

He muttered a few choice curse words under his breath. "CeCe is the queen. I bow down to her quick wit and stunning beauty. It's her stage, and the rest of us are merely players."

"You may enter."

He pulled back the sheet and my breath caught in my throat. Here kneeled the boy I loved so much, even the sun felt cold without him under it. I had no idea how I'd gone years lying next to him, telling stories, making jokes, snuggling against him, but never kissing or touching. Not like we had in the woods. Present me wanted to shake some sense into past me for all the things I could've had sooner if I'd only been honest.

I held out the hem of my Camp Three SixTeen shirt, the one Priscilla had forced over my head after Peter had refused to give back my button-down. "I chased a guy who wasn't worth it to Jesus camp, had the most mind-blowing sex with the guy who's worth everything, ended up getting kicked out, and all I got was this stupid T-shirt."

He glanced at the underside of the trampoline. "Is this a story?"

"No stories today." I patted the place beside me. "I wanted to talk to you before my dad gets home and my eternal summer grounding starts."

He hesitated for a moment before sprawling out next to me. "You're not changing your mind about us, are you?"

"Not a chance." I took a deep breath. "But I do have some things to say."

"Okay. I'm listening." He frowned and laced his hands under his head.

"I didn't want to stay there without you, but that's not the only reason I left." I laid my head in the crook of his arm. "I love my cabinmates, like, so much. Going in, I thought I wouldn't have anything in common with them, but I was wrong. I'm proud to be like them. But I hate everything that camp stands for, and I guess I get now why Ethan is the way he is."

"That's fair." He untucked one of his hands and wrapped his arm around my waist. "But what does Ethan have to do with me?"

"Because I think I understand you a little more too. After what you went through with your dad leaving like he did. You were right when you called me selfish, and I'm working on that. It took me a long time to find myself again, but I'm getting there."

He touched my hip and my entire body responded. "I can barely keep up with you sometimes, but you're the only person who makes me want to bother trying."

I played with the button on his front pocket. "I ran into Lara on her way out. She told me you called her to apologize."

"You gave me a lot to think about in front of the chapel." He brushed my jawline with his fingertips. "You weren't wrong about me, either, but I'm getting there too."

"Good. Because I'm not going to be the weak link in this relationship."

"You could never be the weak link." He tucked my hair behind my ear. "Not after you climbed on a table and stripped down to your bikini in front of a bunch of Christians at the most conservative camp in the state. That's pretty badass."

I pushed off him and sat up. "Who told you about that?"

"Turns out my man Peter snuck a burner phone into camp." Paul pulled out his Android and flicked open his texts. "I've got the whole thing on video."

My voice blared out of his speakers, and I reached for his phone. "Give me that."

"Nope." He pulled it back and stuck it into his pocket. "That one's a keeper."

"Ugh. Peter kept my shirt, too, the little weasel."

"Yeah, that's a squirt rag now."

I closed my eyes and bowed my head. "Rest in peace, faithful button-down. I'm sorry you didn't have a better end to your short, but noble, life."

Paul watched me with a quiet expression.

I wrinkled my nose. "What's that look for?"

"I love you."

The way he said he loved me was so simple, so genuine, so Paul. "Say it again."

He sat up and cupped my face. His thumb glided over my cheek. "I love you, CeCe."

I kissed him then, wanting to taste my name on his lips. He tilted my head and poured everything he felt back into me as we explored this new side of us. And under a ceiling of faded silver stars, the girl who learned to swim in an ocean of her making loved the lonely boy too good for this earth, and he loved her back as it was always meant to be.

The End

Acknowledgments

I have so many people to thank for helping bring this book baby into the world, but first I'd like to thank you, the reader, for following CeCe's story. For the longest time she existed only in my head, but now she belongs to you.

I'm beyond grateful for my amazing agent, Rebecca Podos, who has been my biggest champion for so many years. I wouldn't be here without your unwavering support, excellent insight, and incredible love for my messy, complicated characters.

To my editor extraordinaire, Ashley Hearn, thank you so much for your passion and your vision and for always encouraging me to dig deeper into the heart of this story. Your fierce love for CeCe, Paul, and the cabin eight girls means the world to me.

My copy editor, Kaitlin Severini, is a literal genius and I'm so thankful for her sharp eye. It was an absolute pleasure to work with you.

A huge thank you to the entire team at Page Street, who have made this the most delightful, rewarding experience. Specifically, I want to thank publicists Lizzy Mason and Lauren Cepero, editorial assistant Madeline Greenhalgh, editorial interns Max Baker and Hanna Mathews, production editor Hayley Gundlach, editorial manager Marissa Giambelluca, editor Lauren Knowles, designer Kylie Alexander for the perfect cover that captures the feel of this story in the best way, my publisher Will Kiester, and the wonderful sales team at Macmillan.

Biggest hugs and thank you to my critique partner and literary soulmate, Jen Hawkins, who has read nearly everything I've written and always inspires me to be a better writer.

To Roselle Lim and Kellye Garrett, you both have gotten me through hard times and great times and I love you forever. We'll always be the three dancing ladies.

To my coven of love, Kelsey Rodkey, Annette Christie, Andrea Contos, and our newest addition, Auriane Desombre, your constant cheering, love, and laughs make me thank Santa Plane Jesus every day that you're in my life. Thank you for being CeCe's fans from the very beginning and being there for every step of this journey.

To my early readers, Rachel Lynn Solomon, Jenny Howe, Diana Urban, Laurie Dennison, and Alexandra Alessandri, your feedback was so helpful in preparing for submission and I'm extremely thankful for your encouragement and friendship.

Thank you to my Pitch Wars mentor, Dannie Morin, who was the first person to really show me the ropes and teach me craft, I'm so grateful you took a chance on me all those years ago, and huge thanks to The Clubhouse for being there through all the ups and downs.

Thank you to the Novel Nineteens for being a fabulous debut group. Writing can be solitary, but it feels less so when we can lean on and learn from each other.

I couldn't do any of this without the endless support of my husband and our girls. Thank you for giving me the time to write and for always believing in me. <3

About the Author

Sonia Hartl is a YA author who calls Michigan home, even though she's lived in several different states. When she's not writing or reading, she's enjoying pub trivia, marathoning Disney movies, or taking a walk outside in the fall. She's a member of SCBWI and the communications director for Pitch Wars. She has been published in *The Writers Post Journal* and *Boston Literary Magazine*. She lives in Grand Rapids with her husband and two daughters. Follow her on Twitter @SoniaHartl1.